OFFICER DOWN

THERESA SCHWEGEL

St. Martin's Paperbacks

This is a work of fiction. All of the characters, organizations and events portrayed in this novel are either products of the author's imagination or are used fictitiously.

OFFICER DOWN

Copyright © 2005 by Theresa Schwegel.
Excerpt from *Probable Cause* © 2006 by Theresa Schwegel.

Library of Congress Catalog Card Number: 2005047018

ISBN: 0-312-94211-7
EAN: 9780312-94211-3

Printed in the United States of America

St. Martin's Press hardcover edition / September 2005
St. Martin's Paperbacks edition / November 2006

St. Martin's Paperbacks are published by St. Martin's Press, 175 Fifth Avenue, New York, NY 10010.

10 9 8 7 6 5 4 3 2 1

For my parents

ACKNOWLEDGMENTS

Many thanks to all those who contributed advice, expertise, and direction: Ed DiLorenzo, Len Schrader, Scott Phillips, Ellen Clair Lamb, Dave Putnam, Jeremy Iacone, June Yang, Peter Ho Davies, Katherine Faussett, Lauren Anderson and Kathy Nehls, and Kelley Ragland.

Special thanks to David Hale Smith, my other big brother.

Thanks to Kevin for his relentless optimism.

And finally thank you to my family, to Bop and his eagle eye, and to Joyce, for dealing with it. All of it.

I will keep my private life unsullied as an example to all; maintain courageous calm in the face of danger, scorn, or ridicule; develop self-restraint; and be constantly mindful of the welfare of others. Honest in thought and deed in both my personal and official life, I will be exemplary in obeying the laws of the land and the regulations of my department.

—FROM THE LAW ENFORCEMENT CODE OF ETHICS

OFFICER
DOWN

1

Normally, I avoid domestic disputes, but this girl is standing in the middle of my hallway, and she's hitting herself in the head. With her own shoes. I could turn around, take the elevator back down to the lobby, and notify the doorman. But Omar knows I'm a cop. He'd send me right back up here.

She's my next-door neighbor, unit 1612. Her name is Katie or Kathy or something cute that doesn't quite fit, especially now. She's a small girl with a lot of blond hair and a mouth even worse than mine. She lived here by herself when I moved in two years ago. The first time her late-night partying kept me up, I tried to be reasonable: I slipped a friendly note under her door. The next few times, I made official complaints to the Association. The last time, about a year ago, I invited my co-workers over. They busted her snorting coke with a couple suits from the Board of Trade. Since then, she never says hello.

"You'll be *fuck*ing sorry when I'm *fuck*ing dead, you *fuck*ing asshole," she yells, the profanities accentuated with a swift heel to her head. A forearm full of gold bracelets clinks, echoing her swing. I figure she's high, but when she sees me she pauses, her arms midair, and her eyes are clear with conviction. I try to think of something to say. "Excuse me" doesn't seem appropriate. I feel like I'm in *her* way.

She takes a step back, politely allowing me to pass, like this is an everyday thing. I stand there like an idiot. How can she be so serious when she looks so ridiculous? When I don't take the opportunity to make a break for my place, she turns her attention, her yelling, and her shoes to the door.

"Did you hear what I said, you son of a bitch? Do you even care if I die?"

The door couldn't care less.

I've heard her arguing with this guy through my adjoining living room wall for a few weeks now. Senseless, hurtful arguing. Arguing about arguing. One night after a double shift I thought I could sleep for a week and I didn't sleep at all because I could hear them. *What did you just say? Say it again. I dare you.* I felt like a kid back home with my parents in the next room. And just like when I was a kid, I tried not to listen. I closed my eyes and tried to think about other things. I told myself it wasn't my problem to solve. Back then it became my problem. Now, it's right in the middle of my hallway.

"You think you can find someone better than me?" the girl asks. "Besides your *mother?*" Ouch.

When the girl gets no response, she starts assaulting the door with her shoes. I'm comforted it stands between them.

I look both ways. There's no one else around, though I'm sure they're all listening from inside their condos. Granted, that's where most of them solve their own crises.

By now, the humor of the scene is wearing thin, even when one of her French-manicured fingernails pops off. It just adds insult to insult.

The girl keeps at it, and part of me wants to join her and yell at the guy too. I'm sure he's guilty of something. I work with men. My best friends are men. I know how they operate. The guys who play games can go play them at a bowling alley as far as I'm concerned.

On the other hand, this girl hasn't exactly worn a halo since we've been neighbors. It might not be my best move, but I decide to give this guy the benefit of the doubt. I get behind her and grab her arms to stop her from whacking me in the head. Surprisingly, she doesn't resist me. Maybe she wanted me to stop her. The shoes slip out of her hands and into mine. Maybe she's tired. Maybe she's ready to talk.

Or maybe she wants me to hold her shoes so she can bang her head directly against the door.

In her defense, I know sometimes there's no reasoning with a woman in love. My dad ran around with every woman from here to Gary, Indiana, and my mom always accepted his lame excuses. No matter what he did, she'd always take him back. I guess the good times must have been good enough for my mom. Of course I haven't discounted the possibility that she stayed with my dad just to make him miserable. I'm the first to admit she might have been a little nuts. To her credit, though, I never saw her yell at a door.

"You better let me in, Jerry, or I'll do it!" the girl in the hallway yells, and to this, she gets a response. The door opens, and Jerry, a surprisingly calm-looking individual, tosses a bottle of pills at her. He catches her off guard, and the bottle ricochets off her rib cage like a poorly lobbed whiffle ball. It doesn't make a sound when it hits the carpet.

"Do it, then," he says. "You're crazy." Then he acknowledges me with a neighborly nod and closes the door as quietly as he opened it. The lock clicks. She looks over at me like she wants to confirm we just witnessed an atrocity, then snatches her shoes from my hands.

I pick up the pills. They're alprazolam, a generic anti-anxiety drug. When the girl resumes her raucous battle of footwear versus door, I think Jerry might be on to something.

At this point I decide I'm going to stick with my first instinct and find an acceptable way out. When we get a domestic violence call, the guys usually want me to deal with the woman, like we have some allegiance. It generally doesn't work. In fact, I tend to make women more hysterical, and that's about the last thing this girl needs.

I know I should keep my mouth shut, go home, and get ready for my date. I don't.

"Maybe you should take a break. This whole hysterical thing isn't getting you anywhere." I shake the bottle of pills like a maraca.

She tucks the shoes under her arm and takes the bottle from me. "Asshole," she mutters as she reads the label. "These won't kill me."

"He knows you're not going to kill yourself," I tell her. "You want him to respond to you? You put those shoes on your feet and walk away."

"This is my place. If I kill myself, he'll have to move out." She's clearly not listening, but at least she's talking herself out of it. "He can't afford the rent." She smacks the door a few more times before she runs out of steam and slumps to the carpet.

"Do you have somewhere else you can go?" I hope she says yes.

"Why should I have to leave? He's the one who left the goddamned tickets in his pants pocket. He expects me to be psychic. I spend all day at the Laundromat while he's God knows where, and when he comes back he acts like I deliberately ruined his big plans . . ."

Wait a minute. "You're threatening suicide over a load of laundry?"

Her answering glare is as close to a *fuck you* as you can get without saying it.

I am really no good at this. If I ask about the tickets, I'm acting like a cop. Actually if I ask her anything she'll be defensive. What I really want to do is tell her to take one of those pills so I can get on my way. I can see my door from here, and I can hear my phone ringing. I'll bet it's Mason, wondering where I am. He's not going to believe this.

I stand there and stare at the wall, waiting patiently for her to make the next move. I notice a subtle leafy pattern in the wallpaper. Did they remodel? This is the longest I've ever spent in this hallway.

"Do you have a cigarette?" the girl asks me, though she's not really asking. She knows I smoke. She also knows I'm a cop. And she thinks I owe her.

I hand her my pack of Camels and a lighter.

"I can go get Omar," I offer.

She hands me one of my smokes like she didn't hear me. Great. Two years of successfully avoiding each other, and now she wants to bond.

"Have you ever been in love?" she asks me as she reaches up to light my cigarette.

I make the first drag of my smoke a long one. I'm deciding if honesty will be helpful or the beginning of a conversation that'll have me stuck here all night.

"Yes," I finally answer. I sit down next to her. I knew I'd feel guilty for busting her someday. If I can make sure she's not going to off herself right here, though, I'll be on my way after this cigarette with a clear conscience. She looks so vulnerable, sitting cross-legged in her pink socks. I wonder if they're supposed to be that color. Maybe she screwed them up in the wash, too.

"Are you in love now?" she asks.

"Yeah." It feels good to admit it.

"Does he lock you out of your own damn condo?"

"No. But I don't do his laundry."

"Does he make you think you're crazy? Like everything's your fault?"

"No." There's something so childlike about the way she looks up at me, anticipating the rest of my answer. I give it some thought. "You know, you should think about why you two fell in love in the first place. Was it the way you folded his T-shirts? Or how you cook spaghetti?" I've smelled things burning over there, so I say, "I doubt it. You probably devoted every free minute you had to each other. But now you live together, and everything is reversed. Instead of anticipating what could happen next, you expect things to happen. Instead of making an effort to be together, you resent the time you spend on the couch. And love gets lost in the details. In the bills. The dishes. You take that stuff away, and you still love each other . . ." I'm even impressing myself with this theory, and I think I can get through to her, but then I smell something else burning, and I notice she's using my lighter to singe her arm hair.

Jerry's right, this girl is crazy. I take away the lighter and she starts to giggle. I can't tell if she's laughing at me or at the fact that she's burned off a lengthy trail of hair. Childlike is right.

"Good luck." I give up. I get up.

"Can I ask a serious question?" she asks before I can take a step past her.

I wait for it.

"How do you do it? How do you make it work?"

Just then, her door opens about six inches and hangs there. Looks like Jerry has had a change of heart.

The girl jumps up, leaving her shoes and her pills, forgetting all about me and how I make things work. The funny thing is, she wouldn't believe me if I told her. She'd think *I* was crazy.

The door closes behind them as I approach my place, feeling smart, and also regretting the fact that I've never given anyone the power to lock me out.

2

"This is your personal 911. Leave a message."

Sounds cheesy, right? Not coming from Mason Imes. I wait for the beep.

"It's Sam," I say, "and it's ten after ten. Detective, where are you? I'm hungry. Hurry up. Call me."

I hang up and check myself in the hall mirror again. I've been ready to go for too long, and I'm second-guessing my outfit. Do I really expect a forgiving black dress and knee-high boots to hide the fact that I haven't worked out in a month? Keeping up with the cop lifestyle has been hard lately. There's no such thing as a diet when you're on duty. The caffeine, the nicotine, the fast food, the alcohol; sometimes I feel like I belong in detox with the junkies. I try to combat my intake with exercise, but since the weather has been bad, I've nixed my lakefront running routine. I was up to six miles when the cold hit. Tomorrow, I keep saying. Tomorrow I'll bundle up and get back to it.

I adjust the underwire in my bra. I'm counting on my cleavage to serve as a distraction from my ass, but that doesn't help the rest of my sub-par appearance. My hair looks like it's been pulled back all day (it has) and my makeup looks like a second coat rather than a fresh one (it is). Good thing we're going to Iggy's; at times like these, I live for bad lighting.

Mason is the one who planned dinner; he knows Iggy's is one of my favorite late-night places. It's low-key, unadvertised, and out of the way, and it's been around for too long to be trendy. The regulars are anonymous, and cool enough to know so. The lights are candles, the booths in the front windows depend on Milwaukee Avenue's streetlights, and the bar is barely lit by blue neon bubbles overhead. It's a speakeasy of sorts, at least for people like Mason and me, where the only one watching is the waiter—and that's just to make sure your plate is empty and your drink is full. I've never had a better steak after 10 P.M. I think most people come for Iggy's martinis, poured in at least thirty different candied variations; I don't experiment because I drink whiskey and I don't like dessert.

Mason knows this too, so I'm sure he has promises planned for dessert: whispers that will lead to a nightcap and a long night somewhere nearby, where I'll wake up tomorrow and hail a cab back to my boring life, daydreaming through other people's problems.

At this point, though, I'm starting to feel reluctant. Maybe that episode in the hallway put a damper on the whole dating thing. I don't know if I really want to go out anymore. If I had any food in the fridge I would have already eaten it straight from its carton, put on my pajamas, and settled into bed.

Mason must be held up at work. He knows I hate waiting.

I'm about to make myself a drink when the phone finally rings. I hesitate to answer. I could have a night alone, a break from what Mason is trying to make too serious, but that also means passing up that steak. My stomach growls. I answer.

It's not Mason. It's my boss, Sergeant MacInerny, Twenty-third District, Chicago PD.

"Samantha Mack, Sarge here. Can you come in? William Wade's out with the flu."

Fuck. I can't say no. I mean, I could, but I can't. Wade is a hypochondriac, but he always covers for me and he never asks questions.

"Smack?" Sarge asks, with enough punch in his voice to sound like a command.

"Yeah. I'm on my way," I say and hang up. My night of passion over before it started, without so much as a protest. I put down the bottle of Jameson and head back to the bedroom to change.

The ride north is quick—not many people out on a Tuesday night this time of year. Once winter gets ahold of the lake, it clings as long as it can, offering only a few flirtatious days of warmth. Come April, people get fed up waiting for spring: they ignore the elements, put away their full-length wools and wear windbreakers, and hope it doesn't snow one last time.

I actually like nights like these, when the air is clear and the city lights seem to heat the sky. I take the Inner Drive all the way up to Addison even though there are at least a dozen stoplights. The buildings on Lake

Shore are beautifully coexistent, I think, like people. I take my time before I have to deal with the ugly things.

I get to the station and nobody's in front. I figure I missed roll and head for the locker room. On my way I notice a box of Dunkin' Donuts in the break room so I stop and scarf down two chocolate-iced rings. They're approaching stale, and I hate sweets, but there's nothing worse than starting a shift on an empty stomach.

The coffeepot is empty, so I get a Coke from the vending machine and take it with me. Some dinner.

In the locker room, the guys are all suspended in various stages of undress, listening to Officer Flagherty tell some new dick joke. Flagherty's naked, hairy belly hangs over his belt in a jovial way, just like his bearded chin hangs over his neck. He stops mid-sentence when he sees me, but not because he thinks I'll be offended by his humor. Paul Flanigan, a rookie with dimples cute enough to keep him from a promotion, hides his lower half behind his locker door even though he's in his boxers. He's not used to me. Everyone else is only mildly annoyed because I interrupted the joke. So I say,

"Wade's tummy hurts. Who am I on with?"

They all look around like I just announced the apocalypse.

"Anybody?" I ask.

After everyone's avoided my gaze, Flagherty finally says, "Wade was scheduled with Fred."

"You're joking," I say.

"I was, Smack," he says, "but that wasn't the punch line."

One of the guys stifles a laugh.

"Ha-ha," I say. When he called, the Sarge failed to mention that I'd be spending the night with my ex.

* * *

"Hey, stranger," Fred says. He's waiting for me outside his squad even though it's so cold the wind could tear your face off. His own face has weathered a few winters, though his expressions suggest otherwise. If it weren't for the crescent-shaped scar that frames one of his true blues, you'd think he worked a crosswalk in the suburbs.

"Just like old times, eh?" Fred asks, and the scar, like cold wax, resists moving with his smile.

"Not quite," I say and get in. Valiant effort, but I don't want to reminisce. I strap myself into the passenger seat and straighten my hat.

"What's with Wade?" Fred asks as he gets in the car.

"Flu."

"Going around, I think. Deb's been feeling bad." Deb. Deborah. Debbie. Yuck.

"If you're gonna try to make conversation, you might want to leave her out of it," I say, and stare ahead. My breath gets short, reminding me I need a cigarette. I pull out my pack of Camels and light one. I know Fred wants to protest, but he doesn't. We ride up Lake Shore Drive from Addison in what I hope he would call an uncomfortable silence.

Fred parks the squad outside the Fireside Tap, a little dive on Lawrence where Uptown meets the Edgewater neighborhood and nobody seems too happy about it. I wouldn't call it dangerous, but I carry a gun.

"We slumming for drunks?" I ask.

"Got a snitch, paged me to meet him at the stop across the street. A guy who's trying to get himself out of a little trouble," Fred says.

"You just described the plight of nearly every guy I've ever met." I wonder if he thinks he's included. I light another cigarette with the butt of the one I'm smoking.

"You know that's bad for both of us," he tells me.

"One night's not gonna kill you." I blow a puff of smoke at him.

He cracks his window.

I blast the heat in retaliation.

"It's always a battle with you. I'm starting to think you do it on purpose," he says and waves an exaggerated hand at my smoke.

"You're right, Fred. We ride together once a year now and you know me better than I know myself."

"I'm still your friend."

I take a dramatic pause.

"A friend doesn't ditch his partner." I had that one rehearsed.

"I didn't ditch you."

"No, you got married," I say. To a money-grubbing bitch disguised as a blonde with self-esteem issues, I don't say.

"Deb's not the reason we're not partners and you know it."

"You're going to tell me it was your idea to work overnights? Wasn't it you who said you'd rather check bags at O'Hare than stay up past ten?"

"People change."

"That's one way to put it," I say, and I'm about to give him another way when he cuts me off—

"There he is."

I assume he's talking about the snitch, a little bastard with a big walk who's appeared just outside the El station. You can always tell the ones that work both sides. They act like they can't get in any more trouble. And they'd all stand out in a crowd of morons. Like this guy: it's maybe twenty degrees and he's wearing a slim leather coat, no hat, no gloves. Homeless guys have more layers. And this guy looks right at us—right at our squad, before he jumps over the turnstile and disappears up the steps. Without paying. I'm surprised he didn't kick up his heels.

"Jesus, did he do that just to spite us?" I want to pull my .38 and shoot the guy from my window just to make a point. I reach for my door handle, but Fred stops me.

"I'll go, Smack. You stay here and wait for your claws to retract."

Before I can reply, he gets out of the car and follows the snitch.

Not five minutes go by—I mean, I'm not even done with my smoke and I'm still pissed about the claw remark, and I have every right to be: It was Fred who got me through my rookie year and then dumped me like a one-night stand. It was Fred who said I was his best friend and then didn't even invite me to his wedding. And Fred's the one who taught me how to be a true partner. Then he switched to overnights and left me without one. So I'm formulating a pretty valid argument about the way things turned out when Fred jumps in the squad and says, "It's on!" He hits the gas and heads for Clark Street. His adrenaline is palpable and I can tell it's time to put all the personal shit aside, though I still want to comment on the fact that Deb's not a real blonde.

"Where we going?" I ask.

"You remember Marko Trovic? That scumbag we arrested up in Rogers Park last year? The one who had the hots for his girlfriend's kid?"

"Yeah," I say. How could I forget. Trovic has a problem with women—particularly nonvirgins who dare to leave the house for more than groceries. He didn't much like being collared by me.

"I arrested him again a couple weeks ago," Fred says. "This time I caught him with his hands *in* the kid's panties. She had those day-of-the-week jobs where it says it right there on the undies? Told her she was wearing the wrong day. Sick fuck."

"Great," I say, "now the kid'll have all kinds of issues. She'll grow up to be a stripper who won't work Wednesdays." I actually amused myself with that one, but Fred's not even listening.

"I did it by the book, but he jumped bail. Girlfriend and the whole rest of his neighborhood aren't talking—in English anyway. But Birdie says he's back in town to finish some business."

"Birdie?" I ask.

"My snitch," Fred says. "And if he's right, and we find that son of a bitch Trovic and I get my hands on him, he's gonna need more than some little girl's underwear to figure out what day it is."

I assume this will not be by the book.

I have to admit I'm as excited as Fred about nabbing this asshole. I'll never forget the day we arrested him, though I'd like to. I put the cuffs on Trovic; that was my first mistake. He wasn't about to take orders from a woman. He made his opinion of me known, spewing profanities in my face. His words slurred between English and Serbian, held together by an imprecise "m," like "Jebem ti mmm'majku . . . mmm'merican bitch." I remember his breath smelled like sarma, the pork rolled in pickled grape leaves he was in the middle of stuffing his face with when we showed up. I took as much as I could of his foul mouth, but then I made my second mistake: I asked why he went after little girls, or women at all, if he hated us so much. I suggested he might swing the other way. And I might have said something about him preferring sheep. Fred thought it was funny, but Trovic didn't. And even though he was cuffed behind his back, he managed to grab a kitchen chair and broadside me with it. I hit the ground, and then so did Trovic—thanks to Fred and his billy club. Fred went off on him. I could hear the blunt contact of metal on Trovic's ribs. Trovic didn't fight back, but he kept his lips pursed in a defiant smile, his black eyes locked on me, and not another word was necessary to convince me of his absolute hatred. For weeks I saw his face when I closed my eyes at night. I don't know what bothered me more: that I mistakenly thought I had the situation under control, or that I knew there was no way to diffuse his hate. I guess some arrests stay with you.

We sneak up, lights off, outside a two-flat in Rogers Park. It doesn't look any better or worse than the other houses on this street, but I wouldn't exactly drop my guard. Not just because of Trovic. This neighborhood is tricky: it's bordered by Loyola University on the south and a state-run group home for mental patients on the north. I wonder if Trovic is shacking up with a college girl or a schizo.

It's quiet, the kind of quiet where you know you should just wait a minute, take a second to think—

"2318," Freddy radios in.

"Go ahead 18," says the dispatcher.

"Request backup at 1431 West Jarvis."

"I've got unit 2320 on a stop at Pratt and Western," says the dispatcher, "en route in five minutes." As her voice rips through the air I sink in my seat, afraid we've been found out. A single car a good twenty blocks away won't get them here that quickly.

"Ten-four." Freddy hangs up the radio and sits so still that not even his jacket makes that familiar comfortable squeak when it rubs against the vinyl seat, and I remember all the times we've had like this, when the silence was our bond. I finally look over at him, and he's looking at me, and suddenly he's not the asshole cop who put his love life over the job. He's my old partner, my buddy, my safety net . . .

"Let's go," he says.

I take back what I just said about safety.

I'd attempt to reason with him, but Fred's already getting out of the car, and I have to follow. Just like old times.

I catch up with Fred as he's casing the front of the place, his gun drawn, held close to his leg. I take cover against the white aluminum siding that looks yellow from the glow of a single streetlight. I check my gun even though I know it's loaded. I can see my breath so I hold it as I take a quick peek inside a window to my left. It's dark; all I see is my own reflection. Fred tries the front door and it's unlocked. I know he's going in and there's no time to argue; I'm going in too. I put my hand on his shoulder to let him know I'm ready. He pushes the door open and we rush in together. I buttonhook right; he goes left.

Once we're in I expect Fred to announce our arrival, but he just stands there in the dark, listening, getting a feel for the place, so I do the same. I didn't expect to be handed a map, but the silence in this place makes me feel completely lost. Something isn't right. I feel like someone will flip on the lights and all the guys from the station will yell *Surprise!* because it's an elaborate joke for Fred's birthday. Too bad they already marked last week's occasion with a cake from the Jewel and a group card.

I hear something at the end of a long hallway that runs to the back of the house, some kind of accidental movement. I check for Freddy's go-ahead and with one look he says, *Yes, I heard it too, we're close, someone's back there; go, Sam.* He stays behind double-checking, watching, waiting for the right person to make the wrong move.

Shadows from the wind-blown trees outside bounce around through the windows in the hall and fool me into aiming at nothing. It's like hide-and-seek and my .38 is a heavy toy. There are doorways to my right and I pause at every one, aiming quickly inside as I dart to the other side and listen for some reaction. I don't move again until I'm sure—I'll be damned if I'm gonna miss anyone. When I get to the back, the floorboards creak under my feet. I stop and press up against the wall, away from the worn part of the floor, and pull my flashlight from my coat. I shine the light around the empty kitchen and stop on the back door. It hangs open on rusty hinges. I can feel the cold air just beginning to work its way into the room. Trovic must have gone out that way. Right?

I make for the door, following my instinct. As soon as I move, I hear something just behind me and in a panic I remember there's always one corner you missed or one shadow that moved when you weren't looking, so I whip around, ready to put a round in someone hiding by the refrigerator—but it's Fred standing there, and he pushes the tip of my gun down like I should have known better. I let myself breathe, finally, heavily, but then Fred puts one finger to his lips and another to the ceiling and I hear a subtle shift of the floorboards upstairs, just like the ones in the hall.

Fred takes my hand like a child's and directs my flashlight to the foot of a staircase. Then he turns off

the beam and lets go of my hand. As my eyes readjust
to the darkness, he disappears. I follow in what I think
is his direction and I think I hear him going up the
stairs. I cross the room carefully, and slightly on my
tiptoes.

I climb the stairs more confidently than I feel, one
foot over the other, with the rest of me wanting to turn
around and get out of there. I feel like Trovic is waiting
for us. Why couldn't we wait for backup?

I don't dare turn on my flashlight, though it's aimed
straight ahead with my left hand just as my gun is with
my right. I see a faint light at the top of the stairs, the
night sky outlining a window, and I make that my des-
tination. I pray nothing gets in my way.

Just as I reach the top, I hear a gunshot.

Before my brain catches up with my body I drop to
the floor. I'm on my elbows, trying to get my bearings.
I'm crawling away from the steps and away from the
light of the window toward the pitch fucking black. I
feel along the molding, navigating my way down a
hall, and then I come to a break that must be the entrance to a room. I get on my knees and aim my gun
around the corner. I can't see shit and I can't hear over
my own damn breath so I back up and hold it. Then another shot is fired. I can't place exactly where it came
from or where it went but I know I'm close. I know I'm
right around the corner. That light from the window
behind me only tells me where I was, not where I need
to be. I need to be in that room.

I call out: "Fred!"

I don't get a response, so I cut around the corner,
keeping my back against the wall, aiming my gun into
the darkness. I wait and I wait and I wait and my eyes
are peeled but I can't see a fucking thing in front of
me. Time stretches like a rubber band. I wait for it to

snap. I wait for another shot. I wait for something, anything besides this silence and its horrible implications. I think about screaming, about firing my gun, about turning on my stupid flashlight and standing up and saying, "Okay, you win."

Then I hear Freddy call out: "Smack?" But without the usual conviction.

"Fred," I say, relieved to know he's there. "Where are you?"

"Right here . . ." Which doesn't tell me anything, but I follow the sound of his voice and I can hear him straining to breathe, so I say, "Are you hit?"

At the same time he says, "I got him."

"Trovic?" I ask, and just saying his name in the dark is enough reason to turn on my flashlight. I find Fred right away: he's on the ground only five feet in front of me. I crawl to him.

"I got him, I got that dirty son of a bitch. You'll see."

He grabs my arm and makes it hard to aim my flashlight and my gun from corner to corner of the room, working toward the middle, looking for "him." I hope I'll find Trovic's body. I hope we aren't sitting ducks. We're in a bedroom, and it's pretty much empty except for an unmade bed. I should check the other side of the bed. I should check underneath the mattress. I see a lamp on a nightstand. I should turn it on. I should move, but Fred won't let go of my arm.

"Fred?"

"I'm hit," he says. Shit.

I kneel beside him and open his coat. I feel around his chest, but there's no blood. He's wearing a vest. I go for my radio, but he grabs my hands and says, "You'll thank me."

"No time for that," I say. I've got to get him out of here. With just this flashlight I can't get a feel for the whole room, and I don't know if we're safe. "Get up," I tell him.

He doesn't, so I set the flashlight on the floor, its beam aimed at the bed. I get behind Fred and put my left arm around his chest, my right still free to fire my gun. I press through my heels and heave, trying to pull Fred back to the wall. He doesn't budge.

"Jesus, it hurts, I think it went through." He grabs my arm and pulls my gun down so I stop because I think he's really hurt and I shouldn't move him. I holster my gun and move back around him so he can show me where he's hit.

He squeezes my arm, the slightest indication for me to move closer, and suddenly I don't think this is about getting shot. I get close enough to see him by the glow of the flashlight on the floor behind us. I think he is crying.

"Fred?" is all I say, though I want to whisper I'm sorry, sorry for all the shit we did to each other, and I wish we would have said what we meant before it was too late . . . Is it too late? Can we ever be like we were?

Then Fred says, "Did you ever call John?"

God knows why.

In the middle of what I thought was a moment. In the middle of what he said was a bust. I can't believe, in the middle of all this, he's trying to fix me up with one of his friends. An attorney from Northbrook, of all people. Why is he saying this to me now?

I get on my knees and feel around his chest again. He wheezes. I check his neck. I can't find any blood.

"Jesus, Fred, I didn't call John and I don't want to hear it. Help me. Tell me where you're hit."

"Guess I'd have to be an asshole for you to listen to me," he says, and he coughs a little. Does he think these are his last words? He won't let go of my arm.

"You are an asshole. And I wouldn't be caught dead running around with someone who makes a living keeping criminals in business." I'm trying to get a rise out of Fred, to keep him going. I don't know what's wrong with him. I pray the guys from car 20 are just outside.

"Come on, he'd be good for you." Fred holds his breath, then says through his pain, "He's a great guy. Single, stable . . ." It's more than pain; his voice sounds heavy with regret.

"How about we discuss my love life once we get out of here?" I think he knows about Mason and me, and I'm sure he doesn't approve, but this is ridiculous.

"You have no idea who he is . . . what he can do . . ." Then Fred's voice breaks and he frantically tries to push me away. His eyes plead for help.

I think he's in pain, so I try to calm him. "Relax," I say, "you're going to be fine." But I realize how stupid that sounds when I figure out Fred is looking over my shoulder, at whoever is behind me. I feel the floorboards shift beneath my knees and I know we're fucked. He didn't kill Marko Trovic. And I didn't check under the bed.

"Leave her out of this," Fred says with the courage of a dead man.

I know any move I make will be futile, but I draw my gun just as whoever's behind me pushes me, a two-handed shove so powerful I feel my neck snap as my knees hit the floor next to Fred. I'm off balance, but that doesn't stop me; I turn and fire. The blast from my gun knocks me on my ass and I slide along the hardwood, past Fred. I kick the flashlight and it rolls in an arc. The beam ends up shining on me like a spotlight for Trovic, and I can't see past the light. I know Fred is in front of me just to my left so I fire over him in the perp's direction. I don't know how many shots I get off, but I keep pulling the trigger until all I hear is the click-click-cick of my gun's hammer falling on an empty chamber.

And then, nothing.

I don't move. No one does. I must have hit Trovic.

I scramble to grab the flashlight. I shine it toward the bed. I scan the room, but I don't see anyone.

I suck some air into my lungs. "Freddy," I say. He doesn't answer. I'm afraid to take my eyes off the room. The flashlight's batteries rattle with my shaking hand.

I let go of my empty gun and feel around for Fred's when suddenly a slick, warm liquid trails down my forehead into my eye. I touch it with my finger as though it's someone else's blood. Then a split second later a sharp pain registers in the top of my head, and as I fall to the floor, I think that Trovic must have hit me too.

I lie there and wonder if I'm dead.

3

Okay, I'm not dead, and I know this only because there are people insisting on it, hovering over me and whispering, "She's awake" and "You'll be okay" and "Try to stay calm." I don't know what they're talking about until they get out of the way and give me a chance to see the mess we've made. Spotlights bring the space to life: a dingy bedroom with impersonal, temporary decor like a halfway house or a weekly motel; everything yellowed like old newspaper except the black-red blood on the floor. Officers wear rubber gloves and goggles as they work around me, dusting where there is already so much dust. I see someone drop what looks like my gun into a plastic bag.

"Fred," I say. I can feel him next to me. "Fred," I say again, and I reach for him, but then hands come from everywhere and start to lift me carefully off the floor. Someone says, "You have a concussion." Someone else: "We're taking you to the hospital." I resist, I say I'm okay, and I drop to Fred's side and pull at his shirt, but he doesn't move. I want to hit him and hurt his feelings and tell him I love him and yes, I'll call John, you fucking nag, but they take hold of my arms again and remind me that I have a head injury. They pull me away from Fred and help me outside like I don't know the way. Like I never found my way here in the dark.

Outside, they sit me down in the back of an ambulance and act like I'm dying. And I sit there like a victim. My uniform embarrasses me.

I watch other cops act officially calm, but I can hear them asking each other all of these questions: "Who were they after?" and "Why didn't they wait for backup?" and "What were they fighting about?" I know the answers. But they're not asking me.

Then I see Sergeant MacInerny. I slip off the back of the ambulance and get to him just before the medics try to drag me back. MacInerny puts his arm around me. I don't understand why he's telling me to quiet down because I'm not saying anything. Then I follow his gaze to a stretcher. Covered with a white sheet.

"Marko Trovic," I say, but now that I am talking, Sarge doesn't seem to hear me. "It's Marko Trovic!" I say again. Sarge holds me there firmly, neither one of us sure where I'd go if he didn't, and I can hear the stretcher getting closer, its wheels turning.

"It's Fred," is what I think Sarge says, but that's when it happens: Marko Trovic sits up on the stretcher. Not dead.

An onlooker screams when Trovic throws the sheet off his wounded torso and pulls out his gun. Everyone dodges in different directions and I grab Sarge's gun right out of his holster before he hits the ground and takes cover.

Then Trovic fires. At me.

I feel all six shots burn through my flesh, through my chest, through my heart, and I still manage to shoot back as I fall very slowly, taking in every detail as I go: Trovic's vicious eyes staring from below a thick brow, the heavy gold medallion peeking out of his shirt, his wicked smile defying my bullets. And then, abruptly, all I see is the underside of everything.

As I lie on the ground, I know I must be dead this time. I don't feel any pain. I don't feel troubled. In fact, I don't even mind that I'm dead. My only hope is that Fred made it out okay.

People surround my body and speak in hushed tones and I can't understand them or make out their faces. I would tell them, "It's okay, I am not a hero, I was just doing my job"—if I could, at least to comfort them, but I know they wouldn't understand. Then one face comes into focus. Just one.

And it's Marko Trovic.

I scream loud enough for the living to hear.

"She's awake all right."

A fat, tough nurse wraps something around my arm. As soon as another nurse messes with a bandage on my head, I'm certain I'm still not dead because dead people don't throw up, and I'm about to. Fluorescent lights assault my eyes and a nauseously pink curtain surrounds half of the room.

"I feel sick." Having stated the obvious, I get a

macaroni-shaped dish placed conveniently on my sternum. So I'm in the hospital. I'd rather be dead.

"Breathe," the fat nurse says, putting her hand on my forehead like she can actually stop my head from spinning. I have to say, it helps.

Next thing I know, she opens my gown, exposing my breasts to anyone who cares to look as they pass by, and listens to my heart. Her shirt is patterned with a gaudy mix of lipstick tubes and cosmetic brushes, and her complete disregard for vanity makes me wonder why she chose it. "Vitals are stable, Cerita."

Cerita nods and gets ready to stick a needle in my arm. "How old are you, hon?"

"Thirty-two."

"You look so young. I'd have guessed she was in her twenties," she says to the fat one as she flicks the syringe with her middle finger.

"She ain't had no babies to round her out," the fat one says.

"What happened?" I ask. I stretch my jaw and my mouth feels like I swallowed flour.

"Your brain practically fell out of your head, girl," Cerita says, matter-of-fact. "Doctor stitched you up. Your hair'll hide the wound, though. Lucky you got so much hair." I close my eyes so I don't have to watch her stick me. Guns, okay; needles, no thanks.

"Lucky she's got a hard head, too. That's some concussion," the fat one says, looking at my X ray in a backlit box. So that part of my dream was true, but . . .

"What happened *tonight*?" is what I want to know.

"That's what everyone outside's waiting for you to wake up and tell 'em. You're the most popular patient we had since . . . since that second baseman in here last spring. Cerita, what was his name? That Cub with the broken collarbone?"

"Don't ask me. I'm a Sox fan," Cerita says as she puts a cotton swab over the needle and pulls it from my skin. "This'll keep the swelling down," she says. Then she puts her gear in some kind of plastic pail, a toolbox for all things injected, and prepares to leave.

"Is my partner here, in this hospital?" I ask. Cerita stops. They look at each other like I'm asking to be a part of some secret club.

"Tell that policeman he can come on in now," the fat one says to Cerita. "He's been bugging me."

"Where's Freddy?" I ask as soon as Sarge clears the doorway. As usual, he can't keep up with himself. He's always out of breath, always stretching his neck with a tense hand. I worry about his blood pressure.

"How you feeling, Smack?" he asks me. A question with a question. Not good.

"Do I look all right?" I ask. He's trying to come up with a polite response, so I save him the trouble and say, "I'm fine."

"Doctor says you have a—"

"Concussion. I know that. Tell me what happened out there."

Sarge keeps his distance from the bed and his eyes on the floor. He's pulling a white handkerchief through his rough hands like a magic trick, though there's nothing magic about it. Finally he says, "Fred died on scene."

The reality of that statement escapes me and I try to go back: Fred said he was hit, but I couldn't tell where. We were talking, and there was someone behind us—

"Marko Trovic," I say.

Sarge looks at me like I've lost it. "Who?"

"The guy I shot. The other body. That's Marko Trovic."

"There was no other body."

The reality of *that* statement hits me. Like a bullet. Marko Trovic is alive. Just like in my dream. I sit up.

"Is he in custody?" I ask.

Sarge doesn't want to answer me. He acts like his handkerchief is the most interesting thing he's ever held in his hands.

"He fled." I assume.

"Is that why you two were at that house? Looking for Trovic?" Sarge asks.

"We got a tip. We heard he was there. He *was* there. He shot Fred." When I close my eyes I see flashes of what happened: Fred going for his gun, the look on his face signaling danger behind me, my knees hitting the floor, the split second before I turn and fire. Our lives in my hands.

"You're sure you saw this guy, Trovic?" Sarge asks. I can see Trovic's face all right, his smile a threat, but I can't tell the difference between what I'm remembering and what I was dreaming. Did I see his face when I turned and started shooting?

"I don't know" is my answer.

"We're trying to get to the bottom of this, Sam. At this point it's a little complicated."

"It's simple to me," I say. "Marko Trovic. And if he isn't in custody, somebody better find him."

Sarge takes my hand and eases me back to my pillow. "Relax, Smack. Doctor says you need to take it easy, let your head settle. We won't solve this tonight. Get some rest, and a union rep will come talk to you when you're feeling better."

"Why would I need a lawyer? You're not telling me something." I get the feeling I'm going to get in trouble for some remedial violation, like not waiting for backup.

"It's procedure," he says. "An officer died."

"And I'm telling you who killed him. You put the word out to every cop in this city and they'll have Trovic strung up by his balls before you can pull his file." Cop killers don't have a prayer in this town, and everyone knows it. "He's probably on the run right now. You should have every uniform on the street after him! Put it on the wires, get it on the news . . ." It seems so obvious to me, until Sarge says,

"We're waiting for ballistics."

Ballistics. "Why?"

"All we have to go on right now is the bullet they pulled out of Fred," he says.

"So?"

"So we can't go out and arrest a guy you don't know whether you saw or not when all we have are two issued thirty-eights, both fired, and two wounded officers, one fatally. We need evidence. We need fingerprints and ballistics."

"Trovic shot Fred. And I shot at Trovic."

"Are you sure?"

Wait, what? My head might be a little foggy, but, "I'm sure. Who the hell do you think gave me this concussion?"

Sarge stretches his neck. "We're trying to keep this quiet," he says, "for your sake, and the department. It's already been turned over to the detectives' bureau and I'm on my way to talk to the superintendent."

My sake? The superintendent? Of the city of Chicago?

"You think I killed Fred?"

"Sam, don't jump to conclusions. We just have to

keep procedure intact, and keep the lines open for the higher-ups. We don't want to make any mistakes."

"Your mistake is waiting around for some lab report while Trovic catches the next flight out of here." I sit up again, swing my legs over the side of the bed, and say, "I'll find him myself."

I stand up too quickly and all the blood rushes out of my head. For a moment I feel okay, maybe a little dizzy. Then the pain comes around the side of my head and it's so bad that I can't fake it. Sarge grabs my arm to steady me and it pisses me off, but he won't let go.

"Dammit, I'm fine," I say, and I think I will be if I can just get used to being upright. Sarge puts me back on the bed, sits down next to me, and presses the nurse's call button.

"You're not fine, and you're staying here," he says.

"I have to do something," I tell him.

"How about cooperating? Get some rest. I'll go see the chief and tell him you'll give your statement tomorrow."

"I'll give it to you right now. Fred and I were after Marko Trovic. He killed Fred, and I shot at him. I must have missed. He must have walked out of there. We need to find him."

"Trust that we will do everything we can." Except find Trovic, I want to say, but Cerita appears in the doorway with her bucket of needles and I know this debate is over.

"All right, Sarge," I concede. For now.

I have no idea what time it is. I feel like I've been lying here for days, but the sun still hasn't come up. I'm waiting for my head to stop hurting, and I ask for some painkillers. The nurses don't listen. They just keep telling me to get some sleep.

Yeah, right. Every time I close my eyes I see Marko Trovic.

So I lie in the dark, staring at nothing, trying to remember everything that happened. None of it comes to me in order, and the more I think about it, the less sense it makes.

I keep hearing our last conversation: "I got him," Fred said. "Thank me." Going on about his friend John. "You don't know who he is," he insisted. What was he getting at? And why would he bring it up in the middle of such a dangerous situation? Fred always mixes up work and life, everyone knows that, but he never brings it on the street. He was different tonight. "Leave her out of this," he told Trovic. I know I haven't worked with Fred in a while, but I still know how he works, and this was more than payback for Trovic's priors. Nobody likes a child molester, but tonight Fred acted like Trovic was after his own kid. Tonight was personal, and it had nothing to do with me, the American whore.

No matter what I remember, it's the only way I can figure that things went down the way they did. It was personal, and Fred left me out of it. Marko Trovic is the only one who knows why, and no one is currently looking for him. In fact, they haven't even posted anyone outside my room.

They don't think he was there at all. They think I made this up. They must think I accidentally killed Fred.

I sit up and give myself a minute to get used to the ache in my head. Then I get out of bed and walk around the room a few times, to make sure I'm mobile. Then I cover up with a coat someone brought from the station, and I sneak very carefully down the hall, past the fat nurse, and out of the hospital.

4

The cabdriver hesitates when I climb into his backseat. Must be my outfit.

"Lake Shore and Goethe," I tell him. He sizes me up in his rearview mirror. "I live there," I assure him. He starts the meter. I guess he figures the fare is more important than the circumstances. If he only knew the circumstances.

I tolerate the ride, though the cabbie is heavy on the brakes. A couple of times I think my brain is going to come out of my head and join him in the front seat. I distract myself by watching the sun rise over the lake, becoming circular and solid as it distances itself from the warm colors on the horizon. How many cups of coffee had Fred and I shared at daybreak, mundanely patrolling the Drive during the sun's daily climb? All the moments we overlooked seem so much more important without him.

I see my building in the distance. It's a high rise with bad management and hardly any amenities. I can always find a parking spot, though, and I have a great lake view. I can see the Hancock and the Drake to the south, and on a good day, clear up to the Baha'i temple.

When we pull up to the rotunda, Omar perceptively intervenes to take care of the cab fare and me without so much as raising an eyebrow. He acts like half of the residents show up barefoot. In March.

I follow Omar inside. He's a nice-looking man with chocolate skin and a vanilla smile. He is older than me by at least a decade and I know he's seen it all with blind eyes. I've often wondered what he looks like out of uniform. What he does when he's not opening doors.

He buzzes me in the front entrance, follows me to the elevator, and hands me an extra key. I'm thankful he's the one on duty. He is definitely an amenity.

"You have a good one," he says as the elevator door closes. He might just believe that's possible.

I get into my place and examine my head in the mirror. I take off the bandage and count the stitches. I think there are nine. They look about as bad as they feel. I put the bandage back in place and try to fit my police cap over it. It's swollen. I cringe from the pain. I throw the cap down. I will not cry.

I attempt to put on my uniform, a leftover shirt I only wear when I miss the dry cleaner's drop-off hours. I can't button the top button, it's too constricting. It chokes me. My hands tingle as I undo the rest of the buttons and lean up against the mirror, dizzy from my own body heat. The logical side of my brain is telling me how stupid I am for doing this, but logic has never been one of my strengths.

I slump to the floor and try to focus. I can see straight. I can walk. I can function. I am still alive. And I have to find Marko Trovic. I just have to get up.

I hear sirens outside. The city wakes. Police are working. I should be working. I rebutton my shirt, zip up my pants, and automatically reach for my holster. Then I remember: It's evidence. Just like my gun.

That's when I totally lose it. My body involuntarily collapses, and I curl up in a ball on the floor, convulsing in sobs. What the hell am I thinking? Fred is dead because I *wasn't* thinking. Fred is dead because I dropped my guard. I'm trying to get around it, but it's my fault. Even if Trovic pulled the trigger, I am responsible. And I am the one who's still here.

I have to figure out what happened. I run through the details of the night over and over in my mind, so many times they begin to seem like part of a movie. I'm talking to Fred. I sense danger. I turn and fire. I see Marko Trovic. He shoots at me. I feel the bullets. Fred ends up dead. What parts are real?

At some point while I'm trying to piece together the events, I realize that Mason is here. I'm disoriented; I feel like I'm waking from a dream that was just the same as this: I see Mason standing over me, taller than ever, his five-o'clock shadow grown through another shift, his steel eyes softened by concern.

I focus on the thick veins that run the length of his arms like electrical cords as he picks me up from the floor, steadying me. I feel small. I stand, though I don't feel my legs. I'm lost; I don't know how he knew I was here. I'm numb. I cannot wrap my mind around the idea that Fred is gone. This could still be a dream.

"Sam, are you okay?" Mason asks, and at the concrete sound of his voice, reality confronts me. There are clothes strewn all over the floor. I ripped everything blue from its hanger and didn't even get dressed. The bed is unmade. The lightbulb in the closet burned out. The mail is unopened. I forgot to pay the cable bill. The place is a mess. And I thought I had everything under control.

I begin to sob again.

I fall into Mason's arms and he holds me there and lets me cry, and I cry until it seems silly. Then I tell him, "Freddy's dead," and crying is the only thing that makes any sense.

Mason pulls me closer to him, forcing my runny nose into his shirt.

"Freddy's dead," I say again, like the repetition will make it seem real. It doesn't.

Mason wipes my nose with his hand and kisses my wet mouth. It doesn't bother him; my tears are his. He doesn't speak, he just holds on to me, and the strength of his embrace stands the moment still. I lose my bearings again; this time I am grateful.

As he holds me I abruptly stop crying, like a child who suddenly realizes it's no use. I feel that I am safe here, in his arms, in the silence, completely detached from the unfair world.

Until his radio intrudes with static reality. "2356, respond with location; over," the dispatcher calls Mason.

Mason responds by turning off his radio. He did not come here to investigate. He kisses my forehead and leans against the wall so that I can settle into his chest. I lie in his lap, and he softly strokes my hair. As I drift in and out of consciousness, I tell myself that under the circumstances this is the best possible way Mason can keep the world at bay, for just a little longer.

I don't know when I fell asleep. I remember Mason carrying me to bed. Sometime later, I hear him tell someone that he was in the neighborhood, so he stopped to check my place and found me. I hear him say I'm not in any condition to leave home. He says I need to sleep. I cling to the certainty of his voice and hope that he can make this mess bearable.

When it's quiet for a while, I think he may be gone. Then I open my eyes and Mason is next to me, seated on the bed.

"You going to sleep forever?" he asks. I wonder how long he's been here, watching me.

"What time is it?" I ask.

"Eight forty-five. Thursday morning."

"I slept through a whole day?"

"When you weren't sleepwalking or speaking gibberish."

"I feel fuzzy."

"It's the concussion. You were really out of it, so I called a nurse. She said to give you Tylenol with codeine before I left last night. I didn't want you to make another escape."

"Oh. The escape." He's probably not impressed.

"Sam," he says, "the night nurse at Saint Vincent's nearly had a heart attack when she couldn't find you. She called 911. It went out over all the wires. MacInerny is pissed. He's afraid it'll get to the press. I bought you some time, told them I found you here, sleeping it off, but it's been over twenty-four hours."

I can tell by the way he's looking at me that I'm not going to like what else he has to say.

"They want me to bring you in."

I was right.

Mason hands me a glass of water and two regular Tylenol. "This is what the nurse says to take from here on out. No aspirin, no alcohol." I take them obediently. I feel dumb, but at least he's the one who came to get me.

"I'll get dressed," I say.

I need to be tough. I clench my jaw as I pull a sweatshirt over my messed-up head. Mason tries to help me, but when he puts his hand on my bruised shoulder blade I flinch, because that's exactly where Trovic made contact when he pushed me down.

Trovic.

"You said you talked to MacInerny," I say to Mason as I pull on some jeans. "Did he tell you if they found Trovic?"

Mason has this way of looking at me that stops me in my tracks. This is not that look, but it stops me.

"What?" I ask.

"The word is out about your conversation with MacInerny. About Trovic. I've talked to just about everyone who was on scene. They tell me the only prints they've identified so far are yours and Fred's. They haven't found any other latents."

"So what are they going out with?" I ask. "They can't just give the press a dead cop with no leads." I know what Mason is going to say but I don't believe it, even when I hear it:

"They're calling it an accident."

They're saying it was me. They're not even going to look for Trovic.

"What about ballistics?" I ask.

"Haven't come back yet," he says. "The case isn't closed. It's just a press thing. You know how it goes.

It's best for the family, for the department, if we have an explanation—"

"There was a third fucking person! Marko Trovic— that's your explanation!"

Mason studies me with patient eyes. I know he wants to believe me, but I don't think he does. He gets up.

"I have to take you in," he says. "You'll talk to a lawyer, you'll give a statement to civil liabilities—"

"How can you be so calm about this? Like it's just some little problem, another little hang-up in your grand plan that never materializes? You probably want to take me in just to show everybody what a sleuth you are."

"Don't make me the enemy. Don't make this about us."

"People think I killed my partner, they think I imagined some killer, and you think I'm worried about *us*? Jesus, that's rich."

"Look, Sam, they know I'm here. They're waiting for us. How's it going to look if I don't get you in there? We have to do this right. If they get the idea that you and I are involved—"

"*You're* the one who's afraid they'll find out we're fucking, not me."

"I don't know what happened the other night, Sam, but you have to follow the rules today if you want my help. If you want me to get on the case. If you want to come out of this with your badge."

"Fuck my star. And you, if you think I did it."

Instead of a deserved counterattack, Mason simply turns to leave.

I watch him walk down the hall and I know he won't turn around. I just put a big, fat obstacle between us: my ego. And he won't argue with that. He knows I'm stubborn, because I don't want to depend on him or anybody.

But I can't be stubborn. I need him right now.

"I'm sorry, Mason, you're right . . ." I follow him down the hall into the living room despite the whopping dizziness I feel when I walk without his guidance. My head rush catches up with my feet and I'm about to lose my balance and fall on my face. I look for something to grab on to. The couch is too far away, so I lean on the wall for support. Still, an unbelievable pain envelops my head and brings me to my knees. I can't call out to him because I'm afraid I'll throw up if I so much as open my mouth, so I just shut my eyes and breathe.

Within seconds, Mason is back at my side.

"Oh, baby, oh, no. Are you okay?" He braces me, and his strong hands give me reason to fight the pain. I swallow and try to right myself.

"I'm sorry, Mason," I finally say. "Take me in."

"You shouldn't get so worked up."

"I know." I turn my head and lean into his chest. I feel like a jerk.

"You want to go back to the hospital?"

"No."

"You sure?"

I nod, though I'm not. My head is killing me. My arm is numb. But Fred is dead, and I need Mason to help me find out why.

"Will you help me?" I ask him, knowing the risk of using personal ties, especially those kept under wraps.

"You know I will," he says. "You do what your Sarge says. I'll see what I can find out about Trovic."

"Okay," I say. "Let's go." I want to be as brave as he is.

He helps me up and waits a moment to make sure I can handle standing. Then he walks me to the door and gets me a coat from the closet. A plain black wool coat, instead of the official blue one hanging next to it.

As he helps me with the coat, I ask,

"Mason?"

"Yeah." He opens the door, and when I don't go through it, he takes my hand.

"You love me?"

He leans over and he kisses me and he means it. "No. Not on purpose."

5

The ride to the station is quiet except for the low static and intermittent chatter on the police radio. Mason and I don't talk much, which is just as well. I hate feeling like he has the upper hand. I have to remind myself this is not about our relationship. I will exhaust myself without someone else to talk to, or to be silent with. I need a partner.

Even after all these months together, I sometimes still feel shy around him, more so than when we met. Maybe I'm afraid he'll discover something about me that he doesn't like. Maybe I'm afraid I won't find anything about him that I don't like. What can I say? Everything about him gets me. His smile: his teeth as straight as they could be without any orthodontia. His hands: the skin rough where it should be; his touch still soft. And his voice: when we're lying in bed talking about nothing and everything, and it feels like we're the only ones awake in the whole city. Even when I'm mad at him I can't help but find his boyish curls endearing. Short of shaving his head, he can't get rid of them. I love the curls, in part because he doesn't. Apparently, "boyish" isn't a compliment.

I look at him out of the corner of my eye, so he won't notice. I think he's smiling. It makes me nervous. Why is he smiling?

Was I right —is he going to bring me in like a trophy? Parade me through the station, nodding at the other guys behind my back? *It wasn't easy,* he'll tell them after I'm gone. *She's a handful.* They'll gather like the press around the President, mouths open, taking mental notes as Mason recounts the cunning details of my apprehension. He'll strut around with odorless shit.

Damn him. I have to say something. I know what he's up to. He's not my partner. He works alone.

I turn toward him, prepared to let him have it, but before I open my mouth, I take another look, and I realize I am wrong. He's squinting. Not smiling, rather, trying to see. I should know better; his expressions are calculated to get information, not to give it. He feels me looking at him, and puts his hand on my leg. As we cruise up Lake Shore, the mid-morning sun glares off the lake. I don't say a thing.

When we get to the station, I turn a cold shoulder to my escort. There's no one outside and most of the squads are out for the morning rush, but you never know who's watching. It's risky dating in this workplace. We're all supposed to be on the same side, but we're not. Not really.

Mason and I enter through the side door and take the back halls to Sergeant MacInerny's office. Mason stops outside the Sarge's door and looks me in the eye just long enough to make a connection. Then he knocks.

"Come in," MacInerny calls out. Mason opens the door. Sarge hangs up his phone when he sees me. He looks like he's working on less sleep and an even bigger headache than I am.

"Thank you, Detective Imes," Sarge says. "I commend you for taking time out from your important duties in homicide to retrieve this stray. Sit down, Samantha."

I know I'm in trouble when he calls me that. So does Mason, because he closes the door behind me without setting foot in the office.

"Sit down," Sarge says again. I do. Then he doesn't say anything, and resumes whatever paperwork he'd been doing. I try to focus on something else in the room and let him finish up, but the window behind him is a bright frame that makes my eyes tear no matter where I look. Anyway, I've been in this situation so many times that I've basically memorized the titles on the bookshelves to my right.

I reread the placard on his desk: *The first thing we do, let's kill all the lawyers.—Shakespeare.* I wonder if Sarge has ever been to a play.

I'm picturing him in a box seat at the Goodman sporting a tux, a cream-colored scarf, and theater binoculars when he throws down his pen and takes off his reading glasses.

"I'll assume Imes filled you in on what transpired yesterday morning after you left the hospital," he says.

"Enough of it," I say. "I apologize."

"Too late for that. I've got the captain and half the higher-ups in the district coming at one-thirty."

"Today?" I look at the clock: it's not even nine-fifteen.

"You have something more important to do? You wanted me to postpone, you should have stayed put. They heard about the number you pulled. You're lucky I talked them into a meeting. They want you locked up."

"My partner died. What do they expect me to do?"

"Oh, I don't know, follow procedure, maybe? Understand, Sam: They're not interested in your feelings. They're looking at the facts, and the fact is, you left the hospital without permission. To them this is a case, just like any other, and one that could make a mockery out of the department."

"God forbid a cop should act like a human being."

"Your so-called human reaction could be construed as an attempt to flee." Sarge comes around and sits on the corner of his desk. This is something he does when he wants to keep what he says off the record. Last time he sat there was to give me advice after I threw a fit about Fred's shift change. Actually, I threw a coffee cup through Fred's squad window. With coffee in it.

"Look, Smack," Sarge says, stretching his neck, "I don't think you understand the gravity of what's going on here. If you keep acting squirrelly, someone is going to think this was more than an accident."

"It wasn't an accident! It was Marko Trovic. Why aren't you listening to me?"

"Come on, Smack. I'm on your side, but you've got to play your part."

"Which is what? To pretend it wasn't Marko Trovic?"

"I expect you to give them a coherent account of what happened Tuesday night without theories or antics. You have to tell them what you remember, not what you think. You start speculating, and we're in for one hell of a ride with the DA. They've been waiting for an excuse to put us through the wringer. Your job is already on the line. You tell them the truth."

"If I tell them the truth, I have to tell them I think it was Trovic."

"You can't solve this case, Samantha. You're a part of it. You tell them about this Trovic business, they'll walk out of here with more questions, and they'll direct half of them to the *Sun Times*. We have to keep this among us. We have to let our guys be able to investigate."

"So, the truth, minus Marko Trovic."

"You've got a good four hours to sit here and figure out what that is." Sarge gets off his desk, opens a drawer, and tosses me a pack of Camels. "If I were you," he says, "I'd be nice to them. I'd make it so they don't have to come back."

"You want me to sit here all morning, and then you expect me to pretend I like these assholes?"

Over five hours later I'm smoking the last Camel in the pack and I've just spilled my guts to the Sarge, Captain Jackowski, and an overdressed female attorney with a distracting hairstyle that should be against her profession. Captain Jack has a better 'do. And he's an old balding Polack.

Two fairly inoffensive advisers from Homicide are running the show. One of them acts like he has to pee, the way he fidgets in his chair. I've had at least a pot of coffee since my talk with Sarge and I'm not half as jittery as this guy.

I don't think the other adviser has had any caffeine ever, because he seems perfectly content to respond to my statement by reading every damn word of his report out loud, painfully, in the most monotonous voice

I've ever heard. And he keeps prefacing everything with "Our report." Like this:

"Our report states Officer Flagherty was the first officer on the scene, and ordered Officer Blake to secure the scene while he attempted, unsuccessfully, to revive Officer Frederick Maloney. Officer Hauser tended to your head wound until medics arrived, at which time they determined your vitals stable and transported you to Saint Vincent's Hospital." And: "Our report indicates that Officer Maloney died from a gunshot wound to the posterior mediastinal cavity, a wound that was inflicted from above and behind to an area not protected by his vest."

This is some interrogation. I assume he's working his way up to some piece of information that will contradict my statement, which I felt was a fairly thorough recollection of everything that happened up until the time I was knocked out. (Minus, of course, my belief that Trovic killed Fred. I also left out our conversation about my love life.) Everyone seems interested, though; for once even Jackowski acts like this is an important place to be.

Then the adviser says, "Our report says residue taken from your uniform indicates you fired your weapon, a thirty-eight-caliber service revolver, which was found empty. The bullets recovered from the walls at the scene match the rifling in your gun." I want to rip that damn report out of his hands and see if he has anything to say for himself. At this point, though, I decide to remain civil.

"I told you," I say as evenly as possible, "I fired my gun when I believed someone else was in the room."

The adviser looks mildly irritated, like he's trying to ignore an offensive smell. He turns away from me and says, "The ballistics report concludes that the bullet extracted from Officer Maloney's body *also* matches the rifling in Officer Mack's gun."

Well, that takes care of that. I'm fucked.

"So you don't care what I say. You think I did it."

The attorney settles back in her chair. "The facts show it." She tilts her head and makes sure she has everyone's attention before she says, "What I want to know is whether or not you meant to."

Did she just accuse me of murder? I look around to see if everyone else is as appalled as I am.

"You think I killed Fred on purpose?" I ask.

"You don't have to say anything," the fidgety adviser pipes in, like he's my best friend. But I do, I have to say something to this cocky bitch, and to these administrative drones, and to the guys who are supposed to be behind me.

"You weren't there," I say. "None of you people were there. Don't you hear what I've been saying? I know who did this, and it was the guy who gave me this—" I point to my head. "The fact is, your report is fucked. I did not stick my gun in the back of my own partner's vest and shoot him. It was Marko Trovic, the fucking chauvinist, racist pedophile we were there to arrest." I see Sarge trying to make eye contact with me, but I'm not done.

"He shot Fred. I thought I shot him, but apparently I missed. I also missed the part where you completely ignored the possibility that someone else was in that house at all, and took it upon yourselves to blame me. So here's what I think: Trovic must have knocked me out and used my gun to kill Freddy. Now I have a question for you: Why isn't anyone looking for him?"

The advisers scramble to find some telling page in their report, trying to explain the bomb I just dropped.

"We're just trying to put the pieces together," the one with the monotone says.

"We're following procedure," his partner echoes, but I want to know:

"What kind of fucking procedure gives the guy who killed my partner a good day's head start?"

The attorney revels in the mess she's made while my guys chime in with "This is a sensitive matter" and "We need to decide the best way to proceed" and "We have to consider the family."

"The family? What about *this* fucking family?" I ask, pointing to myself and then the Sarge. I'm getting really riled up, especially when Jackowski shakes his head at the attorney as though he has no idea what I'm talking about.

Sarge puts his hands up like they're a disclaimer. I can't believe he would dismiss me like that. Then he says, "Sit down, Sam."

I don't know what else to do. I have no one on my side. I sit.

"Counsel?" Captain Jackowski asks. "What's the bottom line?"

The attorney pulls out her own report, from which she reads:

"The death of Frederick J. Maloney is currently under investigation. Whether Officer Mack is a victim, a witness, or a suspect, at this time is unknown. What is known is that Officer Mack was present at, and injured during, this incident. Therefore, it is required she take an administrative leave until the situation has been clarified."

They all accept it, even Sarge, like she just read from the Bible.

"You can't clarify anything without me," I say.

The one with the monotone jumps back in with that

damn folderful of papers. "Our report from the hospital indicates a concussion due to blunt trauma to the head. Samples taken from Miss Mack's wound show traces of wood varnish from the floor at the scene."

"I didn't hit my head on the floor. That's ridiculous. I was pushed and I fell on my knees—" I start to pull up my pant leg, but no one even looks at me. They're more interested in looking at photos of my head.

"Further," he says, "the nature of the wound led the doctor to suggest that Miss Mack may experience confusion and other trauma-related effects. He recommends that her condition be closely monitored by a qualified healthcare professional."

"I'll take it"—the attorney throws her pen down—"her story is skewed."

"We're recommending a diagnostic test for post-traumatic stress disorder, as well as treatment," says the adviser with the small bladder.

"That's why you can't look for Trovic?" I ask. "Because you think it's all in my head?"

"We're not looking because the evidence just isn't there," the other one says impatiently. "Scabs on your knees aside . . ."

The monotone shoots his fidgety partner a critical glance and then he says, "Our report states that Officer Flaherty did not find any evidence that supports your claim that anyone else was present at the time of the incident."

"Flaherty couldn't find his own feet if he was wearing shoes," I say. "You need a detective. An investigation. A suspect. Just like they do on TV."

The attorney lets out an overdone sigh to let everyone know she doesn't want to hear my opinion anymore. I know Sarge agrees with me about Flaherty and I think Jackowski does too, but it's his job to be diplomatic, so he smiles at the attorney when he asks, "When can Samantha go back to work?"

"We're going to require a medical and psychiatric evaluation after a period of thirty days," the attorney says, with a distinct emphasis on *psychiatric*. "In the meantime, she should see a state-provided professional, as suggested by your advisers." She turns to me. "Your superiors will determine the grounds for your reinstatement," she says, "once the case is closed."

"So you want me to see a shrink," I say, "and while you figure out whether or not I'm crazy, the killer gets away?"

The attorney looks at Captain Jack like even the dumbest person knows how these things work.

"Well, that's bullshit." I say, and stand up. "I'm not sitting on someone's couch for a month while you guys push papers. If you're not going to find Trovic, then I am. Put that in your report."

No one makes a move to stop me, so I slam the door on my way out.

Once I'm in the hall, I grab my head. I was so pissed in there I'd forgotten about my headache. I start to feel a little queasy and I'm thinking about hiding out in the bathroom, but Sarge catches up to me before I get there.

"Sam, what the hell is wrong with you? I told you to be smart about this. You know our advisers are just trying to make peace with that attorney."

"All those assholes in there think I did it! Those legal guys? They're some pair. They're supposed to help me? They treated me like I was just let out of a straitjacket. And Jackowski acted like he's never seen me before. So did you."

"We're all on the same team, Smack," he says.

"No, we're not. The advisers aren't even in the game. They're on the sidelines taking stats. And that attorney was in a completely different fucking sport."

Sarge looks both ways in the hall before he leans over and lowers his voice.

"You're making a spectacle of yourself when you should be using that smart mouth of yours to pray to God they call this an accident. Do you know what'll happen if this gets turned over to the superintendent's office? You could be in some serious trouble."

I do not feel the need to lower my voice. In fact, I raise it. "You agree with them? You think I should take some time off and come to terms with the fact that I'm nuts?"

"I'm sorry, Sam," he says and puts his hand on my shoulder. "You don't have a choice."

I remove his hand.

"I don't think you're nuts," he says to me as I do all I can to walk away with some semblance of grace. "I just think you need time to grieve. Go see the shrink, let this die down, and we'll make sure you keep your badge."

"That won't bring Fred back."

"Neither will a wild-goose chase for some guy we can't even place at the scene," he says. "Go home, Smack. Take some aspirin. Let us work this out."

"I can't take aspirin," I say, and make for the front door.

6

Here's the part where I feel sorry for myself. "Grieve," as Sergeant MacInerny put it.

I get a bottle of Jameson and a pack of Camels from the liquor store on the corner. I know: no alcohol. Tell that to another Irish cop in mourning.

I go into my place and turn on the TV for company. Then I put on some radio station that doesn't play sad songs, and I set out to forget what I can't remember in the first place.

The first sip of Jameson seems foreign, because it's hard alcohol and it's broad daylight. I'm used to finishing my shift in the wee hours and stopping by O'Shea's for last call. I'm used to the dark. Hell, I'm used to working.

But I'm also used to Fred being alive. I finish my first drink like a dose of cough medicine.

I pour drink number two and then I go through my closet looking for something else to wear. Nothing seems warm enough. I take my drink into the bathroom and run hot water for a bath. I test the temperature with my toes; the water resists a layer of grime on my feet. They need scrubbing after weeks of neglect and long hours in black socks. I run the shower instead. I'll feel better if I can just get rid of this chill on my skin, this residue that sticks to my goose bumps. It hangs on me like the smell of death.

I stay in the shower until I'm waterlogged. When I get out, the steam in the bathroom feels like a cold fog. I wipe the mirror down to see myself. Bad move.

I have always thought of myself as an attractive woman, looking younger than my age. Maybe because I got a late start growing up. Maybe because I was a rookie at thirty, when most cops make detective, and most women have already made homes and babies. Maybe because I work with a bunch of guys who find the opposite sex a fascinating, mysterious being— especially one who's single.

Now, in the mirror, I'm afraid I would only turn heads in fear of making eye contact. My blond dye job is brassy and riddled with split ends, and when I take it out of its ponytail, it parts right where it's shaved bald for the stitches. My lips are chapped and split at one corner. My gray eyes are inset by puffy lids, from crying or the concussion or both. And there are wrinkles. I see wrinkles. I have aged overnight.

I dry off, put on my flannel robe, and get back to my drink. The whiskey is smoother this time, and I feel a little better, but I still don't feel clean. I need to talk to someone. I page Mason. When he doesn't call back right away, I know he won't for a while. I hope he's working. Who will I talk to?

I start to deal with the idea of attending the funeral tomorrow. I should go, but I'm afraid. If I don't go, people will think I'm selfish or I don't care or I'm embarrassed. Or I'm guilty. But I don't know if I can handle it. Maybe I only think I should go so I won't feel guilty about not going. If I don't, maybe I'll regret it.

I'm complicating the simple truth. Fred was my friend. I should be there.

But what if I get there and I'm worried about what everyone thinks? It'll only take a few sideways glances, a whisper from one wife to another. I'll be wrecked. I'll be more wrecked.

I put some water in drink number three because I feel a little tipsy and I don't want Mason to pick up on it when he finally calls. I have to be confident about what happened at the station today, and I have to trust that he's doing everything he can to help me. I don't want him to think I doubt him. Or myself.

The sun is setting and the radio is starting to repeat songs. I turn on every light in the place and shut off the TV. The news is probably starting. I'm probably on it.

"A fatal accident," some reporter will say. My bullet in Fred's body. Case closed.

But how? Fred thought he'd been shot and I couldn't find a wound. Fred said he shot Trovic. I heard two shots. I knew Trovic was there. I thought I shot him. So many gunshots, and then only one wrong bullet—it's like a memory in a funhouse, all backward and impossible.

And none of it matters, because Trovic got away. It was close range, but somehow, I completely missed him. Completely fucking missed him.

Okay, I say *somehow*—I admit I'm a lousy shot.

But I emptied my gun, and Trovic still managed to clear the hell out of there.

But he couldn't have, not right away, because he got around me and knocked me out. He must have been behind *me* when I fired. That's how I got the concussion. And then he must have shot Fred with my gun. But my gun was empty, wasn't it? Anyone who wants to knows we all use the same service guns in our department— supposed to make it easier in the field, if we need ammo. Trovic could have used one of Fred's bullets in my gun. Oh, God, was Fred alive to watch that sick fuck load my gun?

Am I giving Trovic too much credit? He's awful, but is he that smart? And how did he get away? I go over the whole thing again. The pieces fit, but they don't make a picture.

Unless there was someone else. Two guys. Marko Trovic and someone else.

Where the hell is Mason? I have to tell him.

I make drink number four a double, without water, to slow down my brain. I turn off the radio because the songs are like a sick soundtrack to my thoughts. Shiny happy people dancing in circles around my dead partner. And Marko Trovic leading the *Locomotion*.

With the radio off the silence is just as bad, because now my head is making all the noise. The whiskey isn't helping, either. I wish I could stop thinking. I wish I could be distracted. I wish Mason were here.

The phone rings after what seems like hours. When I get up to answer I realize I've finished my fifth drink, so I put all my efforts toward sobriety.

"What took you so long?" I ask Mason, though I know that's no way to start.

"I just left the wake. I take it the meeting went well?"

"They want me on leave. MacInerny agreed."

"Maybe that's not such a bad thing," he says. "What'd they say about Trovic?"

"Nothing," I say. "They think I'm nuts. That I'm confused from the concussion. I think they're hanging this whole thing on my head because they're scared the DA will prosecute on the grounds I had intent."

"Intent to what? Spend the rest of your life in prison? They wouldn't embarrass themselves."

"I'm not so sure," I say.

"Don't worry about the desk jockeys, Sam. I spent all day in the field. I turned that house on Jarvis upside down, and I came up with enough to prove someone else could have been there with you and Fred. And I convinced Captain Jack to let me handle the case. He's got me on a short leash with this Trovic thing, but I think I can swing it."

"Finally some good news." I think about telling him my news, that I think someone else was there with Trovic, but I don't want *him* to question my sanity.

"The funeral's tomorrow at eleven at Saint Matt's," Mason says. "You should be there."

"I don't know if I can." I can't.

"It'll clear up any question about your intent."

While I recognize that Mason's trying to be positive about this, I want him to feel bad. Like I feel.

"Is that all you care about now?" I ask. "The case?"

"Come on, Sam. You know that's not true."

He's right, but I'm feeling defensive. And alone.

"Will you come over?" I ask.

"I can't. I'm on my way back to the station. I don't know how long I'll be there. Besides, I haven't been home in days."

"So you'd rather go home," I say, like home is where his heart is.

"Why are you riding me here? You should be happy about this. I might be able to get you out of trouble."

"And we can't see each other, and we have to keep pretending we don't even know each other—"

"So what's different?" he asks.

"You're right. A normal relationship would be too much."

"This conversation is headed for hell," he says. "I'm gonna go."

I don't say anything because he's right. I light a cigarette.

"Don't drink your way through the service," he says. "Fred'd want you there."

"I love you," I say, knowing the conversation is over, hoping he'll hear enough disappointment in my voice to change his mind about coming here.

"Not on purpose" is his "I love you too." He hangs up.

I take a long drag from my smoke. I don't know why I have to be so flip with Mason. I should be counting my blessings that he's on the case. I guess I don't want to let him think he has any control over me. I've been cool about our relationship from day one. I couldn't even say I loved him when he told me the first time. We had just spent the night together and he was out the door, late to a homicide call. He said the words so offhandedly that I wondered if he knew he'd said them out loud, or that he'd said them to me. My gut reaction: *Why?*

Of course I didn't ask; in fact I didn't say anything at all. But he must've read my mind, because he smiled that smile of his, and he didn't wait around for a response. The next day, he slipped a list of reasons in my locker—nothing fancy, just a bunch of random, perfect observations, jotted in his detective's scrawl. One was *the way you twirl your hair when you're tired.* Ever since then, his "I love you" is a constant reminder that putting your head where your heart belongs is senseless. We didn't fall in love on purpose.

Now, after this, I wonder if he still loves the way I'd eat cold pizza for breakfast, or if my appeal has worn thin. I inhale, another long, lonely drag.

The bottle of Jamcson stares back at me from the kitchen table. I still have ice in my glass. The phone will not ring again. I have to be strong. I have to be ready for the funeral tomorrow. I just have to make it through tonight.

7

When I wake up I'm not sure how I ever fell asleep, or if I made a conscious effort to do so. I'm on the couch and there's a bottle of Tylenol PM next to my empty cocktail glass on the coffee table, so I can put it together pretty quickly. I step on a near-empty bag of Doritos at the foot of the couch when I get up. Must have been my middle-of-the-night meal. I really did a number on myself, because I have no memory of eating them. At least I finally slept.

The sun is up, but it hasn't penetrated the low cloud cover. Lights from the high rise next to mine shine brighter. It'll be a short, gray day. The shorter the better.

I smoke four cigarettes before I finish my first cup

of coffee. My head aches, this time in a familiar way, and I know it's my own fault. All I want to do is take the rest of those Tylenol and wake up next week. I don't want to go to a funeral.

I get dressed. My uniform feels like a costume. It's hot and it doesn't fit and I know I'll smell like a distillery as soon as I start sweating. I button up the shirt just enough so my star hangs flat.

I'm ready to go, but I'm not going. I have another cup of coffee and try not to look at the clock. It's only getting closer to eleven. If I don't leave soon, I'll be late.

I remind myself that Mason is working on the case. Hopefully it'll be cleared up soon, but not soon enough. Not before they bury Fred.

I light another smoke and think about how much Fred detested the habit. I never heard him hassle any of the guys about it, so I don't know why he was always on my case. It was like he had special rules for me. I guess it's because I was his rookie. I'd like to think it was because he loved me.

I swear the only reason I finally leave the house is because I'm out of smokes. Go figure.

Outside it's not as cold as it looked from my window. Most of the snow has melted, and the slush has made a mess out of the sidewalks. I wish it would snow again, to cover up the brown grass. Everything looks dead.

I get in the car and drive up Clark to the White Hen. Inside, everybody acts so busy and normal, en route to better places. I buy a pack of Camels and get out of the way.

I wait to pull out of my parking spot as a stream of traffic rushes by. I think about all these people in all these cars whose lives are exactly the same as they were yesterday and the day before. All these people who didn't kill their partners.

I turn left at Devon. The church is a few blocks up. The steeple pokes out of the skyline like a knife. I try not to look at it.

When I get to the church, I slow down to see who's there. The guy behind me starts honking and I can't very well just pull into the lot, so I drive right past it. I light a smoke and keep driving.

How far would I have to go to get away from all of this? I probably wouldn't make it past the suburbs. My conscience is like a leash. I always seem to be tied to something that requires me to return and redeem myself.

I could run from my problems, but no matter where I go, I'll just end up with a whole set of new ones. I'd drive until I ran out of gas; someone would pull over to help me, and that same someone would steal my hubcaps, my spare tire, and my wallet while he suggested that on some greater level we were meant to meet at this juncture in the road and in our lives, and could he call me sometime?

So I turn around. There's that steeple again. I almost laugh.

When I get to the church this time, I slow down and put on my turn signal. I'm just going to fucking go already, let them all think what they want. Then I see the squads, the officers lined up outside, the flags, and the marquee with his name: "Frederick James Maloney." I'm holding up traffic and no one honks, but I can't turn in. I cannot go in there.

I'm the only one in the bar at O'Shea's this early. Marty, the bartender whose brother owns the building, is splitting his time between me and a few lunchers in the main room. I'm splitting my time between a Jameson and a cigarette. I like this place; it's dark enough so you can only tell the time of day when someone comes in or leaves. The walls are draped with neon flags advertising the latest fruit-flavored cocktail that's probably consumed only by sorority girls at college bars. Photos of the neighborhood in the days when it was mostly Irish blend into the dark walls under the obnoxious ads, along with old Schlitz signs. I wonder if they sell Schlitz anymore. I wonder if they even make it. The place is comfortable. Safe. Probably because a lot of the cops in the district hang out here—which means I'm safe from them today.

Marty ducks into the kitchen with some empty plates. His cheeks are pocked, and I used to think it was the result of teenage acne, but now I'm pretty sure it's life eating away at him, a little every day. I mean, really, to whom does an old, unmarried bartender complain?

"What happened to Vegas?" Marty asks when he comes back.

"I'm sure it's still there," I say and rattle my glass for another round. I'd forgotten about our defunct getaway. Mason and I booked a quick weekend last month, but he had to leave town at the last minute for some case he wouldn't talk about. I should've gone to Vegas by myself.

"You should eat something," Marty advises. "No more booze. How about some chowder?"

"No, thanks," I tell him. Marty slides a basket of saltines down the bar anyway. He flips on the TV above the bar for the noon news. Precisely what I don't want to watch.

The front door swings open and some curly-haired guy shakes out his umbrella. Apparently the snow turned to rain. The front of the guy's shirt is wet where his gut sticks out. I guess the umbrella isn't as round as he is. He takes a seat down the bar and wipes his face with a napkin. I can't tell if he keeps looking at me or at the TV.

Marty comes back with a bowl of chowder. Trying to ignore it, I say—

"What's that guy staring at?"

Marty does his best to avoid answering. It takes me a second before it registers that I'm still in my uniform. Classy.

"Can I have a beer with this?" I ask. Hoping Marty will oblige me, I unwrap some crackers.

"Will you turn that up?" asks the curly-headed guy. Marty does, just in time to hear:

". . . Co-workers and the city mourn the loss of Officer Frederick Maloney." The last thing I want to do is look at the TV, but I can't help it. The cute little newscaster smiles like she's telling us about a parade instead of the end of Fred's life. If only it were mine.

"Our Jackie Davies is at Saint Matthew's Church with an exclusive report. What's the latest, Jackie?"

The screen switches to a bundled-up newswoman standing in front the church. I won't miss the funeral after all.

"There has been a surprising development in the Rogers Park case that rocked the Chicago PD Tuesday night." They cut to a photo of Fred as she continues, "Inside sources have revealed to me this morning that Officer Maloney's death is going to be listed as a case of friendly fire." As I process this information, I see my own photo on the screen.

There I am in my blues, with the dumbest smile: friendly for sure.

Now that curly-haired guy has a reason to stare. I can feel his eyes on me like the bullets in my dream.

"Officer Samantha Mack, pictured here, has a short

but stellar record with the Twenty-third District. Last year, she arrested an Irving Park prowler when she responded to a call at an incorrect address. She transposed the house numbers, and caught the thief in the act. That mistake made her a hero; did her latest mistake cost Maloney his life?"

The stupid dispatcher was the one who mixed up the numbers. I feel like I should explain myself to the guy down the bar and to Marty and anyone who'll listen, but I can't speak when I see, behind the reporter at the church, six officers carrying Fred's coffin down the steps. My partner, gone forever. How do I explain that?

The reporter jumps in the way of the scene and says, "And I quote, 'Maloney died from a gunshot wound.' And that gunshot just may have come from his partner."

I feel like she's staring at me too, through the damn television, so I force myself to look down the bar at the curly-haired guy. He doesn't look away as he sips a draft beer. I can't tell if he sympathizes with me or loathes me. Without emptying his mug, he answers me by dropping a five on the bar, getting up, and leaving. The swinging door offers a brief glimpse of daylight.

Back on TV, the reporter goes on about the police not saying anything definitive and the investigation pending and some other bits of pseudo-information. They do a close-up of one of the pallbearers. It's Mason, in uniform. It's drizzling on his hat and his face is wet, but not with tears. He was selected for his strength.

I tune out the rest of the report, but I can't help watching my partner's coffin being loaded into the back of a hearse.

Mason was right. I should have been there.

Marty puts a Bud Light in front of me.

"Sorry, Sam. This one's on the house."

I nod, though I don't want it. I can't feel the sting of the alcohol anymore. I can't feel much of anything. I don't know what to do with myself, or with what I think happened.

I am an outsider, and the only way I'm going to get back in is to find Trovic, because someone else has to take the blame for Fred's death, accidental or otherwise.

What would Fred do? Probably ask his wife for advice. Not that she'd have a clue; she knows as much about police work as I do about day spas. I doubt she'd want to talk to me anyway, seeing as I'm the reason she's attending a funeral instead of a cooking class.

I shouldn't be so mean. I am sure she's genuinely upset that she has to open her home to a bunch of cops this afternoon. Assuming that's where she'll hold the reception after the service. Assuming someone told her to hold a reception.

I'll bet every cop in the district will be there. And every one of them knows by now that I think Trovic is responsible. Maybe one of them, someone who was at the scene, or someone who worked with Fred, will agree with me.

Mason said I should go to the funeral; would it be a mistake to show up at the reception? If I don't show my face and let everyone know that I intend to make this right, who will? Even if Trovic is caught tomorrow and I'm cleared, I'll still be the one who didn't have the guts to say good-bye. And I owe Fred so much more than good-bye.

If I go to the reception and pay my respects, at least I'll prove one thing: I'm not giving up.

I've had crazier ideas. I finish my drink and head out into the cold rain.

8

T he cold rain is exactly why I don't stop in time and smash right into the back of a very shiny, very expensive Jaguar. The trunk crunches up into the back window like a paper bag. My fault, clearly. And I'm only two blocks from the bar.

We're on North Avenue and we can't exactly pull over; the few parking spaces that exist are always occupied on this street clear out to the expressway. The Jag edges over and stops in the right lane, and I stop behind it, though I'm sure we'll be holding up traffic when the light turns green at Halsted.

The driver jumps out, holding his cell phone like a weapon.

"Sorry," I mouth as he approaches. I root around for my insurance card, but can't find it. If this guy's calling 911 I'm in deep shit. With my luck Sarge will hear the call on the radio. He'll hear me get collared for drunk driving. He'll tell the arresting officer to fire me. Or maybe shoot me on the spot.

The guy taps on my window with his phone, and I am ready to accept full responsibility, but when I get out of the car he flips the phone shut and stands there like he's in trouble.

"I didn't see the light change," he says, or something like it. I'm not really listening, because I'm looking at him, and he's staring at my chest.

He's staring at my star.

I straighten my uniform. "I apologize, I was in pursuit of a suspect," I explain to the citizen. He's out of place with sun-kissed skin, like he just returned from some South American vacation. Dark, unshaven facial hair casually frames his face. He wears overwashed jeans that are probably completely new. He even smells trendy.

I take a step back because I probably smell like a brewery.

"I really didn't want to get the . . . uhh . . ." He smiles at me, raising his eyebrows, admittedly trying to think of a better word than *cops*. "The . . . you know, the authorities," he says, snapping his fingers. "I didn't want to get them involved." He doesn't have the attitude I'd expect from a Jag owner. Or somebody who could be on the cover of *GQ*.

"I'm not much of an authority," I say. "Don't worry about it." I'm hoping my nice-cop routine will get me out of this without too much trouble.

"Thing is," he says, "I don't really want to call the insurance company, either. I just got this car. My premium is already more than my mortgage." He seems almost apologetic, like he's the one who hit me. If I was driving a new Jag and someone rear-ended me, apologies would not be necessary. Sedatives, on the other hand . . .

A car honks behind us and we're starting to hold up traffic. I'm running out of time to get away with this.

"I have a friend who could fix this, at a body shop," I say, more like an order than an offer. I use my smile like a sugar coating. "Of course I'll pay for it."

"So we can keep this between us?" he asks.

I nod shyly. Then I reach into my car, to the dashboard where there's a little notebook with a pen stuck in the spiral.

"Let's exchange information," I say. "Phone numbers."

"I'd like that." He tilts his head and studies me as I write. He knows this was my fault. He knows I could write down a wrong number. So why is he smiling? Does he smell the alcohol on me? Is he flirting?

Another driver behind us lays on his horn, and the guy hands me his cell phone.

"Take this," he says. "I'll call you."

He runs back to the Jag and takes off. I slip into my Mustang, hoping this isn't my only stroke of luck for the day.

I make the rest of the drive to Fred's more carefully, like anyone would who'd just rear-ended a luxury car. I'm fortunate that the guy in the Jag didn't hate cops. Or that he liked me. Whatever.

I take Elston up to Kedzie since these streets aren't as busy, and even if this route is a little out of the way, at least I'm sobering up. As I cut back east on Irving Park to Fred's, I start to feel feverish; I don't know if it's from the alcohol or the shitty weather or the stress. I drive on, hoping my body isn't suggesting that I turn around.

Outside Fred's house I stand on the sidewalk in front of his bay window. Between heavy burgundy drapes, I can see officers milling about inside. I know I look bad. My hair is soaked from standing out in the drizzle after the fender bender. My makeup is wrecked from everything but crying. I look like I walked here. From Peoria.

Sarge helps an elderly couple out the front door and down Deb's icy steps. Appropriate entrance.

MacInerny has prepared himself for me—his custodial expression doesn't change at all between letting go of the old lady's arm and taking mine.

"Smack. Where have you been? We sent Flanigan over to your place—"

"I was out," I say, and as soon as he gets close enough he knows where. It takes the pleasant smile right off his face.

"Jesus. In your uniform?" he asks, without wanting to know the answer.

"I'm grieving," I say. "I gotta talk to you." I want to tell him my theory about Trovic's accomplice.

"Now?" he asks, as if I'm going to say no. "Sam, are you here to pay your respects, or to cause a scene?"

"I'm here for Fred," I say. I'll hold off on the theory.

Sarge accepts this and escorts me inside. As he leads me through the living room, most of the guys avoid my gaze. I guess they can't believe I showed up. I try to keep my eyes on Sarge's back, following him as though he ordered me to. He ushers me to a corner. He's trying to keep me out of circulation.

"When were you planning to fill me in on the case?"

I whisper, since everyone else is. "Am I supposed to get debriefed by Channel Two?"

"There's a procedure, Sam," he tells me, "and you know it. If you want to discuss this further, you should come to the station. Now's not the time. You should be here for Deborah. She's a real mess."

I see Deborah on the other side of the room flirting with Dave Blake, a cop with a rightly disgruntled ex-wife. Yeah, Deb's a real mess. Blake's so enthralled with her I could probably walk up and take his gun without him noticing. Whatever she's whispering must be infinitely more interesting than anything Fred ever said to him.

"It's brave of you to come," Sarge says.

"It's only brave if I'm the one responsible. Look, I don't care what you told the press. I still want answers," though I completely forget the questions when I see Mason and Susan across the room at the buffet table. Susan's diamond ring sparkles as she feeds Mason a pig in a blanket.

"Sam. The investigation is not up for discussion here. Get that through your head or go out the way you came in," MacInerny says.

I should probably take his advice about leaving, but, "No," I say. "You're right. We should talk about this at the station. Sorry."

Sarge looks relieved until he turns around and sees what I see: Mason has left Susan's side, and he's on his way through a swinging door into the kitchen.

"Will you excuse me?" I ask, because there's no way I can continue a conversation with Mason's wife in my sight line.

"Samantha," Sarge says, but I'm already making my way to the kitchen and he can't stop me without drawing attention.

"I'm thirsty," I say over my shoulder. I know Sarge is afraid I'm about to bother the managing investigator in my case, so I watch my time. He's sure to be along soon.

In the kitchen, Mason is opening a beer from the fridge.

"Aren't you working?" I ask him. He hands me the beer, like he planned it, and keeps a cool distance.

"You okay?" he asks. Asshole.

"Wonderful," I shoot back. "Everything is great."

He takes a soda for himself. He's totally unaffected. How does he do that?

"Don't make it worse, Sam," he says.

"I want to meet her," I say.

He laughs. He fucking laughs at me.

"You think it's funny?" I ask, and I put my hand on the door to let him know I'll go, I'll tell her everything, so he changes his tone.

"Come on, Sam, what did you expect? I'm not trying to hurt you. You know who I want to be with."

I believe him, but fuck it. "I want to meet her," I say again.

"Fine. Introduce yourself." He doesn't mean it, because he's taking a step toward me. Just as he extends his hand to me, though, Sarge comes through the swinging door.

"Sam," Sarge says, eyeing the beer in my hand like it's a problem.

I hand the can to Mason, and make that my exit.

In the living room, I spot Deborah moving deftly from one consoling conversation to another—and conveniently away from me. She winds up talking to a guy who's paying less attention to her than he is to her baby grand piano. He's wearing a real nice suit, so there's no way he's on the force. He sticks his head under the lid, checking out the strings and hammers like he's some kind of expert. He must be John, the attorney from Northbrook; when Fred was talking him up one day he said John "moonlights as a keyboard player in a jazz band." Whoopee.

I scan the room, hoping to find someone who wants to acknowledge the fact that I'm standing here. Unfortunately, Deb isn't the only one avoiding me. All the conversation circles closed when I came back in the room. Guys who barely know one another are shoulder to shoulder. I might as well have shown up at Trovic's family reunion. I wish I had a white flag to wave.

Even the civilians aren't interested. A group of men who seem to know one another sit together quietly, in prayer. One of them looks at me like I'm a Protestant. Probably not a good idea to walk up and say hello. I wonder if they're Fred's cousins, or maybe his high school buddies. I assume they know who I am.

When every cop in the room has turned his back to me, I decide this whole thing is a bust. Why did I convince myself to come here? I'm about to make a break for the door when Susan catches my eye. Before I can decide which way to escape, she walks up and offers me her hand.

"Are you Samantha?" she asks.

"Yeah." Shit.

"I'm Susan," she says as she clasps my hand with both of hers, like a politician. Her hands are soft and dry and my palm is sweaty. I pull away when I feel the metal of her wedding band on the back of my hand.

There's no denying her beauty. She is natural, her mannerisms assured, as though no one will judge her. Her eyes are bright, seeing the best in everything, and her smile is genuine, believing it. She practically fucking glows. "Mason has told me so much about you," she says with a voice as warm as a mother's, or a child's. Her hair is pulled back, and when one strand falls forward with the tilt of her head, I know her locks are the true rich brunette they appear to be. Why did I ever dye my hair?

"I hear all the stories—well, you know, the ones I'm allowed to hear." She obviously has no idea that most of the stories she's not allowed to hear involve me without my uniform. I almost feel bad for her. I nod my head and I try to look interested as she goes on: "I've been looking forward to meeting you. It's a shame it has to be under these circumstances. I'm so sorry about your partner. I understand you two were very close."

I look around, hoping for an interruption, because suddenly I don't have anything to say. I see Blake whisper to another guy in uniform, both pairs of eyes glancing in my direction. They're talking about me. My face feels hot.

Why does she have to be so nice? I was prepared to hate her—or at least to find some justification for sleeping with her husband.

Susan steps closer to me. She says confidentially, "I really want you to know, our hearts go out to you. We all know it was an accident. Deborah knows it—she just needs time, I think."

Time to find another guy to push over, I think. On the other side of the room, Deborah hints at a smile as Flaherty refills her wineglass. I must be scowling, because Susan puts her hand on my arm to reclaim my attention. It reminds me of something Mason would do.

"You have a great support group here, including Mason and me," she says. I thought she'd be vindictive like Deb. If nothing else, I thought she'd try to mark her territory.

Mason comes out of the kitchen, looking right at me. My pulse doubles. He approaches us, turns to Susan, and plants a kiss on her cheek.

"You ready to go?" he asks her.

"Only if you are." She latches on to his arm and they stand before me.

"Nice meeting you," she gushes, so sincerely that I think I'm even smiling while she says, "You're more than welcome, if you need anything, you know—"

"She knows." Mason cuts her off, letting me know he's won the battle I didn't mean to wage. Stunned by his nerve, I haven't said a word.

"Take care of yourself, Sam," Susan says. Mason takes her hand and they're off to say good-byes. I stand there and try to recover from the blow.

I don't know why I expected to have any allies in this place, but I didn't expect the only considerate person to be Mason's wife. From the buffet table across the room, Sarge catches my reaction and shakes his head, mid-carrot, disappointed. I want to slip into the periphery. Or out the window. I want out of here.

"Mason, before you go . . ." Deb says, intercepting him on his way to the front door. All the cops in the room watch Deb saunter over to Mason like they're concerned for her welfare. What is she going to do, trip? I catch Randy Stoddard, one of the single officers, eyeing her ass as she steers Mason into the next room. Susan follows behind them without the slightest hesitation.

Two patrol guys compete for Sarge's attention at the buffet, even though the buffet is winning. Flaherty and another cop are discreetly checking the score of the U of I game on TV. Blake and his buddy are sitting on the couch now, looking in my direction. Either they're still talking about me, or there's a clock above my head. I don't need to catch wind of these conversations. Just watching them is enough to know that I'm the only one who wants to know what really happened to Fred. Everyone else just wants to fill in the spaces and move on.

I'm not surprised that when I walk out the front door no one says good-bye. No one wanted me here in the first place. Except maybe Susan, which makes about as much sense as anything else at this point.

At least I know now: I'm going to have to do this myself.

When I get to the sidewalk, I look back at the house. Fred loved that house. He bought it outright from an estate, and he worked hard to breathe life into a place where an old woman had spent her last lonely years. The summer we were partners, he spent almost all his time off remodeling, and all the rest of the time telling me about it. He put in the bay window himself, even though he had never done any carpentry. When I asked him why he didn't just hire someone, he explained, "You can do anything as long as you follow procedure." I think he meant it as some sort of profound advice from seasoned officer to rookie. The next time I picked him up, though, there was a gaping hole in the siding. I bugged him until he finally admitted that his math was off and it screwed up his measurements. He was so embarrassed, he begged me not to utter a word of it to the guys. I didn't, though I did ask if this particular procedure included duct tape (since he used it to secure a plastic tarp over the hole). He said if I kept talking, duct tape would definitely come in handy.

Now, through the windows that Fred eventually installed correctly, I see Deborah and Susan fawning over Mason.

I feel like I need to grieve some more.

9

Things have picked up at O'Shea's. It's happy hour in the loosest sense of the term, since most of the regulars have permanent frown lines. Marty looks relieved to see me alive, since I didn't stick around for his chowder after the newscast. He makes a couple of guys who have been waiting for drinks wait some more.

"Sam, what can I get you?" he asks. I can tell he's hesitant to serve me another drink. He puts a clean ashtray underneath my cigarette when I take a seat at the bar. "You eat yet?"

I haven't. Hollowed by alcohol's empty calories, my stomach gurgles at the thought of food. I need some grease.

"How about some fries?" I say.

His face lights up. "Cheese?"

"Yep."

"Chili?"

"All right." Chili is one of Marty's specialties (specialties being anything he can put in a giant pot and leave on the stove all day).

"Diet plate coming up," he says, and heads for the kitchen.

"And a draft," I call out, hoping he'll serve that first, but he pretends he doesn't hear me and disappears into the kitchen.

I push the end of my cigarette into the ashtray and catch a guy watching me from the other end of the bar. He looks to be about my age, like someone I might know or used to know. Or maybe I don't know him and he just looks like someone else I know. We make eye contact. He paints on a smile, and I know he's on his way over. This isn't a pick-up joint, so I'm not surprised when he knows my name.

"Samantha Mack?"

"What do you want, an autograph?" I ask. His suit and smug manner tell me all I need to know, but he pulls out a badge and tells me anyway.

"I'm Alex O'Connor. Internal Affairs."

"Good for you." I light up another smoke. He sits down next to me without an invitation. Like I expected him to.

"Can I get you something?" he asks.

"Privacy," I tell him.

"Give me a Jameson," O'Connor says when Marty walks by. O'Connor puts a twenty on the bar. Marty looks at me to see if it's okay, but I'm not sure yet, so I don't say anything, and he pours the drink.

"I just have a few questions," O'Connor says.

"So you're not here for the atmosphere," I say. Marty winks, appreciating my sarcasm. He puts the Jameson in front of O'Connor and takes his money.

"I'm not here for your attitude, either," O'Connor says. He's got the intense look of a cop who's never learned his cool on the street. I'll bet most of his trips out of the office are for sub sandwiches.

"Is there a section about attitude in the Officers' Bill of Rights?" I ask.

He doesn't answer. He knows he can't come in here and bug me.

"You sure you don't want to ask your questions officially?" I ask. "On the record? At the station?"

Marty drops off my draft. I turn away from O'Connor and take a sip, but I can feel him sitting there, watching me. He pushes his glass around on the bar without taking a sip.

"All right, what do you want?" I ask. "I'm not psychic, and I'm not in the mood."

"I need your help," he finally says, once Marty's out of earshot.

"I already gave my statement," I tell him. "Didn't you read the report? It's all there."

"There's nothing there that says you shot your partner."

"It's the consensus," I say. "Don't you watch the news?"

"You want to use this time wisely? I might be the only guy who'll help you."

I know what he's doing. He's being the good cop *and* the bad cop. I'm not playing this game.

"You're IA, you'll tack it on whoever you want to tack it on."

"And that's you, apparently."

"Yeah. I shot my partner."

"You're going to take the blame and let my department write it off as an accident."

"It was an accident," I say, trying not to break. If I'm gonna take this up with anyone, it won't be some guy from IA.

Marty comes back with my fries. Oil glistens off the potatoes I can see underneath the overly orange, hand-shredded cheese and I can smell the spicy chili beans. They look so good, but I get the feeling O'Connor's not going to give me the chance to eat them. I get the feeling this whole basket is going to end up in his lap.

"Why are you so loyal?" O'Connor asks. "The money? No. Your district probably pays your snitches more than they pay you. Maybe, hey, maybe it's that code of silence you patrollers talk about—like you're some secret elite fraternity. No, if that were true they'd already have Trovic in a box somewhere, taking a permanent nap. It doesn't bother you that no one's looking for him?"

I consider this, but if the guys on my force aren't behind me, there's no way O'Connor is. He probably got Trovic's name from one of the legal advisers and now he's using it like he's in the know. Like he has a clue. I take a sip of my beer. The alcohol only parches my throat. My fries are getting cold. Still, I'm not talking.

"You're so loyal you'll let someone else get away with murder?"

His eyes are intent on my reaction. I try not to offer one. He slides his glass of Jameson over to me. Before I decide whether or not I'm going to take it, and what it'll mean if I do, Mason comes up behind O'Connor and slaps him on the back.

"Mason Imes. Long time no see," O'Connor says. They're smiling at each other, but they don't mean it.

"O'Connor. The body's not even cold yet."

"I was in the neighborhood."

"Thought you moved."

"Came back."

"Thought you quit."

"Took a promotion."

"You know as well as I do that she can't talk to you now," Mason says. They're talking about me, but they're acting like I'm not even in the room. I'm not sure which one I'd like to punch first.

"Always looking out for the ladies," O'Connor says, prompting Mason to get in his face like they're about to throw fists. I take the Jameson in one shot, slam the glass on the bar, and get up. I can't take any more of this testosterone.

"I'll leave you two," I say. "You deserve each other."

"If you change your mind," O'Connor says, toasting my empty glass as a last-ditch effort.

"If I change my mind, I'll see a shrink," I tell him. I make sure to give Mason the evil eye before I storm out. They can pay for my fries. They ruined my appetite.

10

go home, since the only thing I can do right now is be pissed off.

I sit in my kitchen, waiting for some frozen garlic bread to heat up in the toaster oven. It's a crummy alternative to those fries, but at this point I'll eat anything. Whatever I eat isn't going to get rid of the sick feeling in my stomach, though. O'Connor made it worse. I don't know why he thinks he can bully me. And I don't know what was going on between him and Mason.

And I don't know what's going on between Mason and me. It's no wonder Susan's friendly introduction threw me for a loop. I'd never met her. In fact, I'd never even seen her until today. People think that cops are in this tight-knit group and they always hang out together. That's true. But not when it comes to spouses. Not around here, anyway. Most of the wives don't understand women cops, or they don't trust us. That's how it was with Deb. I shared a bond with Fred that she could never grasp, so I was a threat. Bet she never thought I'd take him away like this. The irony is awful.

I was never after Fred anyway; I was just looking out for him. I didn't want him to get screwed because his heart was bigger than his head. Mason, on the other hand, was already married. He was already screwed, and trying to find his heart again. And he's still married. "Technically," he always tells me. They've been in the process of divorce for over a year, but they reconciled when he thought Susan was pregnant. She wasn't.

While they were separated he transferred to my district, working Property Crime. That was just about the time I was getting fed up with politics at work, during what Sarge called "patrol restructuring" and what I called getting the shaft, because Fred wasn't going to ride with me anymore and it had nothing to do with work. I was even thinking about quitting, and nobody seemed to care. I felt slighted. I felt like they were waiting for me to give up.

Then Mason came along. We met last summer when I did temporary duty on a task force for the first case he was in charge of. I was assigned surveillance with him. We spent a week of overnights checking into a parking garage, pretending to leave, and then hiding in the car, waiting to catch a thief. With nothing to do but sit and watch the entrance, we got to know each other pretty quickly. I felt like a teenager, talking into the morning hours. Mason listened. He understood. He gave a shit. And he gave me the perspective I needed. I did the same for him, since he was going through his own funk with his separation from Susan. We were both heartbroken, and took comfort in knowing we weren't alone. We fell in love in that garage.

We also connected professionally, or, I should say, in our frustration with the profession. Though Mason had years of police experience on me, I was feeling the same burnout he was. We knew putting away criminals was just a temporary fix. Like nuns with straight rulers, we knew as soon as we turned our backs, the bad boys would be up to something else. And we had no way to stop them. We could only arrest them again when we caught them, and wait for them to slip through the system. Again. It made Mason mad; it made me feel useless.

One night we talked for hours about how we'd escape. We'd just pack a bag, get on a plane, and start over. Mason mentioned Longboat Key, a place in Florida where he used to go with his parents when he was a kid. The only part I liked about Florida was Margaritaville, which was nowhere near his childhood vacation spot. I suggested Arizona. My ex-fiancé had an aunt who lived close to the border, south of Tucson. I've never seen more peaceful, humbling scenery. The only part Mason liked about Arizona was the Indian casinos. We settled on California, since neither of us had ever been there. What would we do for money? Mason had always liked the idea of becoming a professional golfer. I said I'd become a contestant on a reality show. Like two kids, we made up the rest as we went along.

And like two kids, our relationship was briefly innocent. But we couldn't help ourselves. Every time we'd talk after he broke the case (he caught the thief impersonating a valet attendant), we both knew there was so much more to say. Our conversations were so intense, so important, that the next step was inevitable. We had to keep it quiet, though, at work especially, because Mason was still in his probationary period and he didn't want to start off at the district on the wrong foot. I didn't care, because my feet weren't even touching the ground.

The first month of our affair turned me around completely. I didn't sleep, but I wasn't tired. I didn't eat, but I wasn't hungry. Time was like a wrench between our encounters, but otherwise life tumbled by me, pleasantly, for the first time in years.

And then, abruptly, it stopped. It was a Tuesday. There had been a mid-autumn cold snap, so I turned on the heat, and I'd just had my down comforter dry-cleaned. It was the first time Mason and I had the same day off in a month, and we'd planned an afternoon under the covers. I was putting clean sheets on the bed when I heard the front door open, and I was certain I wouldn't finish making the bed before we were in it. I was so happy; I felt as though Mason was coming home. I remember thinking things couldn't get any better.

I was right about that. Mason came in and sat down in the middle of the bed while I was trying to tuck in the top sheet. He was so somber I thought he was going to tell me someone had died. I prepared myself for the worst. I got it. Susan had contacted him: She was pregnant.

I insisted Mason go back to her. I wouldn't have it any other way. I loved him, but I couldn't pretend I was more important than his real life. He didn't know where he'd gone wrong with Susan; he didn't know how the love was lost. But he had invested so much of himself in this woman and carried such a huge sense of guilt for not being able to make their marriage work that he had to give it another chance. He owed it to himself. He owed it to his child.

I couldn't stand in the way of the life he spent years creating, no matter how I felt. I called it off. He went back to his wife, and I went into a major depression. For weeks I hid under those covers—the same ones I thought we'd share. Our affair had been an escape for both of us, but I had nothing to return to.

Less than a month later, Mason showed up unannounced. It was Halloween. "Trick or treat," he said. I didn't have any candy. I was still trying to absorb the break-up; I had hardly left the house. I could tell by the look on Mason's face that he missed me. I was afraid I'd have to convince him we were doing the right thing, because I wasn't so sure myself.

Then he shocked me again: Susan wasn't pregnant. Mason thought he could make it work with a child on the way, and when she miscarried, he was determined to see things through. Then he found out she'd lied to him. She had never been pregnant at all. She'd baited him with a missed period, because she wanted him to come back and work on their marriage.

I admit, even though he came back to me, I felt betrayed. How could he have changed his mind about us so quickly? What could Susan have done to make him stay so long? I had to wonder whom he truly loved. Me? Or himself?

Maybe I'd been fooling myself, thinking his feelings were as strong as mine. And after all the drama, I wasn't sure I wanted to be with him at all. But something about him, or maybe about me, made me want to hang on.

So here we are, nearly six months later. Ever since

Mason came back, he's been even more adamant about getting out of here. And even more insistent that we'll be together when the time is right. Yeah, we still keep it a secret. And yes, I know I should stop seeing him. How much do you love someone when you can't share it? I guess I love him that much. There are times when I know that I do. Times that remind me of the nights in that garage.

I have been holding back, though, and it's been to my advantage. I've made the rules. I've called the shots. Until today, that is.

I guess I should have known Susan would be at the reception. I wasn't thinking when I stormed into Fred's. Mason should have warned me, though. He could have at least warned me.

I've finished off the garlic bread and fixed myself a nightcap when I hear the front door open. I can tell by Mason's careful footsteps that he's going to apologize, but I'm not going to make it easy.

He stands in the doorway. I don't get up from the couch.

"I'm sorry about Susan," he announces.

"You're always sorry," I say. "I saw you guys feeding each other—God! It was repulsive! Then I try my best to get out of there, and you go out of your way to hurt me."

"Sam, I didn't mean to hurt you. You showed up there and backed me into a corner. What was I supposed to do?"

"Nothing," I say, "fuck it." I motion him to sit down on the couch but I make my displeasure evident by moving to the other end, lighting a cigarette, and sighing. Twice.

"What's your problem?"

"What's my problem? Everyone thinks I killed Fred is my problem! I'm a mess, I'm alone, and I'm starting to think they're right. You're supposed to be in charge of this case and all I'm hearing is 'friendly fire.' " I take a gulp of my drink to stress my point.

"You think whiskey's gonna make it all go away?"

"Whiskey is *here*."

"You wonder why you're lonely."

I'm thinking of a comeback when a cell phone chimes a generic version of "Little Red Corvette." It's not mine, and I know it's not Mason's.

"Is that you?" Mason asks.

"Yep—" I say and I can't find that damn phone fast enough. I jump off the couch and grab my bag, hanging over one of the kitchen chairs. I whip out the phone and answer it.

"This is Sam."

"Sam with the lead foot?" the guy with the Jaguar asks.

"Yeah, can I call you back?" I say, suppressing a nervous laugh.

"How are you going to do that?" he asks. "You have my phone. Are you in the middle of something?"

"Yeah. Middle of the night," I say. I can't look at Mason.

"Right. I'll call you tomorrow, would that be okay?"

"Sure," I say.

"Great. Talk to you soon." He hangs up. I flip the phone shut and try to act natural.

I sit back down on the couch, this time closer to Mason.

"Who the hell was that?" he asks. I couldn't tell him if I wanted to—I still don't know the guy's name—and even if I did, Mason wouldn't exactly embrace the idea of me taking some stranger's phone.

"It was Wade. Checking on me," I lie.

"Wade. At this time of night," he says without a question. He doesn't buy it. He knows I only use my cell phone for emergencies, if I even remember to charge it and carry it with me, and turn it on and answer it. Right now it's in my bag, but it's dead because I can't find the charger. Mason makes fun of my aversion to technology; he calls it my "resistance to availability."

"I thought I should be available," I tell him. Then I put my feet up and poke my toes between his butt and the couch cushion and change the subject. "Look, I don't want to fight. It's just that I didn't expect to see Susan. I wasn't ready." I hope he'll feel guilty too.

"I didn't think you'd show up today," he says, adjusting his posture to accommodate my feet.

"Why? Because everyone hates me?"

"Because I saw you drive past the church. Come on, Sam. Don't be so selfish. Today wasn't about you, and it wasn't set up for you to get your feelings hurt."

I know he's right, but I still feel like I was an outsider.

"I tried to go."

"You went to the bar."

"I was afraid."

"So you got up your nerve with a couple of stiff ones and showed up at Fred's like a lost dog?"

"You think it was easy for me? I heard on the news—"

"You heard that we're calling it an accident. You knew that. I told you, the press needed a story. I'm working on finding Trovic. You don't trust me."

"I do trust you. I do."

I reach for him. He takes my hand and pulls me toward him and I use my feet underneath him for leverage as I pull myself up and straddle him on the couch. I hug him, feeling his arms around me, and I smell familiar soap on the skin of his neck. He caresses my cheek, then takes my face gently, with both hands, and kisses me for a long time. He pulls away, and with my eyes closed I wait for more. He pulls me toward him and whispers in my ear, "I love you."

I turn and kiss him hard to let him know I love him, too. We hold each other so tight that it hurts my head, but it's worth it. There are tears slipping from my eyes but I will not stop, this is what I've needed, sting and all. His breath and his hands are everywhere, and there is nothing I want more.

I undo his belt and he pulls at my jeans and we can't even wait to get his clothes off or my shirt before I feel him, and I'm relieved to finally be somewhere besides in my head. He is rough but I am thankful to feel pain instead of hurt. I am grateful that this man has the strength to take us both far from this grim world. He guides my hips through his every move and I let him; I am here and in this moment and I can feel what he must be feeling, too. I hold on to him, my arms around his neck; I press myself against him, as though it's possible for me to get inside of him this way, to crawl inside and hide until the world is right again. He kisses me and I know we are connected. I know he can make my troubles go away. I have to believe in something. And I want to stay in this moment for as long as I can.

11

I am calm, finally. Mason is here in bed next to me, resting, and not on his way somewhere else. I feel so close to him, my leg and arm draped over him, my head on his chest, his arm around me. His body jerks, fighting sleep, because he was exhausted and we still made love for hours. He hasn't slept much these past few days. He hasn't left the job. In fact, the captain made him go home tonight. He came here.

I want to let him sleep, but this is too important. The time I have with him is limited. I need to clear my conscience.

"I think I could have saved Fred."

He turns to face me, registering what I said, pretending he didn't doze off. He blinks and squeezes his lids closed. His eyes are bloodshot from being open too long.

"I've gone over it in my head a million times," he says. "If I had called you back when I was supposed to, you wouldn't have taken Wade's shift that night. You wouldn't be in this mess."

"You couldn't have known anything would happen."

"Did you know what was going to happen?"

I guess I didn't. "No."

"You think if you waited for backup, or if you went up those steps faster, or if you had fired your gun one single second sooner, that Fred would have survived?"

"It's possible."

"What if you did all those things, and Fred still ended up dead?"

"I don't know. I just wish I could make sense of it."

"Me too." He yawns. His brooding eyes remind me of my brother when he was a kid, mad at the world because he didn't get what he wanted.

He pulls me close to him again, my head to his chest. I think it's so he can shut his eyes. It's okay; I know he's listening.

"I know why I feel responsible, Mason. Fred said he shot Trovic dead. I believed him. I dropped my guard."

"It was Fred's call. He made the mistake. You did everything you could."

"What if Trovic was hit?"

"I've gone over all the possibilities, Sam . . ."

"But I fired my gun until it was empty. I could have hit him."

"You also could have hit Fred."

I consider that possibility. For less than a second.

I try to push myself away from him but he holds me

there, tight. I thrash around, I jam my knee into his legs, but he doesn't let go.

"It was Trovic. It was fucking Trovic, and now *you* don't even believe me!"

"Sam, stop. Stop it!"

I make another attempt to free myself with a kung-fu move: a ridge hand aimed at his neck that could knock the air out of his windpipe. If Mason didn't block me mid-strike.

"Sam, if you were a black belt I might entertain this. Stop!"

It's no use. He's got me pinned like an amateur wrestler. I cry out like he's hurting me, but he knows he's only hurting my feelings.

"Listen to me," he says. "I'm on your side. I'm doing everything I can to put Trovic in the center of this. I don't know what else I can say. I'm trying to do this right. You have to trust me."

I'm panting, I'm out of breath, and I'm waiting for an opportunity to break free. He doesn't budge. His arms are a vise.

"I don't care if you shot Fred and you meant to do it. I don't care if you had the whole thing planned like a cold-blooded killer. All I care about is getting you off the hook, and if that means finding Trovic, then that's what I'm going to do. I don't understand why you're fighting me on this. I could lose my job, my money, everything we've planned for, and you're acting like I've been spending my time trying to screw you over."

"How am I supposed to know where you're spending your time? You're not here."

"Damn it, Sam, these little stabs at the past aren't getting us anywhere, and I'm not going to justify every single thing I do. Do you want me to solve your case, or do you want me to get a divorce? Pick something to argue about!"

I didn't mean to turn this into a fight. I shouldn't have opened my mouth.

"What am I supposed to do?" I ask. I rest my head on the bed to let him know I'm done fighting. "Tell me what to do."

"You don't listen to your boss, you don't listen to me. You're injured, emotional . . . you're all over the place. You need help."

He lets me out of his chokehold because he knows I'm ready to be reasonable. The fight is over as quickly as it began.

"You're not going to tell me to see the shrink, are you?"

"You know I think those state-funded doctors are full of shit."

"What are you suggesting, then?"

I reach over and pick up my pack of smokes. He turns my leg, inspecting my scabbed knee, and then he squeezes my thigh.

"Maybe you should talk to Deborah about Fred," he says. "You two probably have more in common than you think."

I hope he's trying to make a joke. "What could we possibly have in common? Would she have sent him to his grave if I hadn't?"

"I just think you'd feel better if you told her what you told me. About that night."

"I'd rather see the shrink." I stick a cigarette between my lips.

"All right, tough girl. I know you don't need mental help." Mason takes my lighter from the nightstand. He doesn't smoke. As he lights the flame and the tobacco catches, he looks into my eyes, letting me know he accepts any decision I make, good or bad.

"You're going to go crazy sitting around this place," he says. "Why don't you get out of here for a while? Go stay with Nikki in the burbs."

The last place I can imagine myself is with my childhood pal and her kids. She left the city after high school. She left her spunk somewhere between here and Rolling Meadows. Her husband is nice enough; her kids are birth control. And there are four of them. The youngest one, Isabella, cries every time she sees me. The oldest one, Frank, Junior, thinks I'm cool because he wants to be a cop. He's eight and he never shuts up. If I didn't get stuck answering stupid questions about squad cars, I'd spend the whole time getting the third degree from Nikki about "carrying on" with a married man. And Bella would scream through it all.

"I want to stay here," I say. "I'll keep a low profile, I promise. Just tell me you're making headway."

"I'm working on something," he tells me, reclining subtly to avoid my smoke. "Now that IA's involved, Captain Jack's going to be itching to shut down the case. If he does, I won't even be able to look for Trovic. But I have a connection who owes me at the state's office, and if he can drum up some charges to put out a state warrant for Trovic, it'll put the search above IA's reach."

"You're worried about O'Connor?"

Mason tenses at the name. "O'Connor is working his way up the ladder. He'd love to use you as a rung. He'll use me, too. After you left O'Shea's, he started grilling me about you. Implying that I know more than I should. Suggesting we're together. He'll blow this whole case open if he can prove it. This is his dream come true. You steer clear of him. No matter what."

"I wasn't planning on telling O'Connor anything, Mason." I put out my smoke and snuggle up to him. He doesn't respond; I've launched him into detective mode again.

"We have to be really careful, Sam. Being together is dangerous. I could claim it's just part of the investigation, but O'Connor is suspicious. He could be outside right now, hoping I'm dumb enough to walk out the front door."

"You think we shouldn't see each other?" I want to offer a solution. I want to say something that will appease him. I don't want him to get out of bed.

"I could quit the case," he says. "I can have one of my guys take over. Say I was too close to Fred."

Investigations take about as much time as their crimes these days, and my case will only stay active if Mason keeps it that way. Given the evidence, any other detective would probably be ready to move on.

"You're the only one who can help me." I cling to Mason, hoping to put our pending separation out of my head.

"I know this is tough, Sam. I know you want to be strong."

"I don't want to be strong," I tell him. "I just want Fred to be alive again."

Mason pulls me to him and strokes my hair. He's careful around the stitches. He just stays there with me. We listen to each other breathe.

As we lie there, I want to keep talking, because I don't know when I'll see him again. I know he doesn't want to give up on the case, but I'm afraid that means he has to give up on me. I want him to reassure me that everything will work out, and that we'll be together again when the time is right. But then I think that this moment *is* the reassurance, and that words are redundant.

As I drift off to sleep, I think I hear him say he's leaving Susan. But maybe he just said he was leaving.

12

When I wake up, Mason is gone. My head still hurts despite the fact that I went to sleep sober. Sober, but crooked. My arm is asleep, and I can hardly feel my fingers when I try to touch my head. I can definitely feel my head, though, sore from the stitches. I don't want to know how I must look.

The sun is peeking through my curtains for the first time in days, encouraging me to get up and get going, but I am content to stay in bed for a while to savor the warmth of my covers. For once I think I can let go of the reins and let Mason handle things.

He was right to point out that I keep mixing up my feelings about his marriage and my case. He's so close to both, I guess all my insecurities have come to the surface.

The truth is, I don't want him to think I'm weak. That's why I let him go back to Susan the first time; that's why I kept him at a safe distance when he came back. I'll never let anyone think they can hurt me just because they say they love me. That's what relatives are for. And I'm not going to let Mason believe that my existence depends on him, either. I was all right before we met, and I will move on, somehow, if I have to.

Since Fred's death, though, I've come to regret that I've guarded my feelings. At work, we learn to put emotion aside. That's why most offenders we collar don't like us: They think we don't care. I did the same thing to Fred. I kept emotion out of it, best I could, anyway. But outside of work, it's called pride. And outside of work, I was just a hurt friend.

I should have cleared the air with Fred when I had the chance, but I wouldn't let my guard down. I don't want to make the same mistake with Mason. I don't want to pretend I'm unaffected. I am heartbroken about Fred. I am in love with Mason. Pride doesn't do me any good.

The night Fred died, Mason and I had a date. The way he'd been talking, I had a feeling he had big news. I thought he was going to tell me he'd served divorce papers to Susan. Truthfully, I wasn't ready. I wasn't prepared to let down my guard. I wasn't prepared to take the risk.

Now, I don't have a choice.

The next time I wake up it's to the tune of "Little Red Corvette." I roll out of bed and find the cell phone in my bag.

"Hello."

"Hi, Sam, is this a better time?"

"What time is it?" I ask.

"Almost five-thirty."

I can't believe I slept the whole day. My body must be in recovery mode.

"You busy tomorrow night?" the guy with the Jag asks.

I don't know what to say.

"I'm asking," he answers my silent question, "because I was hoping I could get the number for that body shop."

"I can give it to you now," I say, because that doesn't make sense.

"I was also hoping we could settle this. Over dinner."

Uh-huh. Dinner.

"I should tell you," I say, "I'm seeing someone."

"I should tell you," he says back, "he's not invited."

Okay, then. How do I respond to that?

"What if I put it this way?" he answers the silence again. "You wrecked my car. You owe me. I'm willing to negotiate, but there are terms."

"Besides dinner?"

"Starting with dinner."

"I'll check my schedule," I say. "Call me tomorrow."

"I will. Have a good night."

He hangs up before I remember to ask his name. I stick his phone in my bag and decide to deal with him when he calls back.

The clock on the coffeemaker reads five forty-five. It's getting dark outside. I'm starving, so I start a pot of coffee and root through the fridge for something to eat. Mustard, soy sauce, Hershey's syrup; two Bud-weisers left in a six-pack. All the ingredients for take-out. I go through some menus; then I order egg rolls and a bacon-and-pineapple pizza from Ming Choy's.

"Won awaa," Ming or Choy says.

I have coffee and a smoke and then I hop in the shower.

I shave my legs and under my arms. I use a loofah to wash my wintered skin. I can't shampoo my hair yet, because of the stitches, but the steam helps. I come out smelling like star fruit, or what the bottle claims star fruit smells like. I feel clean.

I put on cotton bikini underwear and a bra and a pair of jeans. I pull my hair back to cover the stitches. They don't look so bad anymore, and my head feels better, clearer. I put on mascara and moisturizer, my favorite evergreen cable-knit sweater and some thick socks. I am doing just fine, I think.

I can't deny that I'm a little excited about having some hot-looking guy after me. Not that I'll do anything about it, or that I'm even remotely interested. I think what excites me is the possibility of making Mason jealous. It's not a competition, really; it's more like a reminder. Fred used to call it "keeping a guy in the bullpen."

I love Mason, but I'll lose my bullpen when Mason loses his wife.

On my way out of the building I notice an unmarked car across the street. Mason was right: Alex O'Connor is watching me. He must have absolutely nothing better to do. It doesn't appear he's going to follow me, but I cut through a few alleys on my way to State Street just to make sure.

I make pretty good time walking down State, maybe because I'd stored up energy sleeping all day, mostly because I don't like anyone keeping tabs on me.

I get my food and cab it back to my place. I can smell the bacon and the pizza dough and it takes all my manners to keep from devouring an egg roll right in the cab.

When I get back and O'Connor is still sitting in his car, I tip the cabbie, cross the street, and open O'Connor's passenger door, pizza in hand.

"What do you want?" I ask.

"Nice place," he says.

"What did you expect, HUD?"

"How do you make that rent, on a cop's salary?"

"I baby-sit on my days off," I tell him. Why did I come over here? My stomach rumbles in protest.

"Your luxury condo, is it part of some beneficial relationship?" O'Connor asks, sounding like a john asking for a date.

"If you call having a dead grandmother beneficial," I say. So Grama had some cash tucked away in her West Side two-flat, and I got it all because my brother never turned up. Doesn't matter how I got it; it's none of O'Connor's business.

"I'm surprised you didn't pick a place closer to the north side," he says. By his tone I think he's working his way toward some assumption about Mason, but I'm already playing enough guessing games, so I say—

"Look, I'm starved. What do you want?"

"Close the door," he says, gesturing for me to get inside the car. "It's cold."

I close the door all right, and head for my building. The heat from the pizza box warms my hands and I can't wait to dig in.

O'Connor gets out of his car and follows me across the street.

"Wait," he says. "We can help each other."

"You're right," I say and his ears perk up. Then I say, "It *is* cold."

"Tell me what happened," he says insistently. "You weren't supposed to work the night Maloney died. Why did you go in for William Wade?" He attempts to get in front of me, as if that'll get me to talk.

"I don't have to tell you anything, I know my rights." I keep walking, even though he's guarding me like we're shooting hoops.

"There are some holes in the report," he says, "and I'm looking into it. I'm helping you."

"So you're sitting outside my building?"

"I'm learning a lot of interesting things sitting outside your building."

"You must not get out much."

"Suppose I hang around the station instead. Start listening to the rumor mill. Start picking up bits and pieces of conversations about the night of Maloney's death. About your relationship with him." He slows down the word *relationship* just enough to piss me off.

"Jesus, you sound like his wife. I was never in love with Fred; I was in line with him. If you'd spent a day on the street you'd understand that."

"How about your attitude, then? Your negligence?"

"I wasn't negligent," I stop him. "It was an accident."

"Oh. Right. But will the gossip spread in your favor? Or will people wonder, will your next partner want to ask you how it's possible to accidentally kill someone who's wearing a vest? Maybe not. Maybe no one will talk about this. Maybe the case'll be dropped before anyone raises an eyebrow."

I don't want to let him think he's a step ahead, but maybe he is. Time to go.

"Let them talk," I say as I get to the entrance of my building. Omar holds the door for me as O'Connor calls out,

"It's easier to tune out, isn't it? Like you don't care.

You think if you keep your mouth shut you won't get hurt. Did that do you any good with your father?"

He didn't need to say that. I turn around and glare at him.

"I read your file," he says.

"Then you know I have a line that should not be crossed. See it?" I draw an imaginary line on the ground that runs between us. I want to whip the pizza at his head.

"You want to know what happened to Fred or not?" he asks.

"I know what happened to Fred," I tell him.

"Then you know why no one's listening to *you*."

"You included." I turn to leave again, with Omar still holding the door.

O'Connor says, "I believe someone else was there, Samantha. I believe someone else killed Fred Maloney, and I think you know who it was."

I pause. I know O'Connor is looking for a reaction, but what do I say? *Jump on board, let's get Trovic!*? I wish I could be as straight-faced as Omar.

"If we don't help each other, your case will be closed, and someone is going to get away with murder," O'Connor says.

"I don't want your help." Without turning around, I go inside. Omar closes the door behind me and I pray O'Connor does not pursue me. I cannot continue this discussion. I am a cop, not a traitor.

I open the fridge and trade dinner for one of those Budweisers. I'm too riled up to enjoy the food. I smoke one cigarette after another and try to calm down.

O'Connor thinks I know who shot Fred. Of course I do. But why bait me?

He had a lot of nerve bringing my dad into this. *Let*

the records show, I should have said, *I did not knowingly participate in a crime.* I had no idea my own father was using me.

The police report should have said something like this: After four years without so much as a postcard, my dad showed up at my door like he'd just been out for cigarettes. For the first time in my life, I knew exactly how my mom felt.

I gave him five minutes to explain. In two, he had me convinced. He had changed, and he was coming back to his family; and that meant me. It also meant my brother, and my dad's second wife Linda, and their kids. He didn't ask me to trust him; for once, he didn't ask me for anything. He gave me a hug and the keys to a new Mustang, and the next thing I knew, I was invited for Sunday dinner with the family. I knew the car was his attempt at an apology; I didn't know he used someone else's money to buy it. I had no idea how sorry I'd be for taking it.

I had the car less than a week before she showed up: Helen Harper, my reluctant benefactor. She came to my condo with the PI who'd tracked the Mustang. They were out-of-towners, I guessed Georgia from her Southern drawl. The detective was a hillbilly in a tie, and he didn't like me at all. He acted like my dad and I plotted to take down the Ford Motor Company instead of one measly Mustang.

My dad always had a way with women. Helen was no different. She was sadly beautiful, with the spent features of an aging starlet. She had money, but the self-bought collection of jewels that sparkled on her fingers meant as much to her as the boxes they came in. She wanted more: She wanted my dad.

Did I know where my father was? Yes. Would it do me any good to tell them? I didn't think so. Helen wanted my dad; so did I. So I lied. I told them he'd skipped town.

Helen's warmth turned to fire. She threatened to involve the "aathoratees." I offered to give her the Mustang, but the PI said I'd need a whole lotful of cars to make up for what my dad took from Helen. I didn't know if he meant that literally. I played dumb anyway, thinking another conversation with my dad would clear this up. If he'd extorted money from her, he'd pay her back, right?

I showed up for Sunday dinner early that week, but there wasn't one. Linda had those tired tears in her eyes, just like my mom, and I knew once again my dad had disappeared.

He was gone, and according to the aathoratees, he took about a half million bucks with him. He left Linda with a diamond ring she had to give back. I have a feeling there was some cash she didn't mention.

I never heard from my dad again. Evidently Helen Harper didn't either, because she forwarded the car payments to me. An attorney in Nashville contacted Linda when my dad died. He'd been living with a girlfriend, and she didn't know where to bury him. That was nearly three years ago.

I finally paid off the car last July.

I force myself to eat an egg roll and I'm washing it down with the last Bud when the phone rings. I know it's Mason. I reach for it.

"Sam, baby . . . what's up?"

I want to tell him. But I don't.

"Just got something to eat."

"How ya feeling?"

I want to tell him. I won't.

"Better," I say. "I slept."

"Good. Look. I ran into a little roadblock. Don't freak out. Jackowski assigned me to another case."

Son of a bitch. O'Connor was right.

"They closed my case?"

"Not exactly. But just like I thought, Captain Jack is pressing us to let it go. He said IA was talking negligence and he wanted it shut, classified an accident, before it got to the superintendent's office."

I wonder if anyone knows O'Connor thinks otherwise. I can't tell Mason.

"I'm not giving up on this, Sam," Mason says. "I've still got that lead at the state's office. I'm going to stay on tonight, see if anything turns up in our favor, but I'm headed to another homicide. Some high-profile Czech nationalist. I've got a few fires to put out before I can get back to this."

"What about Trovic?" I ask.

"I was all over town tonight and I couldn't get any leads. That doesn't mean there aren't any. Be patient, baby. Get some sleep, and I'll be in touch again as soon as I can."

Sleep. After all this.

"I gotta go. I love you."

It is hard for me to tell him I love him, too. But I manage.

As soon as we hang up I pour myself a stiff drink and make a call of my own.

"Four-one-one; city, please."

If I'm going to get to the bottom of this, it looks like I have to find Trovic myself.

"Chicago, Illinois. Last name Trovic. T-r-o-v-i-c. And I need the address." It's the first place I'm going in the morning.

13

Freezing rain spits on my windshield. It's another beautiful spring day, to match my mood. I'm headed west on Grand Avenue, away from the skyscrapers that stand guard over the city, into an Italian neighborhood. This is no Michigan Avenue. Out here, glass storefronts are fortressed by metal gates. There's no window-shopping, and what few people walk the street are as certain of their destinations as the trains that follow the tracks out of the METRA station.

I stopped for coffee at the Caribou on Wells before I came down this way, but the caffeine doesn't seem to be doing the trick. I didn't sleep well, and I'm pissed at myself about last night. I thought about calling Mason back and telling him about O'Connor. Instead, I drank.

I thought about calling him this morning, too. Instead, I dumped all the rest of my booze in the sink, took some Tylenol, and promised myself I'd sober up. My head hurts from too much drinking and my mind has been going in too many circles.

I make a mental list of what I know. One: Mason is still looking for Trovic and he doesn't want my help. Two: O'Connor is using scare tactics because he needs my help. And three: Neither one of them can really help me. I certainly won't get them to compare notes. That's why, four: I have to investigate on my own.

Once I've passed the sparse blocks between expressways, Grand Avenue bends northwest, and I realize my mind's not the only thing going in circles. I cross Chicago, again, and Division, again. As I keep driving farther into unfamiliar territory, I wonder if the address I got from Information is correct, because Trovic wouldn't exactly go unnoticed here. When I pass Homan Avenue, I know I stick out like a white female. I'm the only driver who stops at a red light and, believe me, I didn't want to. As I approach Pulaski, the neighborhood turns white again, and I know I'm getting close.

I park on the street across from the address. The place looks like the landlord abandoned it a long time ago. The building is a three-story walk-up, set back from the curb by a yard full of ignored, resilient weeds. The glass in the windows is warped like it used to be in the fifties. My parents' building had windows like this. My mother spent a lot of time staring out of them.

It's a busy street, but that doesn't make it friendly. Two young kids stop a game of street ball to watch me cut across their playground, though passing cars don't merit the same attention. Another boy stares me down as we pass on the uneven sidewalk. I keep my head up, but I don't look him in the eye. I don't want any more trouble.

I go up the steps to the door and buzz number three. No one answers. I assume Trovic's place is on the third floor, but I peek inside the first-level window anyway. The place is stuffed with big white couches covered with plastic. There's a glass-enclosed, mirror-backed cabinet filled with tacky crystal figurines. The carpet is white, and it looks like no one's ever set foot in the room—until a short, sturdy Eastern-European woman pushes a vacuum through the foyer. Her hard eyes are set on me, telling me she is not the cleaning lady. She is the mother of this house, and I am looking in her window.

I step back to look for signs of life in the upstairs windows. I buzz the door again. No answer. I hear the kids from the street getting closer because one of them is bouncing the ball, and they're talking. But not in English. They sound much older than they looked in the street.

I hold the call button and say, "Hello? Mrs. Trovic?"

"Go away," a female's thick accent says from the box.

"I need to speak with you; I'm looking for Marko Trovic," I continue. Something hits me lightly in the back of the head. I don't dare make a quick move, so I turn slowly and keep my face as expressionless as I can. A group of about six boys has gathered at the bottom of the steps. I say boys, but they're probably old enough to have done jail time. And they're coming out of the woodwork, all wearing black leather coats like a gang too cool for colors. Another guy comes around the corner, does some hand sign to his friends, and then flips me off. I might as well have worn my uniform, with the attitudes I'm getting.

"I don't talk to cops," the voice in the box says.

"A cop?" one of the boys asks. "A cop bitch?"

"Do any of you know Marko Trovic? It's important." I hope they'll respect my sincerity, if not my profession or my gender.

"No-a speak-a ingles-a to you-a policia," says a skinny one wearing a big gold medallion that reminds me of Trovic's. They all laugh and a few speak to one another in Serbian. The only word I know in Serbian is not a good one, and I hear them say it repeatedly.

Then I hear a horrid scraping sound, and I follow it to a big kid standing on the other side of the street, in front of my car. He has long, slick black hair that's either wet or held in place with too much gel. His black leather jacket is a slightly longer variation of the other boys'. It fits only his wide shoulders and hangs open, the belt dangling, letting his stomach protrude. Somehow, he is not cold; it could be the heat of the moment. Traffic blows by him like a soft breeze. He grins slyly, and puts a set of keys in his pocket.

The rest of the boys carry on in Serbian, congratulating one another like they've just overthrown a regime. They're getting too close to me. I turn back to the box for one more try:

"Please, if I could just speak with you, I have some information—"

I stop cold when the front door opens and Marko Trovic stands in front of me, holding a little girl in his arms.

I back away from him and catch myself just before I fall backward down the steps. I didn't think it would be this easy. My mouth hangs open, and I try to cover my astonishment by saying something. Nothing discernible comes out. Did I just gasp?

Trovic is pleased by my reaction and his cheeks swell into a smile that reduces his eyes to sharp slits. He does not look the same as I remember; he is not the monster I built him up to be in my mind. The reality is he's a bloated lowlife whose defiant smile is actually pathetic. I don't see hate in his eyes; in fact, it's more like vacancy. And, I'm taller than he is. I don't remember that.

"What do you want?" he asks. Immediately I know why he does not scare me; he might be a Trovic, but he is not Marko. Marko's use of the language was vulgar and imprecise. He slurred his words. And, if this guy were Marko, he would certainly know what I wanted.

I spread my feet to stabilize my stance and cross my arms. "Marko Trovic?" I ask, just to make sure.

"Marko is not here. What business do you have with him?" So he is not Marko, but rather Marko's spitting image, minus ten years, plus thirty pounds and proper English. He must be a very close relative. The little girl squirms in his arms.

"Papa," she proclaims.

"Papa is not here." He puts her down. "Go on." She skips past me into the arms of one of the boys on the steps. "Go on," he says again, and then I realize he's talking to me. Behind me, one of them bounces the basketball. Every time it hits the ground I want to flinch.

I stand my ground, because if I let these guys scare me away, I'll never get to Trovic. "Do you know where Marko is?" I ask.

"I already told the police; we cannot talk. We do not speak the same language. My brother, maybe he speaks your language for a price, but I will not speak for him."

"You're his brother?" I ask.

"We are a tight-knit family," he says; "you mess with one, you deal with all."

That wasn't exactly the answer I was looking for,

but then the kid with the medallion interjects something in Serbian that causes all the others to chime in. It sounds like they're quarreling, the way they talk over one another. Marko's brother doesn't participate; he just watches me.

Maybe I shouldn't push it, but I ask him, "What are they saying?"

"Our language has so many more swear words than yours," he says, "though the meaning is generally the same."

I don't stick around for a translation.

Thankfully the guys clear a path for me to leave, though they shout at me all the way to my car. I slip in and lock the doors and start the engine. In the sideview mirror I can see a nice long scratch on my passenger door from the long-haired kid, but I'm not going to examine it now. I get out of there quick, hoping Trovic's tight-knit family doesn't extend much beyond the guys on that porch.

Once I'm a few blocks away I wipe the sweat from my forehead and comb through my hair with my fingers. That's when I find the gum one of them threw at me.

I should have known those guys wouldn't tell me where Trovic is, but maybe I learned more from Marko's brother than I would have had Marko been there himself. I don't think Marko's brother knows where he is, and I don't think he wants to, either. He said Marko spoke our language, "for a price," he said, like Marko was stooling for us.

If Marko was working with us, Fred didn't know about it, or he wouldn't have been so hot to bust him. Snitches might not have any sense of allegiance, but we do, and Fred would have stepped aside for the cop who got Trovic to flip.

What about Fred's snitch? If he was willing to give

up Trovic once, he'd do it again. What was his name? The guy trying to get himself out of a little trouble. The guy with the funny walk. The guy . . . ? Shit. I remember everything but his name.

When we met him at the El stop, Fred said the guy had paged him, so he must have talked to the snitch on the phone sometime that night. That means there's a phone number somewhere. Maybe in Fred's locker. Or at his house. Or in his phone records.

I'm done going in circles. I drive up to North Avenue, turn right, and head for the station to see what I can turn up.

14

I fight the church crowd and too many Sunday drivers to arrive at the station past noon. A cold front is pressing up against the lake, and it's starting to snow again. It's usually quiet on weekend days; today the ward's lot is full of cars. Must be people attempting to clarify misdemeanors or tickets on their day off. I park my Mustang in a No Parking zone and go inside.

I pass the front desk and the line leading up to it. I'm glad they're busy, so I don't have to stop and explain why I'm there. I make it past the locker room without running into anyone, but on my way to Records I see William Wade through the break room window. I haven't seen him since before the accident. I didn't expect to see him smiling, let alone laughing his ass off. Paul Flanigan, the rookie last seen in his boxers, is standing at the coffee machine saying something that must be hilarious. Normally I would pass up this chance to socialize, especially since Paul has asked me out every single time I've ever talked to him, but that's exactly why I stop. He's too young for me, but he's the perfect recruit to get me those records. And who knows? Maybe it's a good joke.

When Wade sees me in the doorway, he stops laughing. Paul straightens up like I'm the chief. I wonder if the joke is on me.

"Hi, darlin'," Wade says, his voice from deep in his throat, like a blues singer. He is by far the largest cop in our ward, but he's not fat or muscular or strong. He has big, aching bones that used to be intimidating. Lately, they only slow him down. Today, he looks more tired than usual. He looks like an old man. He probably looks better than I do.

"Thanks for going in for me the other night, Smack," Wade says, like the other night was ordinary. He's got to be kidding.

"No problem," I say. "You were sick."

"I should have been there," Wade says.

"Well, you weren't and I agreed to cover. So drop it." Wade is known for using his conscience like a doctor's note. Like he's allowed to feel bad and therefore get off the hook. I have to admit, he's grown on me since I've worked with him, but I'm not in the mood for his routine now.

"I couldn't go to the funeral," he continues. "He was my friend."

"He was my partner," I shoot back. I'm not going to let him feel sorry for himself.

Wade pushes on his stomach like he's feeling around for a specific pain. I'm surprised he's not checking his pulse.

"Excuse me, I'm still not quite right," he says, and with that, he ducks out of the room.

"Go right ahead," I say. I couldn't have shown up at a better time. I set my sights on Paul.

"How's it going?" I ask.

"Oh, you know. You, I mean, you're okay?" He's trying to be polite about staring at my head.

"Looks worse than it feels," I say, though I'm not sure it's true. The stitches itch like hell and the bruising has spread over my right eye and turned my cheek a mustard yellow. I can't imagine the fluorescent lights in here do me justice.

Paul checks his watch. He doesn't know what else to say, and I don't want to scare him away, so I get right to it. "Paul, I need a favor. I need Fred's phone records."

"You need a subpoena or a warrant for that, don't you?"

"Yes, Paul. That's where the favor comes in." I step toward him, ready to elaborate; he backs away like I asked him to hold a tarantula.

"Oh, you, I mean, I couldn't . . . I'd be . . . you want me to steal them?"

Genius. "No, not exactly. You know how to work the copy machine, don't you?"

Blake walks by the window and I'm afraid he'll pick up on our conversation. I try to act casual, but Paul catches on when I look over my shoulder to make sure Blake kept walking.

"You're not supposed to be here, are you?" Paul grins and I think he's enjoying outranking me.

"You are a smart one," I say. "You'll make detective in no time."

His lower lip quivers just a little. Did I hurt his feelings? I may have misinterpreted the grin; it could have been because I actually paid attention to him. I might have approached this entirely backward.

"I'm sorry," I say. "I'm under a lot of . . ." I look over my shoulder again and see Wade through the window, so I wrap it up. "I'm an asshole. Could you just do it? For Fred's sake?"

Paul doesn't answer. I keep my eyes on him as Wade returns with a bottle of Pepto.

"Coffee's ready," Wade says, and pours himself some.

"Coffee doesn't bug your guts?" I ask.

"Everything bugs my guts," he says. "I choose my battles."

I keep looking at Paul to see if he's gonna come around. He definitely doesn't know what to do with my attention.

"Coffee, Smack?" Wade asks, stirring milk into his mug. "Paul, get her a cup, she looks like she hasn't slept in a week. You feeling okay?"

Wade knows I don't answer obvious questions. He pulls out a chair and encourages me to sit as Paul offers me a mug. I take both, even though I don't want either.

"Cream?" Paul asks.

"Black is fine," I say, and I smile at him. Wade watches Paul fumble around with some sugar packets.

"Black, Flanigan," Wade says, taking the packets from Paul and tossing them back on the counter. Then Wade comes over and sits on the edge of the table, shutting Paul out like a kid in the way of an adult conversation.

"Really. How're you doing?"

"Give me a break, Wade," I say. He wasn't the one I wanted to talk to, and I'm not interested in niceties.

"Wait, Sam. There's something I need to tell you." He leans toward me to be sincere, but he looks at my mouth instead of my eyes. I don't like it. He's too close. "I feel responsible," he says. "I feel horrible."

"Don't breathe on me," I say, "and don't feel guilty."

"At least let me say I'm sorry." He puts his hand on my shoulder. I promptly remove it.

"You just did," I say. I am unable to share a Hallmark moment. This meeting isn't going as planned. I stand up so I can see Paul and say, "Thanks for the coffee." I start for the door.

"Have you considered counseling?"

I almost don't turn around, because I don't think Wade's talking to me. But I do turn around. And he is talking to me. I wait for him to say he's kidding. He doesn't.

"Has everyone around here lost it?" I ask.

"It was just a thought." That he said out loud, to make himself look good in front of a rookie.

"I don't want to know what you think, Wade. You don't come into work when you *think* you might be sick, and you're telling me to see a shrink? You think I should waste my time getting mind-fucked by some tight-ass smart guy who's never held a gun? Is that what you'd do? Or would you be out on the street finding the guy who made this mess in the first place?"

Wade answers me with a swig from the bottle of Pepto.

"Sergeant MacInerny—" Paul starts, but I cut him off.

"Sergeant MacInerny. Don't you have an opinion of your own? Or are you just jumping on the bandwagon, hoping to get Fred's seat?" I'm trying not to yell, but he's obviously not going to help me, so I don't need his input.

Paul looks at Wade, who stands there with this fake overblown horrified look. He still has the bottle of Pepto in his hand. Neither one of them says a word. They're acting like I caught them with their pants down.

Or they're acting like the Sarge is standing right behind me.

"My office," Sarge says.

I never did know when to take a hint.

"Shut the door," Sarge says. I feel like I'm in the principal's office. "What do you think you're doing, Smack?" he asks.

I don't have a cheeky response. He'd see right through it anyway.

I sit down and he parks his ass on the desk, assuming his "off the record" position. I can tell by his lack of anger, or any emotion, for that matter, that we've been here too many times. He flips through some papers. I don't know if he's giving me a minute to answer or trying to make me squirm.

"I don't claim to know the right way to grieve," he finally says, "nor do I want to know your method. But you can't run around the city with a death wish."

"I don't have a death wish." I don't think.

"I had a guy at Trovic's place who saw you." Oops. He tosses his papers on the desk like they're adding to his trouble. He goes on: "*We* are looking for him, Sam. *You* are on leave. I told you, if you want to know about the investigation, you come talk to me. You don't take matters into your own hands. This thing is enough of a mess. The captain wants me to shut it down. The goddamned lead investigator is wasting his time and taxpayers' dollars questioning your sanity instead of the guy you claim is responsible—"

"Mason Imes? I thought he wanted to help. For Fred's sake," I clarify.

"Sam, I think Imes wants this case about as much as I want a colonoscopy." Sarge slides his ass off the desk and extracts a ticket book from his back pocket. "The last thing I need to worry about is you acting like Nancy Drew with a drinking problem."

He opens the book, rips off a ticket, and hands it to me: a fucking parking ticket.

"Seriously?" I can't believe it. Any of it.

"I don't even want to know how your front bumper got that way," he says. "Or your passenger door."

I stare at the ticket. This just became a hundred-and-fifty-dollar conversation.

"I assumed you understood procedure," he continues, "but since that's apparently none of your concern, I'll give it to you plain. I can't let you enforce the law any more than I can let you break it. Either you do what counsel advised and make an appointment with Dr. Atkin down at headquarters to get your head taken care of, or you go home and ponder your next career move. Either way, you'd better not show your face at this station again until you get your act together. I will take your badge before I let you make a mess of this district."

There's really nothing I can say, because he's not going to let me argue. I'm pretty sure he's heard enough out of me.

"Okay" is my smartest response. I wait to be excused. Sarge gives me a disappointed nod and I stay on my best behavior until I get out of the station.

As soon as I'm outside, I wish I had put up a fight. Like Sarge would go see a shrink if he were in my shoes.

Like any cop would. I want to spit on the squad next to my car that's sitting in the same No Parking zone. I rip up the ticket.

Mason's got some explaining to do. Why in the hell would he tell my boss he thinks I'm nuts? He must have been doing it for show, since he's paranoid someone will think we're together. God, this has been a shitty day. I'm ready for a hot shower and a stiff drink. I shouldn't have thrown out all my booze.

I get in my car, rev the engine, and turn up the heat. I'm just about to peel out of the lot when Paul taps on my window. I should have known I wouldn't get out of here without his usual dinner proposal. Doesn't matter what I said to him earlier. Talk about not taking a hint. I roll down my window.

"Where you headed?" he asks.

"I was thinking a short pier somewhere."

"You wanna get a drink?" he asks. He has to be freezing. He can hardly talk because he's trying to keep his teeth from chattering.

"Paul, I've told you. I have a boyfriend."

"I didn't ask to be your boyfriend."

"I can't."

"Can't, or don't want to?" he asks. Normally I'd have driven away already, but there's something about the way he's standing there, fidgeting, persisting. In a strange way it makes him look confident.

"I'm laying off the alcohol," I tell him. "I have to get my head straight, among other things."

"Good," Paul says, "I'll take that excuse." Then he puts his hands on my window frame and leans in.

I back away, unsure of what he thinks he's doing. I hope he didn't interpret my response as an invitation to ask me out for an O'Doul's. He's quickly losing all the cool he'd been building up as he just hangs there, looking at me in this weird, expectant way. I think he's waiting for me to say something, but I'm afraid he's going to put the moves on me through the window. I can feel my mouth hanging open just a little, anticipating a "no." I hope he doesn't think I want a kiss.

"I don't want you to underestimate me," he says. He leans in just a little more, and I have to stop him.

"Don't—"

Then I spot some papers sticking out of the sleeve of his coat, and I realize this isn't a come-on.

"I do know how to photocopy." He drops the papers into my lap.

I stuff them between the seat and the center console and get ready for an awkward moment, but Paul plays it off.

"Guess I'll go see if Wade wants to battle a Budweiser," he says and rubs his hands together.

My eyes dart around to avoid his. He takes the hint.

"Well, good luck." He starts for the station.

"Paul?" I call after him.

He stops and looks back at me, his cool kept in check by the cold wind.

"Thanks. I owe you."

"Next time you're drinking," he says, and winks at me before he hustles back to the station. Maybe he's not so young.

I wait until I get home to look at the records. Most of the numbers are the same: to and from Fred's house. Checking in with Deborah. Ugh.

I recognize a lot of the other numbers: the station, Wade, Mason, Sarge. There are a few out-of-state, and some anonymous numbers with area codes in the suburbs.

I pause at two outgoing calls to the same number

placed on the night of Fred's death. I pick up the phone and dial it.

A bitchy-sounding woman answers. "Fireside." The background noise nearly drowns her out. It sounds like I called backstage at a rock concert. "Hello, Fireside," she says again. As she hangs up, I remember: That's where we met the snitch, across from the Fireside Tap. I just called the bar. I mark the number.

I see another phone number repeated a few times, but not on the night Fred and I went out. I call the number anyway and an operator's recording tells me the line is being checked for trouble, which is the phone company's polite way of saying the bill hasn't been paid. If this is the snitch, I doubt an overdue phone bill will make his list of priorities at this point.

If I could just remember his name. What did Fred call him? Something cute like Tweety. Buddy? Damn. I can see his face, I could pick him out of a lineup, but I have a mental block about his name. I can't think of it.

I call the phone company.

"Hi, I'd like to make a payment on my bill."

"What's the number, please?" a woman asks.

"773-929-4013." I hear her type it into her computer.

"And the name on the account?" she asks. She sounds like she's done this at least a hundred times tonight, and at this point she's either on the verge of falling asleep or into a boredom-induced coma. I hope she wants to make this easy.

"Actually, I'm not sure . . ." I say, "I think it's in my husband's name . . . but maybe it's mine, oh, I don't know . . . Can I just give you my credit card number?"

Silence from the other end. I think she's yawning.

"Hello?" I ask. I hear her typing again.

"Is this Mrs. Burdsell?" she asks.

"Yes."

Birdie. That's it!

"It's in your husband's name, Edward. Go ahead with your credit card number . . ."

I hate to cut her off, but every second that passes is another that puts my case to rest. I hang up and look for a warmer pair of socks.

Then I dig out my old .22 from behind the coatrack. I secure it inside the leg of my boot, pull on some earmuffs, and trudge back out in the snow to find Birdie.

15

From outside, the Fireside Tap actually looks inviting. The windows are fogged by heat and condensation; the sign and surrounding lights are covered with a friendly layer of snow.

Inside, it's evident that the coziest thing about the place is its name. There is no fireplace. There is definitely no warmth. The cold air I bring with me when I walk in is met by cold stares from the regulars. A truck driver couldn't get comfortable here.

"A guy named Burdsell been in here tonight?" I ask the blond bartender, trying to sound like I know whom I'm talking about. She looks like she'd just as soon serve me a fist as a drink if she didn't run the risk of falling out of her low-cut shirt. Maybe it's because she knows I'm full of it, or maybe she doesn't like women in general, but she doesn't look happy to see me.

"Don't know anybody by that name," she says. I catch a young stocky barback sneak her a look, and I know *she's* full of it.

"Must not be here yet." I look around the place like an eager customer. "What do you have on tap?" I grab a stool and light a cigarette.

"I already called for last call," she says, as she pours one shot of everything in the well into a Collins glass for a Long Island. It's maybe ten after ten and from what I can tell, everyone else is just getting started. A couple of guys in the corner are sharing a pitcher, in the middle of a game of darts. Two serious drinkers have a record of empty Scotch glasses on the bar, and money to refill them. There's a full pitcher of MGD on the spill mat.

"You sure I can't sneak one in? While I wait?"

She points to a sign above the top shelf liquor that says, WE RESERVE THE RIGHT TO REFUSE SERVICE TO ANYONE. I get that I'm anyone.

"I'll just wait, then," I say very nicely.

She is clearly miffed by my decision. She takes my cigarette from the ashtray I set it in and puts it out.

"We're closing," she says. "Early."

"What about that Long Island?" I ask, testing her claim.

She puts a straw in the glass and sucks up almost everything but the ice in one try.

"Gotcha." I slide off the stool. There's no point in starting a fight with the wrong asshole. I bite my lip to keep from thanking her for her courteous and helpful service, and decide to let her think she's scared me away.

On my way to the front door, I can see in the reflection of a painted Heineken mirror that she's watching me leave.

I can also see someone poke his head out from underneath a booth at the back end of the bar, and I wonder if that's his pitcher of MGD on the spill mat.

I keep walking, but I'm sure as hell not leaving. I think I just found the snitch.

Once I get outside and down the block, I turn the corner to the alley and light a smoke. It quit snowing but it's still really cold, and it bugs me that I have to play this game. That bartender hated me. I can't believe the last woman who didn't was my boyfriend's wife.

I lean against a wall outside the rear of the bar. I'm in the shadows, so the snitch can't see me when he opens the back door.

"Thanks," he calls behind him.

"Dumb ass," the bartender says and pulls him back into the doorway for a kiss. I can't imagine the sloppy details, let alone what I'm sure is the torrid history of this affair. I'm not done smoking and I don't feel like a foot chase, so I let them finish and wait for him to come to me.

The bartender closes the door and the snitch makes for the street. He walks right by, with that funny walk, and I can't believe he doesn't see me. I could put my foot out and trip him. I'm betting he's not too bright.

"Hey, dumb ass," I say and grab him by the jacket. He's only half-resisting, so it's easy to drag him across the alley.

"Ow! What the fuck?" he whines.

"Your name Burdsell?"

"Huh?"

"You heard me," I say. I slam him against a chain-link fence to let him know I'm not whistling Dixie.

"Who wants to know?"

"The police, that's who."

"I know who you are, and I'm not talking."

"You should be. You already talked your way into getting a cop killed."

"No, I didn't," he says. He's not fighting me anymore, so I let go of him.

"You sent Fred Maloney and me to get Marko Trovic. Fred's dead. Marko's nowhere to be found. You're gonna tell me you pissed off an entire police force to snitch on a child molester? There's more to this, and you'd better spill it."

"Why should I?"

"Because everybody knows you sent us, including Trovic. So tell me what's smarter: to talk to me, or to take it up with Trovic, who thinks you set him up?"

"I don't care what you fuckin' cops think you know. You don't scare me," he says, and starts to edge away from me to see if I'm gonna let him walk away.

"Who are you hiding from, then?" I ask. "You think Marko Trovic will want to hear what you have to say if he finds you?"

"Marko won't find me and I'm not talking," he says, and starts down the alley like I can't stop him. I pull my gun from my ankle and get behind him, pushing the barrel into the back of his neck hard enough to make him change his mind about walking. And talking. He turns around. I'm aimed at his face.

"Marko Trovic isn't gonna come after me. I work for him," he suddenly feels like telling me. The .22 always works.

"So why'd you send us after him?" I ask.

"He told me to."

"We were set up?" I lower my gun just a little as I absorb this news, so I'm not ready when the blond bartender comes barreling down the back steps and knocks me to the ground. Before I can get into a defensive position, Birdie snatches the gun out of my hand, slams me into the pavement, and aims the gun at my head.

"Thanks," he says to the bartender. Then to me he says, "You think you're some smart chick now, running with the big boys. You're gumming up the works, and you'd better watch it or Maloney's not going to be the only one who ends up dead."

I'm looking down the barrel of my own gun, and all I can say is, "I want to know what happened to Fred."

"Like you don't know," he says.

"Fuck you," I say. I don't care what he's pointing at me, I want to get up and beat the shit out of him, but he raises his arm and cracks me, in the eye, with the blunt end of the gun.

Everything goes black when my head hits the pavement. It takes a second before I register how badly it hurts, and then I grab at my face and try to breathe through the pain. It takes all my strength to keep from screaming.

I hear the bartender's laugh echo through the alley as I roll away from where I think Birdie is standing. I hit the fence, pull myself up, and get ready to kick, blindly if I have to, at anyone within range.

I shield my torso with my free hand and open my one good eye. Birdie's gone. So is the bartender. So is my gun. Guess the snitch isn't as dumb as I thought.

I sit in the alley and give myself some time to adjust. I'm not bleeding, so I put some snow on my eye. I close my other eye to stop a tear from falling. All I needed was another knock in the head. Damn it, I'm not gonna cry because of my own stupidity. Countless hours of kung fu lessons and I just got my ass kicked by a guy named Birdie.

Once I can see straight, I let go of the fence, stumble out of the alley, and walk toward the bar. The front door to the Fireside Tap is locked. Just when I really wanted a drink.

I can't believe we were set up. I knew Fred was hot to get Trovic; I didn't know the feeling was mutual. And I don't know if what I just did will make Trovic hot to get me.

I try to think of my next move, but I'm not sure what to do. I'm digging myself a pretty deep hole to get to the bottom of this, and now I'm afraid someone is planning to bury me in it.

16

I stand in my bathroom looking in the mirror. I'm a real sight, with a huge black eye and a scraped-up face. I look like I got knocked to the pavement and hit in the face with a gun.

I'm trying to get some athletic tape straight on the bandage over my eye when Mason shows up in the doorway.

"What happened to you?" he asks. I didn't expect him. I haven't made up my mind to tell him what I've been doing, or whether or not I want to know if he's been doing anything. Call me crazy.

"I fell," I say, with as little agitation as possible.

"On what?" he asks.

I manage a fierce glance through my pain-induced scowl. "You making your rounds?" I ask.

"I am," he says, "but I missed you." I guess he doesn't pick up on my mood, because he grabs my waist like he's ready to sex it up as I try to get out of the bathroom.

I can't take it. I push him out of the way and go into my bedroom.

"What did I do now?" he asks, and I feel like his wife.

"Absolutely nothing." There. I said it.

"Okay, Sam," he says and it sounds condescending. "What's with the attitude?"

"You come here after a shitty blow-off phone call over twenty-four hours ago and you want to know why I have an attitude? You expect me to sit around and wait for you to work on someone else's case, to spend another night with your wife, to tell my boss I'm insane, and then be grateful when you stop by for a piece of ass?"

"Are you just going to be a bitch or do you want to know what's been going on?" he asks.

"I'm being a bitch because I don't know what's going on," I say. I know I'm jumping to conclusions because I have no answers. I'm picking a fight because I lost the last one with Birdie. And I'm scared I'm in over my head.

Mason sits on the bed and invites me to join him. When I do, he takes the roll of athletic tape to help fix my bandage.

"You talked to your Sarge?" he asks.

I nod and the tape gets stuck to my eyebrow. Mason is careful detaching and repositioning the tape.

"He said you think I'm crazy and the case is a waste," I tell him straight out.

"What did you want me to say? That I'm in love with you, and I want to kill the asshole who did this to you?"

I shrug; I guess that wouldn't work.

He tears the tape and folds it over, finished with my head. "You want to know what I told MacInerny? I said, 'Samantha Mack just lost the guy she came up with. She's fucked up in the head. If it was an accident, so be it, but if we don't make sure, we'll be losing two good cops instead of one.' However that was translated to you is no fault of mine."

I can believe that Sarge put a spin on Mason's words, but it's that last part that gets me, because Mason wouldn't say anything like it. He wouldn't say I'm a good cop. If he did, Sarge would know he was bull-shitting, because as far as Sarge is concerned, Mason has no interest in me or in my case. Mason's got to be bullshitting one of us.

"So what's next?" I ask, hoping I can call him out on something more concrete.

"We're going to close it."

Son of a bitch! Did Mason just pick up a shovel and throw dirt over my hole?

"Listen," he says, because he can tell whatever's about to come out of my mouth isn't going to be dainty. "My guy at the state's office is getting the warrant. IA can't touch that. If I can pull in Trovic on another charge, I'll get so far up his ass he'll be begging to confess to Fred's murder. Sam, I've thought through all the options. It's best this way. No internal investigation, no pressure from the chief, no press, no link between us . . . and you'll be cleared."

He smiles at me, twirling the roll of tape around his finger, proud of himself and his plan. And for a moment, I think maybe he isn't throwing dirt over my hole. Maybe he's helping me dig.

But then he looks at me. And in his eyes, I see a flicker of exhilaration. Like he's getting away with something. Like he's lying.

I wonder if his wife ever notices this look. I wonder if I've overlooked it. Because somehow, Mason always seems to get what he wants.

"What happens if you don't get Trovic?" I ask. "There's no investigation, no questions, and no link between us. Sounds like *you*'ll be cleared, and I might as well turn in my star." And there's not a damn thing I can do about it.

"What else do you want me to do?" He tosses the athletic tape on the bed with the offhanded indifference of someone who knows he has control.

"I want you to quit telling me what I want to hear. I want the truth."

Mason gets up. He's had enough.

"Look who's talking about truth," he says. He starts pacing the room. "You're the one flirting with rookies and faggots in Jaguars. You're the one drinking yourself into a pathetic hole. Next you're going to tell me you fell into whoever's fist gave you that eye. It's no wonder you're suspended. Misunderstood. Alone. I mean, look at you."

"You're no help," I say, "if you're watching me instead of Trovic."

He stops and looks at me. For a second I think that if he was ever going to hit a woman it'd be me and it'd be now, but he takes a controlled breath and goes back to his pacing. Maybe because he was thinking the same thing.

"I'm no help?" he asks very calmly, and in a distinctly softer voice, "I'm the only one trying to solve your case. *You* are the one sabotaging my every move. I can't get any of those Yugos in Trovic's neighborhood to talk to me because you went in there and shook them up. In fact, I can't get a line on anyone connected to him because your outburst at the hearing tied everything up in evidence. And all the evidence does is incriminate you. I don't have any legal right to go after Trovic, and you're not making it any easier by snooping around on your own."

His voice has been building with every word, so he stops talking, quits pacing, and puts his anger in check. Then he looks at me, and that damn smile takes over. He can't help laughing at his own words, as though explaining this to me is futile, and the situation painfully ridiculous.

"And you want to talk about us?" he asks like it's the most outlandish request of all. "I got that asshole O'Connor breathing down my neck because he's got a small dick so he thinks he's gotta fuck everybody. I got a boss asking why I'm so interested in an open-and-shut and I gotta convince him how important I think it is to 'take care of our own.' I got a suspect who's probably just arrived at the tropical get-and-stay-away of his choice, and on top of all that I got you, my own little fragile headcase, who asks more questions than a five-year-old. So you're right, I am no help."

Mason waits for me to say something, but my foot's already pretty well lodged in my mouth. And I already have a black eye.

We both stand our ground, me with my silence and him waiting for my apology. He won't look at me, and I don't even know what to say because I feel like I just cross-examined my own witness. I can't tell him that a snitch and some guy from IA put ideas in my head. I can't tell him I doubt him. But I can't tell him that I believe him, either: he said I was a good cop and a headcase with equal conviction.

After a moment the silence wins, and he turns to leave. When he gets to the door he takes one last look at me, and it's then that I can see his eyes are welling with tears. I have never seen him cry.

"Mason, don't leave." I really need to get my head checked if I let him walk out on me. "You're right," I say, "I'm sorry. I know I'm screwed up."

"You hit your head, baby," he tells me, the familiar reason back in his voice. "I'm just trying to make this right." He waits, his hand on the doorknob, and I try to think of something to say.

I want to tell him that someone else hit my head, that Birdie cracked me in the eye with my own gun. That Fred and I were set up, and Birdie thinks I know why. I want to tell him that O'Connor believes someone else killed Fred, too, and that he wants my help. And that I don't have a clue what to do.

I want Mason to give me answers that will point me in the right direction. Details about the case. About his marriage. Anything that will help erase my doubts.

He doesn't say anything. Instead, he answers me in a way that could never be rehearsed, with a look that I can only explain by its effect: I feel it in my heart. It is the simple truth. He believes in me. My doubts are in myself.

I'm halfway across the room to start with a hug and finish by telling him everything. I know we can get through this. I just have to be honest.

Then that generic version of "Little Red Corvette" chimes from my bag, and I am caught again.

"Funny," Mason says, opening the door. The tears stay in his eyes. "I thought you hated Prince."

He slams the door when he leaves.

I don't know what I'm gonna say when I catch up to him, but I throw on my coat and grab my shoes as I go for the door. I bolt down the hall and I'm at the elevator in seconds, but I'm a second too late. I take the stairs.

Sixteen flights later I run through the lobby and out the front door. I get out to the sidewalk just in time to see Mason drive away in a squad car.

Omar's outside too, putting someone in a cab. He whistles for another when he sees me. He hints at a smile when I jump into the cab, and I'm almost offended. Then I realize I'm carrying my shoes. I hold them up through the window, as a concession, as we drive off.

"Follow that car," I tell the cabbie.

"The squad car?" he asks.

"Yeah. The squad car."

17

Can I get arrested for this?" the cabdriver asks me as he sizes me up through the rearview mirror.

I poke my head through the hole in the plate glass divider.

"No. Hurry up, he's turning left," I say.

"Fucking cop. Police doesn't obey law and I'm the one with a ticket," the cabbie says.

"He's my boyfriend." I cut him off to stop him from going on a cop-hating rant, though I could be in the mood to agree. I sit back and put my shoes on.

I wonder why Mason's driving a squad. He always refuses to take an unmarked car because he says it's as obvious as a regular squad, and he doesn't want anyone to get the idea he's hiding (go figure). But he usually drives his own car. We're headed north on Clark and I hope Mason isn't going to the station, because I won't be able to talk to him there.

Then we pass Addison and head west on Irving Park and I know this route, too. I get this increasingly sick and unfortunately familiar feeling in my gut. The heater blows stale air at my face, and I start to sweat. I really hope we're not going to turn onto Fred's street.

We do.

"Fucking cop," I say.

The cabbie nods like he could have set me straight a long time ago.

"Stop here and cut your lights," I say, a block from Fred's. The cabbie pulls over, shuts off his headlights, and hits the fare total. I don't make a move. Mason parks the squad on the street and runs up to Fred's house.

"You getting out?" the cabbie asks. Fred's porch light comes on. I wait.

Deborah answers the door in a bathrobe. And not a depressed widow kind of bathrobe.

She throws her arms around Mason. From the backseat of the cab it's hard to tell if it's a passionate hug, but the cabbie must have a clear view, because he resets the fare to zero.

"I am sorry," he says with a question mark after he says it. "You want I wait?"

Deborah leads Mason inside the house and shuts the door. I feel stupid and I'm about to tell the cabbie to keep driving, but then Deborah pulls those dark red drapes shut and I think about telling him to drive across the sidewalk and through the damn window. I take a twenty out of my pocket and keep control of my smile.

"Don't worry about it," I say. "It's not what it looks like."

"Thank you," he says to the money. I'm glad he doesn't ask any questions, but I still feel like I'm walking a plank between here and Fred's front door. As I get out and make my way slowly up the sidewalk, the cabbie takes his time counting my twenty-dollar bill. I know he wants to see what's gonna happen.

Having an audience in the street is embarrassing. I can't just go up and knock. I figure my best bet is to make like I know what I'm doing, so I head around back through the gangway, because I haven't got a clue.

The grill in the postage-stamp-size yard brings back this vague memory of a summertime barbecue—one of those events I would have skipped had I known any better. We were all having a great time until Deborah had a fit. Fred said it was something about the way he cooked the steaks, but I got the feeling it was because she wasn't the center of attention. We were sitting around telling war stories, and I could tell she was getting jealous. I told Fred that anyone who gets jealous about working a beat patrol has issues. He stuck to his story about the steaks.

I found out later that the real reason Deb was pissed was because Fred had been showing off an old Walther he bought at a gun show. It wasn't that she cared about having firearms in the house; she was mad because he'd spent the money. She was always concerned about money.

The money issue wasn't the only thing that didn't mesh in their relationship. Everyone could see they were polar opposites. She's frilly, concerned with where to get the best pedicure and what kind of cheese to serve. Fred was a real guy. He felt a sense of accomplishment when he mowed the lawn. He considered Cheez Doodles an acceptable hors d'oeuvre.

Fred always stood by his word, though, and he

promised Deb he'd do whatever it took to make their marriage work. He sold the Walther to a buddy in the Eighteenth District. He switched to overnight shifts. And he stopped hanging around with me. I guess he was in love. I was not part of whatever it took.

The tiki lights Deb put up on the back porch are gone now, and the grill doesn't look like it's been cleaned since that barbecue. The moonlight isn't bright enough to bounce off what's left of the snow, so the yard is completely dark. From out here, looking up into the house through the sliding glass door is like watching a big-screen television. What I see inside is like a soap opera, and I wish I could turn it off.

Deb and Mason are sitting on the couch. She's pawing at him with her pretty hands. He's got her laughing through her tears. She opens her robe. Mason covers her up. Consoles her. She kisses him. He stops her.

I'm weighing the consequences of running up the porch steps and banging on the window when something rustles in the alley behind the garage. I instinctively reach for one of my guns, then realize I don't have either one of them, which is probably a good thing since I'm an intruder and I'm pretty sure I want to kill one of those people in there. When a light flashes from the alley, I look for a place to hide. And damn quick.

I crouch behind some bushes that run along the fence to the alley and I swear I hear footsteps, so I listen forever. When it's quiet for a while, I get on my feet. Then, as I sneak between the garage and the fence, I hear the rumble of an engine. I peek around the corner into the alley and see a yellow Chevy truck just as someone puts it in gear and speeds away.

I catch my breath and tell myself it was nothing. Where else are people supposed to park, if not in the alley? The muscles in my legs are stringy—I haven't moved this fast since the night Fred died, and the rush I feel makes me want to puke. I walk slowly back along the fence, into the yard.

Of course when I get there, the goddamned sliding door's curtains are closed, so I'm left with only a part of the story. As usual.

I make my way back around the house and I can't find any other windows to look in, so I force myself to sit in the gangway and wait for Mason to come out. I don't want to talk myself into anything that may or may not be going on in there.

I don't have a watch. It seems like I've been sitting here an hour. Since my brain is working overtime, I'd like to underestimate, but I've had enough time for my fingers and toes to consider frostbite. I remember one winter when Fred and I picked up a drunk who'd passed out in someone's yard. His clothes were wet from urine and he was stuck to the grass, literally. He was homeless, he was disgusting, and he was too wasted to notice he was seriously frostbitten. We'd seen a hundred like this guy, but for some reason I wanted to help him. Fred knew it; I knew we were ten minutes from the end of a long tour, and Fred was ready to go home. The next shift would have to handle the drunk. "It's just so cold out here, Fred," I said. Fred answered me by checking his watch. I took off my gloves and pulled them on the drunk's hands. Fred answered me with a weary sigh. Then he gave me his gloves, pulled the drunk out of the grass, and arrested him. Fred handled the whole thing, all the way through booking, charging the guy with enough to make sure he'd be locked up for the night. Without a complaint, and without another word about it, Fred stayed on an extra two hours. He helped a stranger that night because he always helped me.

I wish I had his help now.

I'm out of sight next to the steps when the front porch light finally comes on. I argue with myself about what to do. I wonder what Deb and Mason would say if they opened the door to me. Maybe I'll stand up and say something accusatory. Or I'll jump up and startle them with a simple "Aha!" Or maybe I'll just come out and ask Mason for a ride.

When the front door opens, I don't do anything at all. For some reason I'm scared shitless, like I'm the one being found out. I'm frozen, and all I can do is listen.

"Mason?" Deborah says.

I hold my breath when Mason stops on the steps. I can see his feet; I don't know if he can see mine.

"Yeah, Debbie?"

A low sound starts in her throat and works its way into a . . . a moan? Is she crying? Laughing? Mason's feet disappear back up the steps, and I strain to see. They're hugging, but I don't know what kind of hug.

I'm still squatting there like an idiot when Mason lets her go and skips down the steps. He doesn't see me. When the front door closes and the porch light goes out, I watch Mason get into the squad.

I have no clue what the hell just happened but I don't think it had anything to do with policework.

I think about running up and tapping on the squad window before Mason takes off, but I know if I confront him now he'll have a perfectly reasonable explanation. And he'll really think I've flipped my lid if he knows I followed him.

I'll have to wait and bring it up next time we talk. Ask him how Deborah's doing. Be polite, ask, *how's she holding up?* If he says he doesn't know, I'll know better.

If I don't say anything, if I wait it out, Mason could wind up sucked into Deb's feminine vortex, just like Fred. I start to shiver. I don't think it's because I'm cold.

What was Mason doing here tonight? Consoling Deb? She must be really fucking forlorn if she's going after my boyfriend.

I think back to the last time I was here, at Fred's reception. The way Mason steered Susan and me in whatever direction he wanted, and the way he followed Deb. I think about that look in his eye tonight, like he knew something I didn't.

Have I been conveniently oblivious? Do I know him at all?

The only thing I do know right now is that I gave the cabbie my last twenty. I have a long walk home.

18

sneak on the brown line El at Irving Park and save myself the walk. There are some benefits to knowing the system. And who's going to arrest me?

My stomach turns as we pass Addison. Even though the lights are off, I can see Wrigley. The station is just past it. I wonder if Mason is there.

The train slides down the track loosely, knocking from side to side as it rights itself on the rails. Three college girls get off at Fullerton, giggling and intoxicated, concerned with where to get burritos and whether or not to bother with an eight-thirty class. A black man in an old coat watches them, probably wondering how they've managed so long without getting mugged. He digs through a plastic bag, produces an or-

ange and peels it, dropping the rind back in the bag.
The smell of citrus reminds me of Longboat Key. I
wonder what it's like. I wonder if I'll ever know.

The train dips underground, now fast and certain on
its track. I get off at Clark and Division.

On Division I walk past at least a dozen bars. Half
of them have been around forever; they're suburban-
male traditions. The other, newer half seems to come
and go in months. They're geared toward younger,
richer, more beautiful people who apparently get
bored easily. I wish I had a few bucks. I need a drink.

I get to my building and a new guy mans the door: a
young white kid with an olive tinge in his complexion.
I decide he's Greek. Though I've seen him before, I
haven't introduced myself. I don't feel like it now, either. He lets me in, nodding his head as a welcome. I
nod a thanks.

The lights are still on in my place and for a second I
hope Mason is here, though I know he isn't. I decide to
go back downstairs to the liquor store, because I don't
think I'll be able to sleep without a little help.

As I grab my bag, my answering machine beeps
once, alerting me to a single message. So, do I play it
now? Or do I get myself a bottle, and some nerve
along with it, before I listen to what Mason has to say?

I push *play*.

"Sam, it's me. Are you there? Pick up." A pause. Is
he formulating a story? "Look, I'm sorry I left. This
thing is getting blown out of proportion. We have to
trust each other."

It's going to take more than that.

"After I left," he says, "I went to Fred's house. Deb's
had guys staying over there, and it was Flagherty's
night, but his kid is sick. So I go over there, figuring I
can maybe get some information while I'm at it. And

she's a total wreck. Apparently some insurance man had been there, asking questions that made her feel like she'd robbed a bank. I tried to comfort her, and— you're never going to believe this—she starts coming on to me. She was so desperate. It was sad. And it hit me, you know, it made me think of you with someone else. I couldn't handle it. Are you there, Sam? Are you listening?"

I am. And he's got me hanging on every word.

"I hope you know I'm in this with you. Just give me time. And trust me."

I want to.

"I'm going home tonight," he continues. "I've got to do some damage control. I hope you understand. I wish I could be with you."

Me too.

"I'll be in touch." He hangs up. Why wouldn't he? He said everything I needed to hear.

I am shivering again. I can't get rid of the chill running down my spine that reminds me of sitting in Fred's yard, wondering if Mason is telling the truth.

And here I am, alone again. So I am having an affair with a married man. When do *I* start to feel cheated?

Instead of going out for alcohol so I can get drunk and emotional, I decide to cut out the middleman. I put on my pajamas, get into bed, pull the covers over my head, and cry myself to sleep.

19

I wake up when the phone double-rings, meaning it's the doorman. I look at the clock: it's just after eight. I hope I don't have a visitor.

"Hello," I say into the phone.

"Good morning, Miss Mack. A delivery for you," the Greek kid says.

"Can you bring it up?"

"Right away."

I'm startled when I catch sight of myself in the hall mirror. My eyes are so swollen from last night's breakdown that I look like a battered geisha. I make an ice pack out of a tray of cubes and a Ziploc bag and I press it to one eye at a time until I hear a knock at the door.

The Greek kid hands me a vase, with floral paper protecting whatever's inside.

"Thanks," I tell him, and hand him a couple bucks. After an awkward pause, he nods and gets on his way. When I put the flowers down on the kitchen counter, I realize I'm not wearing a bra under my off-white pajama tank, and I think the kid saw more than I wanted him to.

I tear the paper off a dozen long-stemmed roses. No card. That's how I know they're from Mason; roses are his apology MO. They are beautiful, the stems so long and the petals so red that they almost look fake. I don't want to draw the parallel.

I feed the flowers their packet of stuff and then I snag some cold pizza from the fridge for myself. I'm three bites in when the phone rings again, this time from an outside line.

I consider hiding, finishing this piece of pizza and the whole rest of the box, feeling sorry for myself and waiting to be rescued. And then I answer anyway.

"Smack, it's Wade. How ya feeling?"

"I've had better hangovers."

"You feel like breakfast?"

"Not really." I drop the half-eaten slice back in its box.

"I'll be at the Granville," he says, "if you're interested."

"Not really," I say again.

"Come on, Sam. Get off your ass and come talk to a friend. We have to stick together."

"Fine," I say. "Give me half an hour."

I hang up and throw on a pair of jeans. I decide a charcoal turtleneck will draw the least attention to the discoloration in my face, but it's tough to pull over my beat-up head. The ice pack didn't do much for the swelling, and the bump on my forehead where Birdie knocked me is the size of a peach pit. Sunglasses are the only solution. I grab a pack of smokes and my Ray-Ban knockoffs and head out. Real peachy.

At the Granville, Wade's in his usual booth, dumping cream into his coffee. The tables are all set close together and crowded with customers. I keep my sunglasses on and navigate around them. The place stinks of grease; the odor reminds me of Wade. He comes here so often he never gets the smell out of his clothes. There's only one waitress, and she's always here, and she's on her own time. People who know this place don't mind. Best breakfast in Rogers Park, they say. Eggs are eggs to me, though, and I wouldn't wait for them.

Wade watches me come in like he knows what's under my sunglasses. He pushes his plate aside when I sit and remove them, revealing loveliness.

"I'm not your father, Sam," he says when I sit down.

"I know." And I know he's going to lecture me like he is.

"That's why I'm not asking."

"Okay, I won't tell you."

"I am not asking," he says again. "But you'd better quit this nonsense."

"I will."

He's not convinced.

"I will," I say again, with a little more feeling behind it.

"When? When you're dead?" Wade stirs his coffee like he's just added gunpowder to it, like it'll explode if he's not careful. I'm thinking he'll explode if he's not careful.

"You look like you're feeling better," I say, trying to avoid a scene.

"You look like you've been through an oil change without a car," he says, to the whole restaurant. No one really pays attention, but I'd like to put my sunglasses back on.

"I don't get it, Sam. You're the sweetest face on the force, with an A-1 bullshit detector and a one-way ticket to the top, if you'd just take it. But you let your damn heart get in the way. And now you want to find this guy Marko Trovic. For what? For justification?" Wade removes the spoon from his mug and points it at me like a threat. "You don't want justice, darlin'. You want to put a fuckin' gun to his head."

Wade puts the spoon aside and pulls up his shirt-sleeve, showing me the scar from the bullet wound on his shoulder for the hundredth time. I figured I'd hear this story again, though, so I give it the appropriate inspection.

"I know how it feels, Smack. Some days I'm still looking for the guy who shot me. Thing is, they can put fifteen guys on your case. They won't stay long. Time goes by, less than a week even. Investigations get old quick. Guys gotta keep up with the crimes. You're not so important, especially if you've still got a pulse. They got four, five people killed in this city every day and somebody's gotta explain every one. You think you're special? You're alive. They don't have time to feel sorry for you."

"I don't want anyone to feel sorry for me."

Wade shakes his head like he believes me only because he has been through the same thing.

"Six years go by and I still think I see his face on the street sometimes. It'll be the same for you. If they do nail him? You'll be lucky if he doesn't find a loophole in today's goddamned politically correct, baby's ass legal system. 'Officer so-and-so wasn't nice to me. He hurt my feelings.' And just like that, a pedophile has a way out because someone asked him the wrong question, or, better yet, a cop finally gave him what he had coming to him. One punch in the mouth, and the guy's back on the street cruising for blow jobs from teenage boys."

"That doesn't always happen, Wade." Ever since he got shot, he's been real bitter about the way things are handled, legally anyway.

"Yeah, sometimes justice is done. So what? Say everything goes as planned, and they catch your man and manage to lock him up. You'll spend every day he's in jail dreading the day they let him out."

Wade flags the waitress, and he might be the only person in this whole place she acknowledges on the first attempt.

"Trust me," he says, "everybody's sorry, but nobody cares. You have to make it right with yourself."

The waitress comes by and takes Wade's plate, though he hasn't eaten much. "They put enough cheese on that, Bill?"

"Sure did. Thanks," Wade says, and I wonder who else calls him Bill.

"You like to order something?" she asks me.

"Coffee, for now."

"Cream?"

"Black's fine."

"Like her eye," Wade says. "Bill" is hilarious.

The waitress winks at him, and I'm sure some variation of this familiar banter goes on between them every morning. She walks away, her plump lower half forcing her hips right and left with every step. She's probably a grandmother; some kid's favorite lap.

"You were saying?" Wade asks.

"*You* were saying," I correct him.

He leans in close and I can guess from his breath that he ate all his sausage. "You're a good cop, Sam. I knew it from day one. It's in your blood. Remember your first week? You skipped your brother's arraignment to help me nab that arsonist up at the Wilson El platform."

"He was lighting *people* on fire. You needed help."

"So did your brother."

"I couldn't help him." My brother had been arrested for shoplifting at a mall out in Dundee. "I knew he was guilty." I didn't know he'd never talk to me again.

"Admit it: the Job came first."

"I was a rookie," I say. "I didn't know what was important then."

"Yes, you did."

Wade sits there, waiting for me to object, watching me like a pretend wise man.

"What are you getting at?" I ask.

"You're not going to like it."

"Say it anyway."

"You won't listen."

"Try me."

He waits as the waitress brings my coffee and refills his mug. He takes a sip, careful it doesn't burn his tongue, dragging out his response like he's letting me in on some profound philosophical truth. Then, finally, he says, "Give it up."

"I won't let Fred go this way. I owe it to him to find out the truth."

"Fred's dead, darlin'. That's the truth. When are

you gonna let go of this cop shit and accept it? You hide behind your star and you're gonna regret it. Just like with your brother. Sometimes, Sam, you have to let go of the Job. Take it from me, you won't find peace looking for someone else to blame. If you want forgiveness, you have to deal with what you have left."

"What's left?" I try to ask myself. There's not much of an answer.

"Come on, Sam, you're young. You still have a chance. You can change. Become somebody. Get out of this garbage life. Be a teacher, or a counselor—"

"A minute ago you said I was a good cop."

"A week ago you weren't in the middle of this shit."

"I'm not quitting."

Wade takes a cigarette from his breast pocket and holds it between his teeth.

"You're in over your head. With the Sarge, with Jackowski. With Internal Affairs . . ." He trails off like I'm supposed to agree.

"Yeah, so?" I ask.

"So, it's a losing battle. IA just wants everything sealed up nice and tight so they keep their hands clean. They're not solving cases; they're making ad campaigns for the city. They probably came up with that friendly-fire bit the news guys used like a slogan."

"But a cop was *killed*," I say, hoping he won't be offended.

"No, a cop *died*. By another cop's gun. Case unfortunate, but closed."

"It's not that simple," I say. I lean in and look him in the eye so at least he'll feel bad if he lies when I ask, "Did you know Trovic was working with us?"

Wade cracks something close to a smile and I realize he's surprised by my naïveté, and not by this bit of information. "So what," Wade says, "you want to tell the world that Fred was associating with a scumbag? You want people to remember him for that?"

Trovic was working with *Fred?* Wade can read the astonishment on my face though I'm trying to pretend I already knew what he just told me.

"Trust me, Sam, your poking around is only gonna make it worse. You can't clear your name by stirring up shit. You want to end up like me?" Wade's eyes turn soft and haunted. "Let it go, Smack."

Yeah. Right.

"Even if I do," I say, "IA will keep asking questions. Alex O'Connor won't leave me alone."

"Neither will Paul Flanigan, from what I can tell," he says, completely changing the subject. He's either had too much coffee or he's thrilled with the idea of my dating the rookie, because now he's wielding that spoon like a magic wand.

"Don't start," I tell him.

"If I were your father, I'd like to see you with a kid like that. He's a good kid."

"*Kid* being the operative word," I tell him. I take my time lighting a cigarette. I think Wade has his suspicions about Mason and me. I don't think he likes Mason, and he probably has good reason; but after last night's scene with Deborah, I don't want to know. I'm guessing bringing up Paul is Wade's attempt to get the dirt on my love life without mentioning Mason. Like his teasing will give me the sudden urge to admit that Mason and I are together. Like he doesn't know in the first place. Funny, the way we sit here with smiles and pretend neither one of us even knows Mason.

"If you were my father," I finally say, "you'd tell me to stay away from cops."

"And you definitely wouldn't listen."

Wade pulls on his coat and fishes around in his

pockets. He knew he wouldn't get any secrets from me, and somehow I knew he wouldn't have any answers.

"I heard somewhere," he says, "that there are two ways you can go: in search of happiness, or in search of relief. One is a hell of a lot more rewarding, I'm sure."

He takes out a bottle of pills and washes one down with the end of his coffee. I wonder if they're for happiness or relief.

"That why you missed work?" I ask.

"You don't live to be as old as me without a few days off," he says. "Today's not one of them. I gotta go." He puts a ten on the table as he scoots out of the booth.

"I'll buy," I offer, "as long as you forget that shit I pulled yesterday at the station."

"You going to pick up Sarge's lunch, too?" He doesn't think twice about taking his ten bucks back. He rubs it between his fingers. "Some people will do anything for money," he says. "A lot of people, actually." He puts the ten away and stretches his bad shoulder. He usually kisses my head, but this time he just touches my swollen cheek. "You're fighting with yourself," he says. "How can you win?" He stands up and winks at the waitress before he heads for the exit. "Stay out of trouble."

Great advice for someone with nothing but troubles. Maybe he was talking to the waitress.

When she comes to refill my coffee, I order breakfast. While I'm sitting there waiting, I think about what Wade said. Is it really possible that Trovic was working with Fred? Is that why Birdie assumed I knew why Fred was killed? I wish Trovic would turn up, because he's the only one who knows the answers.

Wade doesn't seem to think the answers will make

me feel any better. What would I do if Trovic is found? I'd be relieved to know he was locked up somewhere, but I wouldn't be able to do anything. I'd have to watch him go through the court system, my own hands as tied as his. I'd pray he gets what's coming to him. But convicted or not, will having someone else to blame for losing Fred be any consolation?

Maybe Wade is right. I'm fixated on Trovic so I don't have to think about Fred. My partner died. Have I cried for him, or only for myself?

I know it's time to own up to my feelings about Fred. I also know I have to settle my doubts about Mason. When my omelet arrives, I choke it down along with the thought of going to talk to Deborah.

20

I pull up in front of Fred's house and sit in the car while I finish my cigarette. A couple of young kids run from a school bus into the house next door. Even though the sun is out, the temperature has dropped again and frozen everything that melted, leaving no snow and no place to play.

I approach Fred's steps carefully, because the pavement is still covered with ice. I'm surprised nobody has jumped at the chance to throw down salt for Deb.

I knock on the door and hope she isn't home. At least then I can tell myself I tried, and go back to my place and come up with a plan that doesn't involve sympathizing with a woman I can't stand who might just be after my boyfriend. No matter how I try to convince myself that talking to her about Fred will make me feel better, I think I'm only here to fuel my suspicion that she's not so upset he's gone.

I'm about to head back to my car when she answers the door. As usual, she looks like she walked off the cover of a magazine. Today she's wearing too much makeup. I wonder what she's covering up. She stands there and waits for me to say something.

"Looks like you're holding it together better than I am," I say.

"I'm just better at faking it," she says, and turns back inside. She leaves the door open, so I assume it's okay to follow her.

We go into the front room and she sits on the couch by the bay window. I sit on a dining room chair that hasn't been moved since Fred's reception.

"You look good," I say, even though this is the first time I've noticed her age.

She doesn't say anything. She looks out the window like she's sitting in a convalescent home.

"I, uh, I wanted to apologize . . ." I start, but I don't know how to finish.

"What?" she asks, bringing her attention into the room. "I'm sorry, I've been a bit distracted."

"I can understand," I say, though I don't know if she'll take comfort hearing that from me.

"There were footprints in the snow," she says, "all the way around the house. Now that the snow's melting . . ."

I cross my legs and tuck my feet under the chair and I wonder if it incriminates me.

"It was probably just some kids," I suggest.

"I guess I'm not used to being here alone," she says. "This is the first time the house has been empty since they notified me."

I don't know what to say to that.

"I don't hate you," she says, looking out the window again. "I have to believe God has a plan."

"Some plan," I say. "I wasn't in on it." I'm trying to be polite, but I'd almost rather she blame me than Him. I don't buy it.

A phone rings somewhere in the house, saving me from a sermon. The corners of her mouth curl up just enough to clue me in: Either she wants me to know she's happy to get a break from me, or she doesn't want me to know she's happy about whoever's calling.

"Excuse me," she says, and I do. Gladly.

As I'm sitting there, I notice a policeman's coat lying on the piano bench. I shouldn't snoop, but it's not like I'm going through her drawers. I figure it's Fred's, and I'm hesitant to pick it up, but when I walk over and get a better look I see IMES stitched into the breast pocket.

Next to the piano is a cardboard box full of what must have been in Fred's locker. I'm just about to look through it when I hear her coming back, so I tink a few keys on the piano and act like I was just waiting patiently.

"Some investment company," she says about the call. "They've been calling at all hours, wanting to know where I'm going to put the benefit money, the pension. They didn't waste a second." I, too, wonder what Deb's going to do with her new income.

She sits down again and adjusts an uncooperative bra strap. It's then that I notice she's not wearing her wedding ring. She didn't waste a second, either.

"When the money comes through I'm going to get out of this place," she says. "There are too many memories."

"I guess you'll want to start over," I say. With at

least a quarter of a million bucks, I estimate. "Where will you go?"

"My brother lives in Florida. Maybe there."

I don't have anything nice to say about Florida. I'm sure she and Mason had plenty of things to share about it when he was here. I decide to cut to the chase.

"About the accident . . ." I start, though I'm still not sure where I'm going with it.

"Mason told me it was quick and painless," she says. "He said Fred never knew what hit him, and that he didn't suffer," which is not true. I saw him suffer. The way she assumes Mason knows what happened creates some allegiance between them that I don't like at all.

"Mason make you feel better?" I ask.

"I beg your pardon?" She can tell from my tone that I'm talking about more than consolation. "Mason was one of the officers who stayed with me," she says. "I didn't see you breaking any records to come here."

"I'm sorry."

"You killed my husband. You should be."

It takes every ounce of love I had for Fred to keep from getting up and punching her in the nose job.

"I can see through a lot of things, Deborah, including your little sympathy ploy to get Mason."

"And my windows? You see through them?" She gets up. "I didn't expect you'd come back here, let alone apologize for what happened to my husband. I see now that you're looking for some kind of pardon. You will not get it from me. You will not get anything else from me." She motions me to the door. "Get out. I don't expect to see you again. Ever."

"Fine with me," I say, standing my ground near the piano, "but stay away from Mason."

"Isn't that what you always wanted to say to me

about Fred?" she says, and under all that makeup I'll bet there's a smile. "My relationship with Mason is no more your business than my marriage was. I know you don't like me, but Fred is gone and I no longer have to put up with his opinions, or yours. Now just go."

She puts on a wool coat and begins buttoning it up from the bottom.

"You late for a hot date?" I ask.

"I am going to the crematorium," she informs me.

"Out with the old . . ."

"Starting with you." She opens the front door and invites me to leave.

On my way out I notice a wall in the hallway full of nails. A box of photos sits at my feet, and on top is an official police picture of Fred.

"You can get rid of everything but your conscience," I say. "If you have one."

I'm barely out the door when she slams it. So much for making peace.

I shouldn't have tried to play nice. We were never friends and I didn't exactly see it happening in this lifetime. I should have gone in strong and asked Deb if she had any knowledge about Fred's dealings with Trovic or Birdie. Asked if she'd noticed Fred acting differently in the weeks leading up to his death. I should have interrogated her like a detective instead of a suspicious girlfriend.

I don't need another clue to figure out she's a conniving bitch. What I need are clues to figure out what happened to her husband.

I get in my car, drive around the block, and wait for her to leave.

21

I watch Deborah pull out of the alley, and then I pull in. I park next to a row of trash cans between her house and the neighbor's.

My promises to Mason and Sarge to stay out of the investigation went out the door with me, at Deb's request. I have a hunch she's getting over Fred pretty quickly, the way she spoke so assuredly about her "relationship" with Mason. With Fred gone, she gets what I think she's wanted all along: the opportunity to be more than a cop's wife.

I don't know if Deb is aware of Fred's ties with Marko Trovic. But if she is, I think she's trying to keep it quiet so she can take the money and run. If anyone finds out she knows about Trovic, they might also want to know why she was so willing to let me take the fall. I was his partner, his friend . . . why wouldn't she push for justice? And what if her insurance company heard she failed to disclose information that was relevant to the case? They might be more suspicious than I am.

I'm guessing she'd rather have the cash than the killer, and she doesn't want me or Trovic or anyone else slowing her down. I'm sure this trip to the crematorium is already cutting into her schedule.

I'm casing the place, checking windows and trying to figure out the best way to get into the house, when I peek inside and notice that most of the rooms are bare and there are boxes stacked everywhere. Deborah is either packing, or she's having one hell of a garage sale. Either way, I'll bet whatever didn't make it into those boxes is in the trash. Maybe I won't have to break in after all.

I follow my footprints where the snow has melted to the grass. I left a pretty obvious trail last time I was here. I might not have been so smart that time, but I think I'm doing some real cunning detective work now. I make sure no one's around before I open the lid to the first trash can. I'm ready to find some secret documents or some overlooked piece of evidence that will turn this whole thing around.

I throw some newspapers on the ground as well as a Glad garbage bag full of plastic utensils, paper plates and food people brought over to ease Deb's burden. The pungent smell of perishables kept warm by decomposition cuts through the air.

I take out empty Franzia wine boxes and wonder how anybody can drink Chablis. Then, underneath a second Glad bag, I find what looks like a Chicago postman's trunk: a whole bunch of sympathy cards. Like from the entire city. At least a hundred cards, addressed to "The Family of Officer Maloney," or some variation, pitched into the trash like junk mail—many of them unopened, like Deb couldn't be bothered. Now I know for sure she didn't care about Fred, and I want to go up to the house and break down the door and toss the place until I find something that proves it, but I just can't believe all of these cards . . .

I look up at the sky. The clouds seem so far away and the significance of this "trash" seems so unfairly small. I can feel my eyes start to burn, the familiar prelude to tears. I look back at the house, dark and empty. Fred is not there. All the work he did to make the place a home will be forgotten, just like these cards. Just like he will be.

For Fred's sake, I decide to open the cards. I think I qualify as family.

I take them all out of the garbage can and put them on the hood of my car. Then I climb up and sit there and I go through each one. Condolences offered to the widow of a fallen officer, to a stranger, for a hero. One from a woman in Schaumburg says, "In Hours of Dark Despair, God's Love Will Light Your Way." Another, signed by kids from a second-grade class in Crystal Lake, is a crayon drawing of what I think is a cop. It says "His Badge Stands for Courage" in grown-up lettering. I put each one back in its envelope like I'm safely tucking away his memory, because every card is another reason that Fred was a cop. And every card is another reason I have to find out what happened to him.

I'm in tears. I'm sobbing over one from an officer in Morris when I come to an envelope with a familiar return address. It's Mason's.

This is the first one that makes me question the legality of my actions, but it's already open, so I pull the card out.

The cover reads "In This Time of Sorrow" and blah, blah, blah—I skip it to get to the important stuff. Inside, a handwritten note reads:

Deb,
As the wife of an officer, I know there is little I can say to console you. We've talked before about how the job is like a love affair we try to ignore: we don't think about it when he leaves for work, and we can't fathom it even after we know it's happened; worse, we always have to think it could have been avoided. They say that to be killed in the line of duty is honorable, but there is no honor in losing a husband. I share your sorrow and hope that the person who took Fred finds her way to acceptance and absolution.
      May God bless you, Susan Imes.

Acceptance? Absolution? What the fuck is she talking about? She's saying I killed Fred. Her husband says he's working overtime to prove I didn't. I'm saying nobody gives a shit who killed Fred, and this whole thing is a sham.

I slide off the hood and I want to rip up the card and throw it back in the trash, but I wind up sitting down on the ground, my back against my right front tire, reading it again. I reread the part that pisses me off: *... hope that the person who took Fred finds her way ...* and now I'm crying because I just can't believe it. Susan acted so virtuous when I met her, and all the while she thought I was the fool. She sounds like Deborah with her righteous bullshit. *Our hearts go out to you,* she said to me. My middle finger goes out to her.

I'm trying to stuff the damn card back in its damn envelope when a kid from the house next door comes around the corner and catches me sitting in a heap in the middle of a bunch of trash.

"Are you a bum?" he asks me.

I am a mess. I wipe my nose with my glove. "That's not a nice thing to call someone."

"Are you?"

"I'm a police officer." I stand up and dust off my pants.

"Are you looking for clues?"

"Something like that. Go back inside."

He kicks the gravel around with his big snow boot, eyes on the ground. I don't have the patience to talk him into going away, so I begin to put the cards in some kind of order to take them elsewhere.

Then the kid announces, "My dad doesn't like cops." Little shit.

"Good for your dad," I say.

"He says most of 'em are crooked."

"Like your teeth?" I ask.

The kid isn't sure it's funny.

"Was Mr. Maloney crooked?"

"No," I say, "Mr. Maloney was not crooked."

"Then how come you're going through his garbage?"

"This isn't garbage."

"Are you crying because Mr. Maloney is dead?" he asks, like dead just means "gone on vacation."

"Yes," I say. The kid follows me around to the trunk, picking up cards that fall along the way.

"Did you love Mr. Maloney?"

"Enough with the questions, all right?"

"Sorry."

I open the trunk and dump the cards inside. The kid throws his handful in too, and we stand there like we're watching a campfire.

"Yes. I loved Mr. Maloney," I tell the kid.

"You shouldn't cry," he says, and bends over to pick up a dropped envelope. He hands it to me. Of course it's the one from Susan. "My dad says if you love someone and they love you, that they're always by your side, even if they're dead."

"How about if they're married?" I ask him.

The kid shrugs. "I didn't ask him that."

I toss Susan's card into the open trash can and tell him,

"You should."

"Jey-iff-reeee," a woman calls from next door, and the kid's eyes light up.

"I gotta go." He runs away as fast as his big boots will let him. "I'm coming, Mommy!"

I watch him cross the yard and think about how simple happiness is to a kid. A cup of hot chocolate with marshmallows. A cartoon. A snow day. Tears forgotten as quickly as they're shed. And love, as easy as a handshake. Then, somewhere along the way, things get complicated. Innocence is less attractive; it becomes ignorance. Fred always used to say, "Ignorance keeps us in business." As I get into my car and head for Mason's, I wish I didn't know better.

22

The sun is setting quickly, marking the day and night contrast between the city proper and its neighbors to the north. I drive up Sheridan Road, past Cavalry Cemetery, into Evanston.

I feel like I'm on patrol, taking in every detail: the big lawns, the tree lines, lanterns instead of bright halogens along the streets, the cutesy mailboxes shaped like barns. The land of brick homes and big windows, extra garages and long driveways. The suburban dream, with the city for its backyard. I can't say I'm not envious. I light a cigarette.

I turn off Sheridan, drive two blocks toward the lake, and slow to a stop in front of Mason's house. The place could be on a postcard. All the elements are there, from the decorative curlicue fence to the huge front window, where a dozen long-stemmed roses sit center stage. I wonder if she accepted his apology. I wonder if I will.

A silver Lincoln Navigator sits parked in the driveway, and I finally get why Mason's been driving that squad: He traded up. He told me he wasn't going to spend the money. Maybe he's trying to tie it up in assets.

Headlights come up from behind. A truck flashes its brights and gives a quick honk, so I hit the gas and drive on, but I haven't seen enough.

I do a U-turn, head south on Sheridan, and park in a lot next to the lake. People park here to use the bike trail, but it's getting late and it's pretty windy, so I'm the only one here. I'm sure most people in this neighborhood are tucked into their cozy homes with their well-adjusted families for the night. I'm sure Susan is cooking the perfect casserole. I pull on a hat, zip my coat, and get out of the car.

As I walk up the path, the air off the lake feels like an ice pack against the few parts of my skin that are exposed. My eyes water and my lungs feel asthmatic when the wind hits me head-on. I adjust my scarf and check behind me for cyclers or joggers before I turn onto a dirt trail—a schoolkids' shortcut—that runs up against the residential backyards. A few houses down, I disregard a sign that boasts PRIVATE PROPERTY. Part of it is supposed to be mine, and I'm here to make sure of it.

I stay along the perimeter of the yard until I reach the base of the wooden deck. Staying in the shadows, I follow the rim of the deck to its steps. I get on my hands and knees and crawl up a few steps, and when I see the coast is clear, I move quickly and position myself behind a big Weber grill. From here, I have the perfect view into Mason's house. Into his other life.

Through those floor-to-ceiling windows I'm sure Susan loved when they picked out the house, I can see her preparing a salad in the kitchen. Mason has his feet up on the coffee table in the adjacent room. He's absorbed in a basketball game on his big-screen TV. I can't help but think of him fondly when his left foot moves to its usual internal tick. It moves even when he's sleeping. When he sleeps with me.

Susan absentmindedly slices an onion and I wonder if they've run out of things to say. They continue like this, without speaking, for so long that I'm even starting to get interested in the basketball game. This is not how life would be if I was in that house. Mason would be wrapped up in me.

Susan finally says something, but Mason either doesn't hear her or he doesn't care. She repeats herself, and this time I think I can almost hear her, so I know Mason heard, but he still doesn't respond.

So Susan, with carrot and knife in hand, walks out from the kitchen and stands directly in front of the TV, blocking his view. Mason waves her out of the way like a bug, because there's less than a minute left. She holds the knife like it'll make a difference, but obediently steps aside.

Mason finally acknowledges her during a time-out. He takes the carrot out of her hand and eats it. Whatever he says to her sends her back into the kitchen, and I don't think the onion is what finally makes her cry.

For a second I think I hear something out in the yard, but it's either the wind, or a squirrel, or a twinge of guilt. I shouldn't be so delighted to have stumbled across a fight. I'm not so sure it's Susan's fault.

I can't take my eyes off Mason, sitting there so comfortably. I wonder if he wishes he were with me. There he is, in his big beautiful home, and here I am, on the outside.

I had the chance for a life like his once. I could have been settled, going through the motions of a marriage, thankful for a secure household and content with neighborhood gossip. I could have been a wife, hoping to be a mom; believing my life's meaning would be clear, like memories in photo albums. I would live for Christmas. I would chuckle at the fact that I know less about my mate than his co-workers and more about basket weaving than anyone should have the right to. I would bake bread.

Maybe there is happiness to be found in that life, but I will never know. I didn't have a tradition to follow, and I wasn't willing to sacrifice passion. The last man I had a serious relationship with was wonderful, but he was also terribly safe. He had a plan, and if I had stuck to it, I could have ended up living right next door to this place, trading recipes with Susan. I didn't like putting my life on a schedule. I would have traded one spur-of-the-moment kiss from him for our entire relationship.

My ex-fiancé, before him, was no less grounded. He was older than me and smarter by a couple of college degrees. He was an intelligent guy, a perfectionist. He had ideals and the money to back them up. He promised marriage would give me the freedom to do whatever I wanted, except what I wanted was the freedom to change my mind about the marriage. I was young. I didn't want to get stuck.

Inside Mason's house I see safety. I see stability. And I see misery. Mason has more emotional investment in what's on TV than in the woman he married.

Susan acts like fixing a salad is the worst chore in the world. I wonder what made them give up. I wonder if I would have, too.

When the game is over, Susan returns with an envelope.

She holds it up in front of him, and for the first time ever, I think Mason is caught off guard. He motions for her to hand it to him. She refuses. He stands up and takes her by the arm. She tries to keep the envelope away from him, but he pulls her down on the couch and rips it out of her hand. What he says then I can't tell, because he's in her face and his lips are hardly moving. Whatever it is, she stops crying, calmly gets up, and returns to the kitchen. Mason tucks the envelope into his back pocket, picks up the remote, and changes the channel.

I feel like a spectator, and I have to stop myself from yelling "Look out!" because all of a sudden Susan runs back into the TV room with the bowl of salad and dumps the entire thing right on Mason's head. We both wait for Mason's reaction.

Mason calmly stands up. He runs his hand through his hair; lettuce falls to the plush carpet. He brushes himself off, celery and all. Then he takes the bowl from her and sets it on the coffee table. He turns off the television. And then he leaves. Just leaves her standing there.

Susan collapses in tears to what must be the slam of the front door. Her tears give way to stillness, and she listens, as I do, to the Navigator's engine rev in the front of the house. It is sad to watch her there, as her world comes down around her.

I break for the bike path and hope I beat Mason to my place, because I think I just watched Susan discover the divorce papers, and no matter how I feel about it, I know I'll be first to get the news.

◆ ◆ ◆

I jump in my car and I'm backing out when I notice a
yellow Chevy truck sitting idle in the next spot. It has
to be the same truck I saw in Deb's alley last night.

As I'm looking at the truck, I start to roll forward
when a pedestrian hits the hood of my car with his fist.

"Jesus, you almost fuckin' hit me!" the guy says. He
keeps walking, but he looks back at me like I meant to
do it and that he'd be willing to come back and argue
about it.

Best thing I can think to do is get out of there as
quick as I can, and see if the yellow truck follows me.
As I weave back and forth between two lanes going
south on Sheridan, I try to blow off the feeling I did
something wrong. I didn't see the pedestrian. It's not
like I meant to hit him. And I didn't actually hit him.
He didn't have to be so hostile. Some people are just
assholes.

I see the yellow truck's brights in my rearview mirror. He's tailing me, and once we get to Lake Shore
Drive I wish I could bust him for driving with Class B
plates (pickups aren't allowed on the Drive). I speed
up, trying to lose him, and I think I set a record when I
pull off at North Avenue, until I hit a stoplight. The
truck pulls up on my right again, and I can't convince
myself it's a coincidence.

The truck is too tall for me to see in the windows,
which are tinted anyway. The driver revs the engine
like he wants to race. It can't be Marko Trovic.

When the light turns green, I let traffic in front of
me go ahead, and I wait for the yellow truck to move
forward so I can get over to the right. Instead, the
driver waits for me to move. I floor it and try to get
ahead of him, but the damn truck rides right along next
to me, like a big yellow bully, speeding up and slowing

down to block me into the left lane when I need to be in the right.

I don't know what this guy's deal is, but he's definitely doing it on purpose, so I make an illegal left over a double yellow and pull into the Shell station. The truck keeps going. I sit there for a minute and tell myself that I didn't do anything wrong. And that it wasn't Marko Trovic.

I decide to take alleys and side streets back to my place. Along the way I remind myself that some people are just assholes.

When I get to my building, I park across the street and double-check to make sure my car is locked. I look both ways on the street even though I'm sure I lost the yellow truck. Maybe he wasn't following me after all, and my imagination is bumping into my brain. Concussion, that's it. I've probably seen the truck around town; it stands out like a four-wheeled banana. I look over my shoulder on the sidewalk.

Omar lets me inside the entrance.

"Will you keep an eye on my car?" I ask, even though I know he always does.

"I sure will."

He calls for the elevator, and as I'm waiting, he asks, "You know someone in a yellow truck?"

I look outside just as the Chevy rolls by the drive.

"Nope," I say to Omar, but he knows better.

The truck stops out front and its engine booms through the circular corridor.

"You can't park there, man . . ." Omar says. The elevator door opens and Omar urges me inside. "Excuse me, Miss Mack. You have a good evening." As the door closes, I see Omar take a walkie-talkie from his desk and start outside. I'm relieved to let him deal with what is most likely my problem.

◆ ◆ ◆

When I step off the elevator, the hall light on my floor is out, which is weird. I use the ray of light peeping out from under the shoe girl's door as a guide to my own, telling myself all lightbulbs burn out eventually.

I hear the shoe girl's TV advertising some new talk show for men. I'll bet women will tune in religiously. I guess some people need all the help they can get.

When I stick my key in its lock, I stop.

The door is already unlocked. I didn't see the Navigator out front.

Then, *ding*—the elevator door opens. I wait.

No one welcomes me into my place, and no one gets off the elevator. I don't have a gun, or handcuffs, or a radio, so I stand in the hall and consider making friends with Miss Shoe.

I was out of it when I left today; I might have accidentally left my door unlocked. Then again, Omar wouldn't send the elevator up empty.

I leave my keys in the door and start down the hallway. Maybe it's Mason. Maybe he wants to surprise me.

"Hello?" I say, like if someone *was* there and wasn't getting off, they'd answer. Just before I can tell if anyone's inside, the door closes. So it's not Mason. It's someone else who wants to surprise me.

Just then, the door to the stairwell behind me opens. I move out of the way like I'm dodging a bullet, and I shout, "Don't move!" in my best cop voice. It works, because whoever's on the other side of the door lets it slam shut.

I grab the knob and lean back with all my body weight. The handle turns. I hold tight.

"Open the door!" a man shouts, banging on the door. It's definitely not Mason. Oh, God, if it's Trovic . . .

I let go of the door with one hand, still using my

body weight to keep him in the stairwell, and lean over, pressing the elevator call button to bring it back up from the lobby. It's my only way out.

The man keeps banging. "Hey!"

I wait. And I wait. And I wait. I hear the elevator *ding* more clearly as the car rises—four, five, six . . . then the banging stops. The shouting stops. And the *dinging* stops—at the floor below mine. Is he catching the elevator?

I have no choice. I let go of the door and break for my place. I run so fast I can't tell if anyone's behind me, and I pray no one's in front of me. I throw open my door and grab the keys and get inside and slam the door shut and dead bolt the lock. I leave the lights off and peer through the peephole, and I don't make a move.

Until I see O'Connor.

He stands there and catches his breath before he knocks.

"Samantha Mack? You'd better be in there."

I catch my own breath and remind myself: Some people are just assholes.

23

I'm relieved it's someone I recognize, but I'm not happy it's the last person I want to deal with.

"What do you want?"

"I want to talk to you about Marko Trovic."

I look through the peephole. O'Connor pinches his side like he's got a cramp.

"You can't ask me questions without a warrant."

He pulls one from his coat and presents it to the peephole.

I unbolt the door and hope he'll make it quick. I don't want Mason showing up while O'Connor's here. A guy from IA would kind of ruin the moment.

"Does that warrant say you can stalk people?" I

leave the door open for him and he follows me into the kitchen.

"Sounds like you're paranoid," he says. "Or guilty."

"I can't be paranoid when someone is actually following me," I say.

"Your face looks better. Your head clearing up any?"

I don't answer because I know the less I fight, the better. I turn on the burner for a half pot of coffee that's been sitting there since the other day. I can drink anything—it could be brewed with lighter fluid—and it'd taste better than the acrid blend they serve at the station. I hope O'Connor is picky.

He takes a seat at my kitchen table. I clear off a pile of mail so he won't look through it.

"What do you want to know about Trovic?" I ask.

"I've been reading over your statement. I think you're hiding something."

"Is that a question? I don't really feel like shooting the shit." I get out two mugs for the coffee. I'm afraid he'll stay longer if he thinks I'm in a hurry.

"Fine." O'Connor flips the pages of a steno pad. "Question: You said in your statement you didn't know you were a suspect. So why were you so quick to leave the hospital?"

"I was upset." I should probably stick to short answers if I want to get him out of here.

"Did you have any contact with Mason Imes the night Fred died?"

"Nope."

"And you say Fred Maloney was tipped off as to where Marko Trovic was hiding out, and it was Maloney's goal to apprehend Trovic."

"Yes," but I don't add that I still don't know why.

"You arrived, you went into the house, and shots

were fired. Did you witness an exchange of fire between Fred Maloney and Marko Trovic?"

"Yes."

"You did."

"Shots were fired," I say, backing up a little since I don't remember the specifics of my statement. "I thought it was Marko Trovic."

"And then you tended to Officer Maloney, unaware that, in your estimation, Trovic was still alive."

"I don't know if Trovic was there," I say. My insistence that he was is probably the reason O'Connor's asking questions. Damn report. "I had a concussion. The doctor said my memory could be inaccurate."

"Could you identify Marko Trovic from a photograph?" he asks. He doesn't care about my excuses.

"Yes. He's been in and out of the system since I started in the district."

I pour myself some coffee while O'Connor produces a booking photo of Trovic, staring dead ahead at the camera.

"That's him, all right." I recognize those eyes.

"How about this one?" O'Connor asks, and flips over another picture of Trovic.

This time Trovic stares dead ahead at the camera because he is just that. His eyes are about the only thing I do recognize. The rest of him is a bloated, bloody mess.

"I'll ask you again. Did you see Marko Trovic that night?"

"I . . . don't remember . . ." I say, wondering if an affirmative answer makes me a suspect. I take the photo to get a closer look while O'Connor keeps firing questions at me—

"You don't remember because you were knocked unconscious sometime after Fred was shot? Or you don't remember because that's what Mason Imes told you to say?"

"Marko Trovic is dead?" I ask, and I think I'm happy about it.

"Sure looks that way. You ready to start talking?"

I sit down and put the coffeepot on the table. I stare at the photos, trying to be blank-faced and determine what O'Connor has on me. He knows I think Trovic killed Fred. Why would Mason have told me to bring Trovic into this? "I fucked up," I finally say. "I thought Trovic was dead. Trovic shot Fred and I got hit in the head. It was an accident," I tell him and myself. I don't think I'm lying.

"So now all of a sudden Trovic shot Fred? It wasn't you?"

"It was my gun."

"I guess accidents happen," he says, though I can tell he doesn't mean it.

"I don't know what happened to Trovic," I say.

"You sure? You want to confer with Mason?"

"I don't know what you mean. If you think I'm lying for Mason, that's your problem."

"That *is* my problem. I just don't know why you didn't go with the friendly-fire scenario from day one. You made a big mistake when you brought Trovic into this."

"Trovic brought himself into this." I stand up, pick up the coffeepot, and pour O'Connor the last of it, grounds and all. "Guess I'm out. Are you finished?"

"Not quite," he says. "Trovic's body was found in Florida."

"So? The word's been out. He knew we were looking for him. And I'm sure we weren't the only ones. He was a scumbag. I guess someone just beat us to the punch."

"Three weeks ago," O'Connor says.

Wait. "What?"

"They found his body three weeks ago," he clarifies. "Marko Trovic was dead before your partner was."

I almost drop the coffeepot in his lap.

O'Connor studies me, waiting for my reaction, but I don't move. I don't know what to say. He takes the coffeepot from my hand and puts it on the table. I sit back down and try to comprehend how badly I just got fucked over, and by whom.

"That's why no one has been looking for him? You IA guys knew he was dead and you were just screwing with my head?"

"You know how it works, Mack. You don't have to trade tips with suspects. Even if they are lovesick cops." He takes a sip from his coffee. The taste doesn't faze him.

"If this is about Mason Imes again, you're off the mark," I say, keeping my voice steady. "I hardly know him."

"You might be right about that," O'Connor says, smirking. "I apologize, I guess I'm just jealous because he never sends me roses. Come on, Mack, you're not much of an actress. I'm not interested in your sex life anyway."

"Then what did you come here for?"

"I think you know who killed Fred Maloney and I think you know why. All this Marko Trovic bullshit has been fabricated to make us think you don't. You want to tell me the truth now? Or are you going to save it for your lawyer?"

"You'd better go," I tell him, because I don't know what the fuck he's talking about, but I do know he's not on my side. In fact, I think he's just become my enemy.

"Okay, I'll go, but let me just make sure I have this

down." He flips through his notes, though he's not really consulting them. "You don't remember what happened, so you run around blaming it all on a guy who was already dead. Your captain is quick to call it an accident because he'd rather have one cop on med leave than a half dozen in jail. No one turns up anything in your district's so-called investigation, which just happens to be run by your boyfriend. The case wears thin, and people want to forget, including the widow, who seems to enjoy consolation. And so the only one left wounded is you. Does that all seem fairly accurate?"

"You forgot the part about the hard-ass at Internal Affairs who's out to get me.".

"Now that *is* paranoia. I'm after your boyfriend." He gets up and puts his cup in the sink. I hope this means he's leaving.

On his way to the door, he stops. "One more thing. Mason booked two tickets to Miami yesterday. You invited?" He smiles just to make me mad before he tucks his steno pad in his coat and lets himself out.

I whip my mug in his direction. It hits the door and then the floor, but it doesn't break.

Who the hell does O'Connor think he is? First he says he wants my help and then he says I'm a liar. Before he believed someone else killed Fred; now he accuses me of making up my story about Trovic (okay, I admit that looks pretty suspect now). But O'Connor also accused the captain of calling Fred's death an accident to protect other cops. If I did kill Fred, on purpose or not, what does anyone else on the force have to do with it?

I'm lighting a cigarette when it all hits me: the tickets to Miami. Trovic's death. Mason and me. Protecting our own. O'Connor thinks Trovic's death and Fred's death are connected, and he must think everyone from the chief on down is covering it up.

O'Connor must be harassing me because he thinks I'll flip. He wants me to go against Mason.

This has to be personal. O'Connor had that look in his eye—just like the one Fred had when he talked about Trovic. And O'Connor was more than pleased to tell me about Mason's trip to Miami. O'Connor wants me to think Mason is using me—like he isn't trying to.

Mason's got two tickets, so what? Who else would he take? After the argument he had with Susan tonight, I'm pretty sure she isn't home packing her swimsuit.

Unless . . . no. The thought is so ludicrous I laugh out loud. Deborah? She did say something about Florida. Damn O'Connor for making me think it's remotely possible.

I get my coat. I'm not going to believe anything O'Connor wants me to until I talk to Mason.

24

Mason obviously isn't home with Susan, and he didn't come to my place, so I reluctantly head north to drive by Deborah's. I know Mason could be anywhere, and I could have paged him, but a phone call isn't going to be enough to get O'Connor's ideas out of my head. I have to see for myself.

My heart sinks when I turn onto Fred's street and see a squad out in front of the house. At least it isn't the Navigator. I slow down enough to get a look inside the house's bay window, but the drapes are drawn. I park in front of the squad, jump out, and peek into its window instead. A pack of Benson & Hedges sticks out of a drink holder on the driver's side door. Flagherty is the only one I know who smokes those cheap ones. It must be him. I go back to my car and hope I can get out of there quietly.

From Fred's house, I head for the station. I drive south on Damen through a Hispanic neighborhood. Every time I take this route, I think about MariCarmen Matias. She was a good girl in a bad neighborhood, and I had hoped she'd beat the system. She was filling out an application to UIC's nursing school when I questioned her about her brother, Javier, a small-time gangbanger we busted dealing heroin. MariCarmen wouldn't talk; she didn't want trouble. Trouble turned out to be her brother's friend, Cid. Cid got MariCarmen hooked on him, and on heroin too. The next time I saw her, her bright eyes were glazed, and nursing school was as far from her mind as her swollen belly. She was too caught up in getting high to even notice she was pregnant.

The last time I saw MariCarmen, she was lying on this street, passed out and bleeding everywhere. Cid told her if she could handle heroin withdrawal for a few days, she'd reduce her tolerance for the drug and get a better high. He didn't tell her that her unborn baby couldn't endure withdrawal. On her way to get a fix, she spontaneously aborted the baby, right here on the street. MariCarmen survived, but I wouldn't call that beating the system.

I make a left on Addison and bring my mind back to the present. I am aware of my surroundings. I can recall each block's details, and mentally check off the order of things. I know this route better than I know myself. Though I guess that's not saying much at this point.

I shouldn't be letting O'Connor sway me. I never had much luck with relationship advice from people I respected; I don't know why I'm interested in what some guy off the street thinks about Mason. I mean, I'm perfectly capable of ruining my own relationships.

O'Connor could be trying to trick me. He could have been twisting his facts, trying to get me to crack. Still, I wish I knew why he's after Mason.

When I get to the station, the Navigator is parked outside. I hope Mason is in there working on my case. Maybe he already knows about Trovic, and he's got a new lead. Maybe he found Birdie and got him to talk. Or maybe he doesn't have any leads, and he's tying up loose ends so everyone can get on with their lives, including the two of us. Together. In Miami. I'll bet the tickets are sitting in the front seat of the Navigator. I'm just being impatient.

Or maybe O'Connor is on to something and Mason hasn't been looking for Trovic; he's been stringing me along, hoping the whole thing will go away. Hoping I'll give up, and O'Connor will too. Of course I would believe him; I believed him when he promised he was leaving Susan. More than once.

Now I'm the one twisting facts. Mason wouldn't lie to me. He wouldn't waste his time. Why should he? I could walk, and so could he. I'm not his wife. O'Connor should be bugging Susan. Maybe, though, O'Connor's pursuing me because I'm the one Mason loves. I'm the one who can hurt him. I just wonder why O'Connor wants to.

An hour goes by before Mason leaves the station. I've talked myself into and out of both his complete guilt and his total innocence, and I'm probably giving him too much credit in either case. I've given it too much thought, which is why, when he gets to his SUV, I jump out of my car and announce, "Marko Trovic is dead."

"I know," Mason says. "I just got the wire report." He looks around for possible witnesses. "You shouldn't be here."

I've been sitting in my car long enough to know no one's around, but I don't want to push it, so I keep my distance.

"Mason, you have to tell me what's going on. I found out Trovic was working for Fred. And Trovic was killed before Fred. O'Connor came to see me, and he tried to pollute my head with this conspiracy theory that's crazier than me accusing a ghost of murder. You're right about him; he'll take down the whole district if he can. And he wants to start with you."

"I told you," Mason says simply. Doesn't this worry him?

"What are we going to do?" I ask.

Mason opens the door to his Navigator. "You," he says, "are going to go home and wait for me." He stands behind the SUV's door, shielding the smile he can't hide from anyone who might be looking besides me. "I'm busy right now. I'm in the middle of a murder. And a divorce."

I was right: Those were divorce papers I saw. Susan is finally out of the picture and I am going to Miami. I want to jump from where I'm standing into his arms and let him spin me around until I'm dizzy, but I play it cool since O'Connor is the one who told me about the trip. Mason reaches for something inside the SUV. I wait for him to hand me my ticket out of here.

Instead, he comes out with a pair of gloves. For himself.

"There are some details that need to be ironed out in Florida."

"In Florida," I echo like an accusation, which it is, because at that moment it occurs to me that Mason got the tickets before he knew Trovic was dead. Or, he knew Trovic was dead and didn't tell me. And, he didn't invite me to Miami.

Just then the front door to the station swings open and Paul comes hustling down the steps toward us.

Mason says, quickly, "I can explain everything but I can't do it now."

"Who's going with you?" I ask, hoping for a quick "You."

"We'll talk later" is what I think he says instead, through tight lips.

"What?"

"I said I think you'd better go." Mason raises his voice and it probably sounds pretty stern to Paul.

"There a problem?" Paul asks.

"No. She knows she's not supposed to be here. She's going home." By the way he says it, I'm guessing I'm supposed to meet him there. "Let's go, Flanigan," Mason says, and slams the door to the Navigator. Mason pulls on his gloves, one at a time, without so much as a glance at me. Paul obediently joins him, and I'm still standing there when they hop into the adjacent squad and drive away.

I don't resist the urge to stop at the liquor store but I only buy a pack of smokes, some gum, and a Coke. I have to have my wits about me when Mason shows up.

I know it's terrible, because I should be concerned about O'Connor and Trovic and Miami, but all I can think about is the divorce. Mason is finally going through with it. A week ago I would have told him I wasn't ready, but after everything that's happened, I don't want to keep our feelings a secret for another minute. I've questioned Mason's every move since Fred died, and he's always answered. I've been assuming the worst, and he keeps proving me wrong. And despite all my doubts, he still has faith in me. In us. I should have it, too.

I turn on the TV and half-watch a rerun of *Double Indemnity.* Fred MacMurray is falling for Barbara Stanwyk and her anklet while he's trying to sell her insurance. MacMurray helps hatch a plot to kill Stanwyk's rich husband so she can collect on his policy. She assures MacMurray they're in it together, "straight on down the line." MacMurray follows through, even though he knows better.

We all know better.

The last thing I remember is MacMurray's boss complaining about the little man inside him that's giving him a sick feeling about the blonde. I know exactly what he means.

I'm asleep on the couch when my phone rings. I reach around in the dark for the cordless.

"Mason?" Assuming he's calling to say he's on his way.

"I think we should talk," a woman says on the other end.

"Who is this?" I say, but I know. It's Susan Imes.

"Meet me at Clark and Devon. Stacks 'n' Steaks. Back booth. Half hour." She hangs up.

I don't think she's hungry for pancakes.

I pull into the parking lot of Stacks 'n' Steaks, a neon, twenty-four-hour restaurant that looks like it was transplanted from Atlantic City. The bus stop on the front sidewalk is unusually crowded for this time of night, and I have to walk around some homeless people who loiter outside like moths around a lightbulb.

Inside, I walk past a group of drunk kids. One of them has her head down on the table, already regretting too many kamikazes. The waitress looks like she's been here since breakfast; I don't think she's expecting a tip from the kids, or anyone else.

Susan sits in a back booth, staring out at the street. The neon lights around the window steal her previous glow and amplify the circles around her eyes. She doesn't greet me when I arrive.

"I hate the city," she says. "Its filth."

"I doubt you came here to talk about cleaning up the streets," I say.

I look out the window, thinking I'll see whatever litter she's referring to. I do a double take when I think I see that long-haired Serbian kid who scratched my car. I slide across the cracked vinyl seat to get a better look, but he disappears around the corner before I can make a positive ID. I'm left staring at a big bearded homeless guy who carries all his belongings in a collection of plastic Dominick's bags. He's having a really intense conversation with nobody.

"You didn't exactly pick the best part of town," I tell Susan.

The waitress comes over, serves Susan a cup of tea, and waits for me to say something.

"Coffee. Thanks."

"I can hear Mason," Susan says to me.

"What?"

"You sound just like him."

I don't know if I'm supposed to thank her or what, so I let her do all the talking.

"I want to ask you something," she says, as she dunks her tea bag wearily. "Do you think you're the only one? 'We'll get out of this place. We'll get away from all this. When I get the money.' You think I haven't heard that before?"

The waitress brings my coffee, saving me a response. We both acknowledge her politely. It seems kind of wrong, two grown women talking so calmly about the one man they love, like there was a solution to be found over coffee at a breakfast joint in the middle of the night.

"This has happened before," she says. "We've been through it. What Mason's not telling you, and what I want you to know, is that I know. Everything. And I think you should know that you're only going to get yourself in trouble. Like Fred."

To that, I must respond.

"You don't know anything about Fred."

"Maybe I don't. Not as an officer, anyway. I can't say I know anything about the way a person would act in the midst of a police situation—"

"You obviously have an opinion about it." I saw her sympathy card.

"I'm sorry Fred is gone."

I don't want to, but I believe her.

"I did not come here to fight," she says. "I am speaking to you as a woman. As a human being. And I am asking you to stay away from my husband."

"He's really leaving you this time." I try not to smile.

Then Susan smiles. Not vindictively; rather, it is the smile of someone who is right.

"I know Mason better than anybody," she says. "And this"—she holds up her wedding ring—"may not mean anything to him. Or to you. But this"—she pulls that envelope from her handbag—"must mean something."

She opens the lip of the envelope: plane tickets. So they weren't divorce papers, and my name isn't on one of them. Then why was she so upset at their house earlier?

"We're going to look at property," she says. "Mason went down nearly a month ago to research a new housing development."

That's where he went when we were supposed to go to Vegas? Looking at homes in Florida?

"Why did you call me here, if you're so secure?" I'm annoyed by her confidence.

"Because if I were in your shoes, I'd want the truth." She takes the tea bag from her mug and takes a sip.

"Which is?"

"Mason and I will also be going to Miami to see my mother. To tell her I'm having a baby."

What do I say to that? That's impossible?

"That's impossible," I say.

"Unfair, you may think, but not impossible."

"Mason loves me," I insist. I feel like a kid arguing over the outcome of a board game, because the result is the same, no matter who cheated.

"No one loves anyone on purpose," she says. The words sting, because now *I* can hear Mason. "It's time someone told you the truth, Sam. Marko Trovic is not a killer. Fred is not a hero. And my husband is not yours. I'm sorry."

"You don't have proof," I say, offering to play the board game again.

"Friendly fire," she says and gets up. "That's all it was. You'd best be advised to keep it friendly."

Susan puts a few dollars on the table and leaves me there. Stunned.

25

I don't remember lighting the cigarette I'm smoking. I vaguely remember leaving the restaurant. I'm standing in the parking lot when one of the homeless guys asks me for change. I fish around in my bag like I'm supposed to and pull out my wallet. I give him ten bucks.

I find the Jaguar driver's cell phone in my bag and use it to call Mason.

"This is your personal 911. Leave a message."

I don't.

In my car, I try again.

"This is your personal 911. Leave a message."

I hang up.

◆ ◆ ◆

In front of my place, before I get out of the car, I dial once more.

"This is your personal 911. Leave a message."

I can't.

This time, when I hang up, the phone rings back at me.

"Hello?"

"Hello, Sam. You in the 'middle of the night' again? Or in the midst of some important police business?" the Jag driver asks.

"No."

"When you didn't answer last night I thought I might have to call 911."

I think of Mason. I can't respond.

"Are you free tonight? You care to meet for a drink?"

I don't want to.

"Remember, Sam, these negotiations are supposed to be on my terms. I shouldn't be feeling desperate here."

I do. "Tell me where."

I try Mason one last time before I go inside the Raven Tavern.

"This is your personal 911. Leave a message."

I take a deep breath and wait for the beep.

"I wanted to talk to you about your wife. I should have figured out by now that you won't answer my questions, but I really want to know: Have you been waiting until the last possible moment to break my heart? I don't want any more promises. I know the truth." I hang up and prepare to drown my sorrows.

A large black bird made of metal is perched at the head of a wrought-iron fence, watching me as I make my way down a set of stairs. The entrance is below the street, marked by a wooden sign without lights. It says, simply, THE RAVEN. The bar is dark, nestled in the basement of a gray stone two-story. A psychic reads tarot cards on the first level, and a law office occupies the second. I think this place offers better counsel.

My first sip of Jameson doesn't do enough. My first glass scratches the surface. I don't see the Jag driver and I don't care. I just want to make everything go away. The bartender, a young guy with an unkempt beard to make him look older or grungier, doesn't give me a second glance when I order a double.

A twenty-something woman in a tight velvet shirt approaches the bar.

"I'd like a Midori sour," she says.

"You got ID?" the bartender asks.

She looks through her purse with no luck. "I'm sorry, I'm such an airhead. I think I left it in my other purse."

"You leave your phone number in there too?" the bartender asks. After a moment of silent bargaining, he hands her a pen. She writes on a napkin; he pours her a drink.

I light a cigarette and hope it'll kill me.

"Hello, Sam," the guy says when he shows up. "How are you?" I can't even look at him.

"Do you really want to know?" I ask.

I finish my third drink and toast it to the bartender for another.

"Have a drink," I tell the guy.

The bartender brings me another Jameson, and my friend a martini.

"You look good out of uniform," he says. Before I

came here I changed into a sexy black dress, one I'd never worn out of the house, to make sure there'd be no question. I also put on dark eyeshadow. Lots of mascara. He won't see the real me. He wouldn't want to.

I take the olive from his glass and run it seductively around my lips. I can smell his cologne, and the memory of someone who used to wear it sobers me. I should not have come here. I cannot follow through. I put the olive back in his drink.

"I have that number, for the body shop," I say, preparing to retreat.

"I don't know if that'll be necessary," he says. "Why don't you come outside with me, and assess the damage?"

Right in the middle of the bar, he runs his hand along the inside of my thigh, and I know it's too late to call it off.

"Are you comfortable?" he asks me.

I'm not. We're crammed into the front seat of the Jaguar. Every time he moves, my knee bangs into the dash. He turns me away from him to caress the back of my neck. I look out the window at the city lights as I let this man feel my body, put his arms around me and take my breasts into his hands. I let him touch me where he thinks it will have an effect. It means nothing. Not even when he turns me around again and places his hand below my chin to get a look at me, like Mason used to do. I cannot look back at him.

"You are so hot," he starts. I kiss him so he'll stop. I am not here to talk.

He rips off my nylons. I have no reason to be inhibited. I no longer have anything to hide.

I moan as he pushes himself on me, the weight of his body forcing my head between the car door and the seat. I feel my stitches catch on the fabric of the head-rest. I hold on to the seat belt to right myself as he pulls me back on to him, his hands on my shoulders. He begins to thrust; again and again he drives forward, into me, and I resist as long as I can before I move against him. I cry out for the death of my partner, for the end of my relationship with Mason, for myself. I am alone again, no matter whom I am with.

"You can't get enough, can you?" he asks, his ego fed by what he thinks is my insatiable desire for him. I feel him inside me like others in the past, others I thought would love me; the feeling is no different. I have deluded myself. I tear at his back with my nails. I strain into another position. I want this man to hurt me. I deserve it.

"Harder," I say, but the only thing I feel is the ache of my heart.

When I get home, I call Mason. I have to end it.

I'm so afraid that I almost hang up when he actually answers.

"Hello?"

"I need to talk to you," I manage to say.

"I told you we shouldn't talk," he says. I assume he's at the station.

"Look, I saw your wife."

"You saw Susan?" he asks.

"I'm really messed up, Mason." I don't want to do this over the phone, so I say, "Can you come over? We have to talk."

He doesn't say anything.

"Hello? Mason?"

"Sorry," he says after a moment. He sounds distant. I think he knows I know.

"Please, Mason. Just come. I have to do this now. It can't wait. Hello?"

"I'm on my way."

26

I try to preoccupy myself while I wait for Mason. I notice the coffee I threw at O'Connor has stained the hardwood in the foyer. I can smell the syrupy remnants of alcohol in the empty bottles of whiskey that never made it past the kitchen trash can. In my bedroom, the comforter and the sheets are tangled at the foot of the bed. I pull the sheets toward the head-board and tuck them under the pillows. Under the pillow Mason likes.

I won't let tears fall now, though I have every right. I've lost the two most important men in my life in less than a week. I'd like to think both Mason and Fred were trying to protect me, but now I know: The truth will always surface eventually. In the end of a life, or the beginning, the truth is unstoppable and crushing. Especially when you don't want to believe it.

I leave the bed half-made and go in to the bathroom to get a look at myself in the mirror. I had covered the bruise on my face pretty well with makeup, and fixed my hair to cover the stitches. I have a brief impulse to let my hair down, change out of this revealing dress, and be the person Mason wants me to be. Instead, I smear on more lipstick. I can't be that person anymore. I can't feel how I want to feel about him.

I know Mason will be here soon, so I sit down in the kitchen and smoke a cigarette. I can smell the scent of that other man on me. My lipstick leaves a scarlet stain on the filter. Like blood, I think. Like a letter.

Mason taps on the front door and I think, what the fuck, don't be polite all of a sudden. I want him to be mad. I want him to be a jerk. I want him to make this easy.

I open the door and I can't imagine the look on my face compared to the one on Paul's. He and Wade stand there gaping like I've been set on fire.

"Sam. We gotta bring you in," Wade says.

I have to cover myself—they've never seen me dressed like this. I must look like a prostitute to them. I try to hide behind the door, but Wade pushes it open and steps inside.

"Wade, what's going on?" I say as he grabs my arm.

"Paul, get her a T-shirt." Paul doesn't know which way to go, so he just stands in the doorway and gawks at me.

"Paul. Quit standing there like a dope. Get in here." Wade points him toward my bedroom, and Paul complies. Wade stands there with his hand on my arm like I'll bolt if he doesn't.

"What the fuck did I do?" I ask. "You're acting like I just killed someone."

"You don't have to tell me anything. In fact, it's better if you don't," he says.

"Let me get dressed," I plead. "I can't go up there like this."

"Paul is bringing you something," he tells me.

"Is this because of Fred? The case? It's O'Connor. What did he tell you? He thinks I had something to do with Marko Trovic's murder." I can't think of any other reason they would do this.

Paul returns with a shirt and gives it to Wade.

"Come on, Wade. What's going on?"

"Help me, dammit!" Wade commands Paul. "This is embarrassing enough. Get her coat."

"Wade, please don't do this," I beg as we struggle with the shirt.

"Come on, Smack. I don't want to have to cuff you," he says.

"Cuff me? For what?" I ask, still trying to wriggle my wrists from his grasp.

"Susan Imes has been in a car accident," Wade says.

I stop fighting him. "Is she okay?"

"I don't know."

"What does this have to do with me?"

"I don't want to know." I let him pull the shirt over my head and I stand there, compliant, because I am in shock. I barely hear him when he says, "Paul, find her star."

When they escort me out of the building past Omar, he won't look at me, and it's not because he doesn't see me. I look like I'm getting picked up for a sex crime.

Outside, the air feels clean in my lungs. I didn't realize I felt so nauseated. My legs are weak and I don't know how I manage to put one foot in front of the other.

Then they put me in the backseat of a squad. Wade straps me in and shuts the door. I feel like I'm looking through a stranger's eyes, at someone else's skinned knees in front of me. I see my hands shaking, but I barely feel them. Do they make me look guilty? What am I guilty of?

Wade and Paul are silent in the front seat. Paul drives. When he pulls out of the rotunda onto the Inner Drive, I see a city crew cleaning up the gutters, working their way toward Lincoln Park. In a few weeks, tulips will pop out of flower boxes all over the city. Tourists on Michigan Avenue will marvel at the order and cleanliness. Construction will update the face of the skyline. And on the surface, it'll be magnificent. Only a few of us will know how dirty it can be.

I wish I could roll down the window. I feel like I'm suffocating. I can't register that I'm sitting here, where I've put so many bad guys. Ignored their excuses. Presumed their pleas for lenience were only a part of their scheme. Treated them like they were guilty of something, sometime, and this was simply the payback.

I see Paul's eyes in the rearview mirror. He looks at me like he expects I have something to confess.

"I didn't do anything," I tell him.

"Save it for the station," Wade says. They look at each other, and then back at the road in front of them.

So this is my payback.

Detective Nehls sits across from me in the interrogation room. His balding head shines in the overhead light as he peers at the report in front of him through reading glasses. He was just promoted at Christmastime. Some people think he didn't deserve it. Fred thought there were too many spaces open; he said Nehls couldn't have been luckier if he'd fallen into one of them. I never had a problem with the guy. Until now.

I see the flashing light on the video camera in the corner and I wonder who's watching behind the scenes. Nehls keeps his eyes glued to his papers. I think he's mortified by my cleavage. Embarrassed by a cop with bare legs.

Paul stands by the door like a hired security guard.

Nehls rubs his forehead. "You met her at Stacks 'n' Steaks on Clark and Devon," he repeats again. I've told him twice. "You left there at approximately one-thirty and drove home, where you changed clothes. Then you proceeded, via Clark Street, to the Raven Tavern on Lincoln Avenue. You arrived at said location no later than two-twenty."

"That's what I said."

"To meet a guy who drives a Jaguar whose name you can't remember."

"It's not that I can't remember. I don't know it."

"There seem to be a number of things you don't recall lately, Mack, and people keep ending up dead, or damn-well near it."

"I didn't go after Susan," I tell him.

"A witness claims a black Mustang ran her car off the road just past the intersection at Peterson and California at one-forty."

"You can't hold me here for that."

"In light of recent news, I don't know that I can agree with you."

"I told you I met her. How does that incriminate me?"

MacInerny pokes his head in the room and summons Paul. Paul slips outside the room, keeping a grip on the inside handle and the door slightly ajar. I speak up so Sarge can hear. "You find Mason. He'll tell you all I didn't do it."

Paul comes back inside and waits for Nehls's okay before he says, "Susan Imes is in critical condition. Detective Imes has gone to the hospital."

"What did he say?" I ask. "He told you it wasn't me."

Paul acts like he didn't hear me while Nehls checks his notes again.

"Imes claims you expressed interest in him the day he started here. He says you had a brief affair that he ended late last year. He says he agreed to take your case, but not your sexual advances. Shortly thereafter, he claims you threatened him. Says you threatened to ruin his career and his marriage."

That mother—

"He's lying," I say. I can't believe it. "Mason has been trying to get rid of his wife, not me. He said he was divorcing her. He could have done it. He could have run her off the road." Nehls looks at Paul again. They clearly think I'm lying. "Do you think I'm making all this up?" I ask, and I think the answer is yes. They figure I've lost my mind. I must sound like a raving lunatic.

"Let's deal with the facts," Nehls says. "First of all, Imes does not own a black Mustang. Second, even if he did, he was working, and driving a squad. In fact, when he arrived here at the station, Imes had a suspect under his arrest who backs his whereabouts. Suspect says Mason was pushing him around at the very same time the accident occurred."

"Mason accused me?"

"Your name was the first one out of his mouth when we broke the news about the hit-and-run. He felt we should intervene."

"I have to talk to him."

"I think you've done plenty of talking." Nehls hits a button on an audio recorder and I hear myself say, "Look, I saw your wife."

"You saw Susan?" Mason asks.

"I'm really messed up, Mason. Can you come over? We have to talk."

He stops the tape and waits for my explanation.

"I was going to break up with him," I tell Nehls. "You're taking it out of context."

"You mistook Mason's involvement in your case for some kind of personal interest in you," Nehls says, as though it's so pitiful he can't bring himself to believe it.

"Mason did have personal interest. We've been seeing each other for almost a year." No reason to hide it now.

No reason for Nehls to believe me, either. He takes off his glasses and wipes the top of his head with his sleeve. He's got wet rings under his arms, too. I don't know why he's so stressed, because he acts like he's got this whole thing figured out. Thanks to the "facts." Thanks to Mason.

"Come on, Detective, do you honestly think I tried to kill Susan?"

"It doesn't matter what I think. What I know is that you are on leave, with orders to go to counseling. You haven't even made an appointment. Not one. You've been caught interfering with an investigation. You're suspected of stealing classified information. You're hanging around the station. God knows what else you've done that's been overlooked around here. Your sergeant has tolerated your behavior because he felt you were traumatized. He didn't think you'd do anything as crazy as this." Nehls packs up his paperwork. "I'm going to the hospital. Flanigan, take her downstairs." He means the holding cells.

"But I'm a police officer."

"Captain Jackowski won't employ a cop who doesn't follow the rules. Even if you're innocent of these charges, you're still guilty of that."

"You can't put me in jail."

"You're a suspect, and we're holding you like any other suspect."

He's not going to believe that Mason set me up. I hardly believe it myself.

"Get her out of here," Nehls orders Paul.

Paul comes toward me, so I make one last appeal, "I didn't do it. The only thing I'm guilty of is being stupid enough to fall in love with Mason." I know it sounds pathetic. It is.

Paul stands me up.

"Since when is it illegal to fuck a co-worker around here?" I ask Nehls.

He waves us away without looking at me. "You're a disgrace."

All the lights are on in the block and I recognize two of the three women behind bars as we approach the gate. They watch me with hateful eyes.

"Paul, you can't put me in here. Put me in the single," I say.

"Shh," he says.

"I'm the reason two of them are in here. I helped bust them last week. They know me. Come on, put me in the single. Please," I beg, "they'll tear me apart."

"Keep quiet," he says and moves me past them. He knows I'm right.

In the next cell I get a glimpse of Birdie, sitting there picking his fingernails. The little shit nods at me like he's not surprised. He was probably in this thing with Mason from the beginning. From the night he sent Fred and me to get Marko Trovic. I grab the cell bars.

"You're working for Mason. You're the one he arrested tonight. You're his alibi. You liar!"

Birdie whispers something to his cellmate, who laughs. Paul peels my fingers from the bars.

"Let's go."

I let him pull me away. I'm in enough trouble.

Paul locks me in a single cell and he doesn't stick around to make conversation. I'm pretty sure he's finally lost interest in asking me out.

Once he's gone, I almost wish he'd put me with the other women. At least then I wouldn't be alone in here, trapped in my head, imagining the horror of what's happened. Susan. Pregnant and dying on the side of the road. I can't shut my eyes without seeing her—the first time I met her at Deborah's, her face flush with color and what I thought was naïveté, and then again tonight, her radiance gone, worn away, in part, by me. She acted certain that Mason would stay, but she was holding on to all hope that I'd go away.

At least she's alive. Thank God she's alive. I hope she can remember what happened, and that she'll clear my name, because Nehls didn't believe a word I said. Did my story sound that far-fetched? As ridiculous as saying a dead man killed Fred?

Why did Mason blame me? I don't know who ran Susan off the road, but I have a terrible feeling that Mason does. He told me he was going to divorce her. He told her she was going to Florida. I think he was going to get rid of both of us.

Susan was right: It was friendly fire. Maybe she didn't know she was in the line. But I didn't think I was either.

I stay awake and think about how to fire back.

27

The sun comes through the slit of my cell window and I have not slept. I can hear the station manager bringing breakfast. Like I could eat.

I paced around my eight feet of space all night, going over everything that has fallen apart in the space of a week. Sometime after dawn, I had a revelation: I thought I loved Mason. I thought we had an honest relationship, kept in check by the lengths we had to go to just to see each other. But on the night Fred died, when the shoe girl asked how I made my relationship work, I didn't have an answer. I had an opinion, I had an idea about how love should be, but it wasn't complete. Just like my relationship with Mason.

I couldn't explain how the relationship worked because it didn't. I knew I'd never take Susan's place, and at first I didn't want to. Who would trade the mystery and the excitement that goes into an affair for an ordinary marriage? I thrived on our secrecy like it was intimacy. I believed our love was rooted in honesty and acceptance. I was right, but only because Mason was honest about being married, and because I accepted the situation.

The truth is, Mason's been getting everything he wanted all along, and Susan and I have had to share. I've been settling for part of him. I thought it was the better part. Now I know he is a liar, and a coward, and all of him wouldn't be enough.

I do have an idea about how love should be. And I deserve more.

"Samantha Mack," O'Connor says, tapping on my cell bars. "You ready to talk, now that you're not a moving target?"

"Not to you," I say. "You can't hold me in here anyway. I didn't do anything."

"That's what they all say."

He unlocks the cell door and lets himself inside. I can smell his aftershave, and I notice a few nicks on his neck where he slipped with the razor. He reminds me of a guy I met in college, a seemingly vulnerable guy whose steady girlfriend broke his heart once a week. He had girls lined up to commiserate, and I always wondered who was the bigger sucker.

"You're not exactly innocent," O'Connor says, and holds up a photograph of me in Fred's backyard, spying on Mason and Deborah.

I resume pacing.

"What were you doing?" he asks.

"You think I'm gonna tell you? You're probably the one who took it," I say. "Following me around, waiting for me to slip up. You're a jerk."

"I hate to disappoint you, but I'm not the guy who's out to get you," he says.

O'Connor holds up another picture of me, this time behind the Weber on Mason's back patio, looking in on him and Susan. I want to slap the picture out of his hand.

"I get it," I say. "Where'd you get them?"

"Mason sent them over this morning. He says he hired some guy to follow you when he thought you were getting a little insistent about ending his marriage."

"The yellow truck." I thought it was Trovic. Then I thought it was O'Connor.

"Don't know what he drives, but the guy followed you to Fred Maloney's, and Mason's, and to a bunch of bars. You know, you shouldn't drink so much."

Now he shows me a picture of me at O'Shea's, drunk and leaning over the bar saying something to Marty. I'm wearing my uniform.

"Jesus, what are you, an AA sponsor? Did you come down here to intervene?"

"The thing about intervention, Sam, is that it doesn't work unless the person is ready. I just came down here to let you know what's going on. We're not going to do anything about these photos until the case agent gets a look at your car. If there's no damage, there's no case against you. You'll be released."

"There is no damage to my car," I tell him.

"Witness wasn't even sure it was a Mustang. Most likely they'll list it a hit-and-run."

"An accident," I say.

"They do happen."

"Mason set me up," I say. "You saw this coming all along."

"I tried to tell you," O'Connor says. "Like I said. Intervention."

"How did you know?"

He sits down on the bench. "Mason and I go way back. He hasn't changed. Doesn't have to. There's always someone he can get to. First it was me, and who knows how many in between. Now it's you."

"What did he do to you?"

"Put it this way: Jail would have been nice." O'Connor hands me a pack of Camels and some matches, and this time I don't care if he's trying to persuade me. I pack them, unwrap them, and take one out.

"He never told me you two had a past," I say.

"I'm surprised, I thought he was proud of it."

"So . . . ?"

"So, I am the reason Mason is a cop. He is the reason I'm not."

He stares ahead, at the wall, and he looks like a different person. Maybe because he isn't in my face with questions. Maybe because now I'm ready to listen. I sit down next to him and light my smoke.

"We were in the Academy together," he says. "We bonded because we both hated one of the instructors. This guy had it in for us; for Mason, mostly. Mason was a smart-ass with connections. I was just smart. We pooled our resources.

"We studied together, partnered for all the drills, looked out for each other. We were a team. Mason practically lived with my wife and me, since our apartment was so close to school. We spent as many nights telling stories as we did memorizing the manuals. My wife would cook dinner for us, quiz us before tests, drink beer with us on the porch."

O'Connor runs his hands through his hair. He doesn't like where this story is going.

"Long story short," he says, "I worked my ass off while Mason bullshitted his way through the oral board, strong-armed his way through the PA test, and copied my answers on the exams. I didn't care. I thought we were friends, and we were going to be cops.

"The night we found out we'd made it through, we went out to celebrate. I got real drunk. My wife had to come pick us up. They dumped me on the couch and went out on the porch." O'Connor looks at me, and I can guess what he doesn't want to say. I take the cigarette out of my mouth and crush it with my shoe.

"I saw them with my own two eyes, out there, his hands . . ." His unemotional pitch wavers. "I saw how much she wanted him. I knew how much he enjoyed it."

O'Connor stands up, the memory taking over. "I stormed out past them. 'It's not what you think,' I heard my wife say. I got a good look at Mason, standing there like he had every right, like I was the pathetic one. I did the only thing I could do: I walked away. I got on my motorcycle, one of those CBR crotch rockets? I made it down the street and out of the neighborhood before I lost control. I wrecked the bike and shattered my tibia beyond repair. Next day I had a badge and no way to walk the beat. I was assigned to Admin. I could never patrol."

O'Connor sits down again like he feels the pain in his leg.

"What hurt the most was that I let it happen. I had shared everything with him. Even my wife. And I walked away."

"Did you stay married?"

"No. They both denied anything happened. But nothing was ever the same. My attitude was never the same. I thought I was going to be a detective and I wound up being a secretary. I don't blame her for leaving. I turned out to be a real jerk."

"Mason has that effect on people, doesn't he." I take out another cigarette and light it. O'Connor leans back and sticks his hands in his pockets.

"So you're healed; I mean, you don't limp or anything," I say.

"It's been ten years. I'm used to it."

"But you're not over it."

"This isn't revenge, Sam. This is my job."

"Where is Mason now?"

"Hospital, last I heard."

"Is Susan okay?" I don't want to ask.

"Did you know she was pregnant?"

"She told me, yeah."

"She lost the baby."

"Oh my God."

"Mason says that's your motive. He's sticking to his story, he thinks you're responsible."

"What about *his* motive? I could tell you details about our relationship. He told me he was going to leave Susan. Just last night he told me he asked her for a divorce . . ."

By the look on O'Connor's face, I'm guessing I sound as crazy as everyone thinks.

"What about my case? Can you follow up? Mason said he put out a state warrant for Trovic. He said he had a connection at the state's office . . ."

Same look.

"But you know we've been seeing each other," I say.

"You both denied it." O'Connor takes his hands out of his pockets and uses his right thumb to rub his left knuckle, just below where he might have worn a wedding ring. "Face it, Mack. He lied to you."

I stamp out my smoke. The sick thing is, there's a

part of me that still thinks Mason has a good reason for all of this. I guess no matter how I add up the lies, I still don't want to accept the big one: He said he loved me. And I believed it.

"How does he get away with all this shit?" O'Connor asks.

I look at the photos of myself that O'Connor left on the bench. I think about Mason's perfect home, and Susan's huge diamond ring. I am so stupid.

"He takes control," I say. And I let him.

"That's right," O'Connor says, "it's the control. That's why he's taxing. He gets to run the show. It's a power trip."

"Taxing?" I ask.

"He's on the take. He's been extorting money from drug dealers since he started at your district. Charging them to stay on the streets. He's got a string of guys in your ward caught up in it."

I'm trying to process this without emotion. He's a bad guy. *He's a criminal.* I didn't know.

"If you know all this, why haven't you arrested him?" I ask.

"He's good at what he does. The jobs we could nail him for have been too small. He'd either get slapped on the hand by your captain and take his business elsewhere, or pass it off to one of his front men. We want him, and we've been waiting for him to go bigger."

"Seems like everyone's been waiting for him to do something," I say. "Why don't *you* do something?"

"You think I've been following you around because I want a date?" he asks.

"How was I supposed to know all this? You weren't straight with me before."

"I thought you were working with Mason."

"I guess I was." I kept our affair a secret. I looked

the other way when I didn't like what I saw. And I believed everything he said, because I thought he believed in me. I thought he loved me.

But I know I convinced Mason of at least one thing: He thinks I love him, too.

"You think I can get to him," I say to O'Connor.

"Do you want me to say it again? I need your help."

So this is it. I resisted IA to be loyal to my coworkers. I resisted my superiors because I wanted to be loyal to Fred. I almost forgot my duty as a police officer because I wanted to be loyal to Mason. And all along I've been resisting my intuition: Mason is a liar.

I point to O'Connor's badge. "Gimme that for a minute. The snitch down the hall owes me."

O'Connor doesn't budge.

"You *are* a cop," I say, "and you're a better one than Mason. Trust me. We can get him."

O'Connor studies me, maybe looking for a flicker of duplicity in my eyes, like the exhilaration we've both seen in Mason's.

Then he takes his badge from his shirt pocket and hands it to me.

28

Birdie sits backward on the floor, up against the bars, biting what's left of his nails. His cellmate is asleep.

I reach around and grab Birdie's shirt collar through the bars, pull him back toward me, and flash O'Connor's badge.

"You let Mason chase you down last night? Is that why you're in here?" I ask.

"No," Birdie says, trying to scoot away from me.

"Bullshit! Start talking."

"You can't do this. You're locked up too."

"I'm a cop. You don't know what I can do."

He practically chokes himself trying to get away from me. "I turned myself in," he wheezes.

"For what? You better have a good story, or I'm gonna introduce you to every last one of the guys locked up in this place and tell them you're a two-face. You want to make some new friends?"

"It's not safe out there," he says. "Trovic's guys are pissed. You fuckin' cops killed him, and they think I knew about it."

I let go of him.

"You *did* know about it. You said he told you to call Fred. You said you talked to Trovic *after* he was already dead."

"So I didn't talk to him exactly. But the order came from him—from the people he works with. I didn't know he was dead, I swear. I did what I was told and sent Fred to meet him. Look, I'm not saying any more, and I don't have to. I'm already in jail." He straightens out his collar.

"Fine. Get him out," I tell O'Connor, who follows my lead and takes out his keys to open the cell. "I know some guys who'll love to meet you, Birdie."

His cellmate stirs, and Birdie gets anxious.

"Come on, man," he says to O'Connor. "I don't know any more than you."

"You know who Mason brought in last night," I say. "It was a bullshit arrest."

Birdie doesn't say anything; O'Connor sticks his key in the lock.

"All right, all right," he says. "Hold on a minute." He checks to make sure his cellmate is still asleep. Then he sticks his face between the bars and whispers to O'Connor, "I heard it was some guy from the south side, some grunt who works for the guys who are about to score a deal with Mason. I heard the guy was released ten minutes after they brought him in."

"Mason's alibi," O'Connor says.

"Don't ask me," Birdie whispers.

"What deal?" I ask.

With his face against the bars, Birdie can turn only his eyes to me. "Don't act like you're not in on it," he says. "I seem to remember you coming after me, trying to scare me with your twenty-two."

I can feel O'Connor's eyes on me. Birdie senses he's starting trouble. He continues, his focus back on O'Connor, "Word on the street is, she tried to pin Maloney's death on Trovic 'cuz she's in with Mason. They wanted to make it look like Trovic was alive so no one would suspect he wasn't. She's probably in here hiding from Trovic's guys, just like me."

"So what if she is?" O'Connor asks.

Birdie puts his forefinger to his lips because O'Connor is not whispering.

"They've been on the take for at least a year," O'Connor says without lowering his voice. "What's the big deal about this one?"

Birdie takes his finger from his lips and points it at me. "She wasn't supposed to be part of the picture. Mason doesn't pull this off, the bosses will lose their product, and they won't stand in the way if half of Serbia comes after his ass. And hers, too."

I feel like they're talking about the stats of a game where I don't know the rules. And I am the stakes.

"I thought I had a big mouth," Birdie says. "You guys are all playing each other out."

"I'll put you on the street in front of Trovic's guys right now and let them play *you* out," O'Connor tells him. "Or, you can tell me when and where this deal is supposed to happen."

"Don't do this to me," Birdie says, and walks away from the bars. "I'm not a rat. I just wanted to pay my debts." He looks back at his cellmate again. He's still sleeping soundly. Birdie weighs his options.

I decide to help him make up his mind. The key's still in the lock, and O'Connor doesn't stop me when I go for it. I throw the cell door open and grab Birdie by the back of his shirt. I bend my knees and use all one hundred and thirty pounds of me to push him against the bars. He holds his head back, so I grab his hair with my left hand. From this position I could do some damage, starting with a decent hook to his ribs.

"Spill it."

O'Connor shrugs at Birdie, letting him know I'm right.

"Some heroin out of Florida," he says. He quits resisting and his face smashes into the bars. "Ow!"

O'Connor steps in close to him. "Is that why Trovic was in Miami?"

"Yeah," Birdie says. "Trovic set it up, real sneaky, through a friend he met on vacation. Some cruise line out of Miami that stops in Cozumel. I heard he scored like ten kilos. But Trovic wound up dead before he could bring back the black tar. Mason Imes intercepted the stash. He's been in charge ever since Trovic disappeared. All I know is that it's the big one, and after this, all bets are off."

O'Connor signals me to let go of Birdie, but I don't.

"We'll keep you in here. You're safe in here," O'Connor tells him. "All you have to do is tell us where and when."

"I told you everything I know!" he shouts. His cellmate sits up suddenly and stares at us, unsure what to make of the situation. I let go of Birdie. He leans against the bars, holding his jaw. "You bitch, you nearly busted my front teeth."

"Now we're even," I say, pointing to my eye.

◆ ◆ ◆

I grab on to the bars outside my cell to stop O'Connor from locking me up again.

"Let me out of here. You need me, you said so yourself," I say.

"I can't," he says.

"Come on, O'Connor, who else do you have? Every other cop on this force will look the other way. If they're not in with Mason, they're scared shitless of him. I'm telling you, I can get him."

O'Connor mulls this over. He looks at my pack of Camels like he wants one. I don't think he smokes.

"If I get you out, we do this my way. You wear a wire."

"No way. Mason knows me too well. He'll figure it out in a heartbeat. And if I turn on him now, and the deal Birdie was talking about is botched, we're all in trouble."

"If Mason knows you so well, what would he expect you to do, once you're released?"

"He'd expect me to prove I didn't go after Susan. I'd find out who took those pictures. But this has nothing to do with what Birdie told us. There's no time to chase some bottom feeder PI—"

"That's exactly what you're going to do."

"Why?"

"To buy me some time."

"You want me to be a diversion?"

"You're working on clearing your name. Mason will believe that."

"After I find the PI, you know what Mason will expect me to do?"

"No. What?"

"He'll expect me to find *him*."

"Oh no. You stay away from him. You give me enough time to get a handle on this junk deal and then we'll bring you back in." I can't tell if he's afraid something will happen to me, or if he wants to get Mason himself.

"Okay," I say. I don't sound very convincing.

"Sam, promise me . . ." O'Connor starts. For some reason he's hesitant. "If I let you out, promise me you won't say a word about this conversation."

"What conversation?" I smile, the first time I've smiled at him. He has never smiled at me.

"We could both get into some serious shit if we don't do this right. I'm not supposed to be working with you. I'm not even supposed to be talking to you anymore because I couldn't get you to talk before. Division will have my badge if we don't bust Mason."

"Look at it this way," I say. "If I turn up dead, you can nail him for that."

O'Connor isn't comforted.

"You can't walk away from this one, Alex," I say. "It's your job."

When O'Connor finally closes and locks my cell door, I'm on the outside of it.

29

O'Connor says he'll talk to the case agent and take care of Nehls. O'Connor may not be my ally, but we have a common enemy. And he can make things happen.

Thankfully, the station is pretty dead when I leave. O'Connor walks me out and hails me a cab. It's sunny, and almost warm outside, and Addison is alive with bikers and joggers headed toward the lake. I wonder how many of these people are having affairs. I'm probably the only one stupid enough. O'Connor watches as my cab pulls away, and from the look in his eye I can tell he's hoping he didn't just make a huge mistake.

* * *

The back of one of the photographs has a Wolf Camera logo, so my first step is to find out where they were developed. The first Wolf Camera I visit is a place the size of a magazine stand, stuffed into a building on Rush Street. I present the photos to an older guy behind a counter stacked with processing envelopes.

"Any idea how I find out where these were developed?" I ask. I hope he cooperates since I don't have my star to back me up.

"If they're ours," he says, "there's a routing number." I hand him the picture of me outside Mason's and he glances at the image. Then he looks at me. "Who's following who?"

"Please, this is urgent," I say. "I'm a police officer," He isn't sold.

"The person who took these could be in trouble," I lie.

"You're a cop?" he asks, wanting proof.

The only evidence I can give is the photo of me in uniform at the bar. I hand it over; he is clearly not impressed, but he turns over the photo and punches some corresponding numbers in his computer.

"That's our Chicago Avenue store," he tells me, and I know exactly which one, so I grab the pictures and dart out.

"Thanks," I say over my shoulder. I can see him shaking his head in the mirror that covers the security camera. Guess I won't be coming back here for my film processing needs.

"You see the guy who picked these up?" I ask a college kid wearing a tag that says "Tim." This Wolf Camera is bigger, and the space seems unnecessary.

"We can't give the names of customers . . ." Tim

starts, so I lean over the desk and show him the picture of me at the bar.

"Look. I'm a cop. The guy who took these is stalking me."

He looks at the photo, then at me, then at every corner of the room. I wonder if his decision hinges on store policy. I size the kid up, stand between him and the store's security camera, and put a twenty on the counter. Tim considers the money.

"Comes in once in a while with this type stuff," he says. "Don't know his name."

I put another twenty on the counter.

"I don't know it," he insists.

"Can't you look it up?"

He looks up at the security camera. I take that as a no.

I pick up both bills, take the photo, and turn to walk out.

"He drives a yellow truck, right?" Tim says.

I stop.

"He was just in here yesterday. Dropped off a roll . . ." Tim flips through a stack of envelopes and pulls out a processing slip. He puts it on the counter and taps some keys to open his register, waiting for the cash, just like a regular transaction.

I give him the forty bucks and buy the name: Bruce Zahner.

I find a phone booth outside a Streeter's Pub on Chicago Avenue and open the attached phone book to the end. I search the z's until I find a few Zahners. Three with first letter *B*. One within ten minutes of here.

I hail a cab.

The cabbie takes me west down Division Street, away from the upscale brownstone condos and toward the fat ugly warehouses across the river. I stop him a few blocks past the address and walk back to a warehouse facing the river.

I knock. No one answers, so I try the door. It's open.

When I get inside, the lights are on, but the place is strangely quiet.

"Hello?" I say. No one answers. I should have told the cabbie to wait.

If this guy is a private eye, he isn't very private about it. All his equipment is in plain view. Photographs of people who definitely weren't posing for them are strewn over a worktable. A telescope sits dismantled on the floor. A roll of paper hangs from the fax machine; its green light blinks.

"Hello?" I say again. I flip through some papers on his desk, but it all looks irrelevant to my case.

"Who are you?" A skinny woman in acid-washed Levis catches me off guard when she appears from what I thought was a closet. She exhales smoke with every breath.

"I'm looking for Bruce Zahner," I say.

"So am I," she says. She jams a cigarette into her mouth and looks me over with shifty eyes. Or maybe her eyes are steady and the rest of her is shifty. She taps her foot and rhythmically wipes her left hand on her jeans. Either there's music playing that I'm not hearing, or she's strung out.

"Who are you?" I ask.

"Who the hell are you?" she asks right back.

"My name's Mary," I lie uncreatively. "I'm a dissatisfied customer."

"Join the club," she says. "I'm Janine. Bruce's exgirlfriend." She proceeds through the office to what I figured was another closet door. I follow her down a hallway.

"Have you seen him?" I ask.

"Not for a couple days. I should have known he wouldn't be here. He never shows up during normal hours. Sets up this business to look for people, and always the people who come here are looking for him." She opens a heavy door and its weight nearly pulls her along with it. "Says he don't have money. Cheap bastard. Look at this."

I step into a garage that's practically consumed by that big yellow truck. She coaxes me on like she's giving a tour. "Said he had cash coming in under the table, then he goes, gets this shiny car like he's doing surveillance for Donald Trump. To 'keep everybody he owes on their toes,' he says. Moron. And, he owes me money."

She flips on an overhead light, and I see, parked on the other side of the truck, a 2002 black Mustang. It looks better than mine.

"He owe you something?" Janine asks.

"An explanation."

"You're telling me. I ask him maybe he could share the wealth, pay people back instead of blowing it all at the gambling boats like last time . . ." She keeps rambling.

I walk around the car. There are no scratches. Vehicle paint and car body repair tools line a workbench on the passenger's side. There are Avis rental car stickers on the plates. The chemical smell of paint hangs in the air.

This is the car that ran Susan off the road. This man tried to kill her. There's no denying it: Mason hired Bruce Zahner for dirty work.

I need air. I find a door that lets me outside to a gravel parking lot. It's heavy, like the one on the other side of the garage, and I put my weight into it, head down, and push.

That's when I see the blood. Or is it motor oil? Little specks on the floor that get lost in the gravel outside. I prop the door open and touch a spot on the floor with my finger. It's not oil.

"When did you see Bruce last?" I ask Janine, moving on to examine the gravel.

"Two days ago," she says. "I should have known. He's probably too broke to get back from the casino in Elgin. Last time he was there I had to go get him myself." Janine follows me past a row of Dumpsters, though she's moving more slowly than her mouth.

I kneel, searching for evidence, but the blood trail is more like a dead end. Looks like I'm going to have to find out what's in the Dumpsters.

"I should have left him when he lost all the rent money at some off-track betting place," Janine continues, kneeling with me like she's helping, though I don't think she has a clue what I'm doing.

I stand up and open the lid to the first Dumpster and the rancid smell nearly makes me puke. It isn't death; it's more like a Porta Potti. Without looking inside, I drop the lid and move away as fast as I can. About three feet past the last Dumpster, I notice a rut in the gravel. A groove, like something had been dragged toward the river. I follow the subtle path.

"He had this big sob story, and he had the nerve to ask me to spot him a hundred . . ."

I try to block out her jabbering. I feel sick. I stop at the edge of the parking lot where a concrete slab stops the path. I lean over a metal rail that separates the property from the river below. My head spins and I want to tell Janine to shut up. I close my eyes and spit and breathe and try not to vomit. Mason framed me. Mason is responsible for killing his unborn child. I have to find Bruce Zahner.

Janine comes up next to me, still babbling: ". . . I told him if it wasn't for me, he'd be . . . dead . . . he's . . . he's . . . Bruce!"

I think she must be shouting to him across the river. I grip the rail and stand up straight to find out.

"Oh my God! He's dead!" she howls. She's pointing down to the river.

There, the body of a curly-headed man floats, snagged on a rock in the slow-moving current. His beady eyes stare up at me, and I remember him from O'Shea's. And then I throw up.

"Oh no! Bruce! No!" Janine starts to climb over the rail. I wipe my mouth, grab hold of her leg, and pull her back.

"Don't go down there, you'll hurt yourself. Can you stay right here?" Janine collapses to the gravel. I watch her and take a second to recover.

"Bruce," she whimpers.

"I'll call the police," I lie. The last thing I need is to be caught here. "Janine?" She looks up at me in a complete daze. "I'll be right back."

I'm shaking. A cold sweat sticks to my skin. I run back into the office.

I leave the door open to keep my eye on Janine and I find a phone to call O'Connor.

"Where are you?" I ask when he answers.

"Still at your station," he says. "Just finished questioning Officer Flagherty. Only thing he admits is a healthy fear of his wife. You know her? If he had any knowledge of corruption around here, I think she would have slapped the cuffs on him herself. He's in the doghouse just for agreeing to sit nights at Deb Maloney's. So where are you? I ran into your Sarge. He was close to a coronary. He talked to the agent who impounded your car—something about a trunkful of sympathy cards—"

"Forget the cards," I say. "I found the guy. Bruce Zahner. Office is on Division, west of the river. He's floating in it."

"In his office?"

"In the river."

"Anybody else see him?"

"His ex-girlfriend just found him. He's got a black Mustang, all patched up, looks just like mine. It's parked in his garage. Rental plates. And the yellow truck I thought was yours? It's here too. It was him. This is proof."

"Possible proof he was hired to follow you. Not that he was hired to kill Susan."

"If he's responsible for Susan's accident, and we can link him to Mason, that's solicitation of murder. It's at least conspiracy to commit, right?"

"Don't get ahead of yourself. Wait for me there. We'll trace his steps. Find a loophole. A mistake. Do this by the book."

"You know as well as I do we won't get him that way," I say.

"There are other cops involved, Sam. This is bigger than you know."

"I don't care who's involved, O'Connor. I'm the one who keeps taking the blame." I think I would taste bile in my mouth even if I hadn't thrown up.

"Give me the address," O'Connor says. "I'll be there in ten minutes."

Through the doorway I see Janine is out of her daze, waving her arms around and yelling at passing cars. One has pulled into the lot, and the driver is already out of his car, dialing his cell phone.

"Cops will be here in two," I tell O'Connor. "You want me to be a diversion, don't let me get stuck in this."

"Fine. Tell me where to pick you up."

"That won't work. If other cops are involved, word that we're working together is bound to get to Mason if you leave the station. If you aren't getting any answers there, I'm going to find out who else is working with him. *You* be the diversion."

"Dammit, Mack, I don't like this—" he starts.

"I'll be in touch," I finish. I hang up and go out the back, down the alley to Halsted.

If I'm right about the PI, it's true that Mason intended to get rid of Susan and me. Or at least he wanted to make it look that way; if anyone thought I was working with him, blaming me for attempting to kill his wife would certainly dispel the idea.

Why does everyone think I'm working with Mason anyway? Both O'Connor and Birdie said it's because I tried to pin Fred's death on Trovic instead of calling it an accident.

That means nobody believes it was accident. That means someone besides Marko Trovic wanted to kill Fred.

I catch a cab and give the driver Fred's address. He heads north and I wish he'd move faster, because I need to find out the truth about Fred before Mason catches up with me.

30

I didn't handle our last meeting well, but I'm ready to confront Deborah about Fred. If she knows anything about her husband's death, she's going to tell me. I'll choke it out of her if I have to.

The cab drops me in front of Fred's. Though the front window is dark, I think twice about going around to the back. I knock on the front door instead.

Some teenager answers the door with paint on his face and T-shirt. He's smoking a cigarette. He's got muscles that don't go along with his young face. He doesn't look at all surprised to see me.

"You the cleaning lady?" he asks.

I wonder if something about my appearance begs the question.

"I'm looking for Deborah," I say. I try to be nice about it. "I'm a . . . friend."

The kid nods like I insisted the Cubs will take the Series this year (agreement is the only courteous option).

"She moved," he says, looking me over.

"Are you moving in?" I ask.

"Nope. I'm cleaning the place out for her. I was expecting help."

I want to ask who he is. I want to get inside the house and see what Deb is up to, and I want to know where she went. I should have said I was the cleaning lady.

"Could I trouble you for a cigarette?" I ask.

"Yeah," he says, "they're in the back. You want to come in?"

He holds the door for me to join him. I cross the threshold like a vampire. Little do you know, kid.

I follow him down the hallway, taking in as much information as I can. In the front room, everything is gone except the piano. The dining room is empty, too, except for some boxes. The hallway walls are bare.

"So you're my mom's friend?" the kid asks.

"What?"

"My mom. Deborah." This is Deb's son? Deb *has* a son? What the fuck?

I try to play it cool. "I knew her husband, actually," I say. This is incredible.

"Which one?" the kid asks, carelessly flicking ash from his cigarette.

"Fred," I say, probably failing to hide my astonishment. "I was talking about Fred."

"Well, I guess you know he's not here either," the kid says. He means it as a joke, I think. It's a good thing I already threw up.

"Do you mind if I use the bathroom?" I ask.

"Go ahead," he says. "I'll be in back."

I manage to hold it together until I get in the bathroom, close the door, and sit on the lid of the toilet with my head in my hands. My breath shortens. I suck in gulps of air. The faucet drips, keeping arbitrary time. Drip. Drip. It would have driven Fred crazy. If he were alive he would have spent his next day off at the hardware store and under the sink.

I get up and run the faucet. I splash cold water on my face to keep myself from crying. Fred didn't tell me he had a stepson. I'm starting to think he didn't tell me a lot of things.

Maybe I didn't know Fred at all. I have to talk to this kid. He might be my last chance to find out.

In the back room, Deb's son is painting over a spackled wall.

"That's a nice color," I say, to let him know I'm there. I realize I'm standing where the couch used to be. The couch where Mason consoled Deborah. The thought disgusts me.

The kid hands me a fresh cigarette along with the one he's smoking. "I'm outta matches."

"Were you close to Fred?" I ask, lighting my cigarette and returning his.

He picks up a roller and runs it through a tray of pale blue paint. "We didn't get along. I live with my dad. No offense, but for a hard-ass cop, Fred had no backbone. Especially when it came to my mom."

"He loved your mother," I say, though I would have agreed with the kid if Fred were still alive.

"I know. And then he goes and gets himself killed on the night shift that my mom convinced him to take for more money. I'll never be like that with a girl, I don't care what."

"I thought Fred switched shifts because your mother

had a problem with his old partner." The kid paints the wall in determined, hard streaks, up and down.

"The only problem my mom had was with Fred's paycheck. Bet she feels pretty shallow about that now."

I doubt it, so I don't respond. I look around for an ashtray with my hand under the end of my cigarette, though I wish Deb were here so I could put it out in her eye. How could Fred have loved such a fraud?

He quits painting to recoat his roller and notices my predicament.

"You could ash on the carpet," he says, "I'm gonna get it replaced anyway."

"What's wrong with the carpet?" I ask.

"What's wrong with it is that it looks like someone stole twenty sick sheep and stuck them to the floor," he says. "My mother has very expensive, very bad taste."

I agree with a tap on the filter of my smoke. The ashes flutter to the floor and get lost in the thick shag. Makes me wonder what Deb did with Fred's ashes. Makes me mad.

"Where, exactly, did Deb move?" I ask.

"Naples," he says.

"Italy?" I ask, though I get a bad feeling from the blank look on his face.

"Huh?"

"Naples, Italy?"

"I don't know about Italy," he says. "She's in Florida."

Florida is shaping up to be pretty crowded. I'd better get on my way.

What about Fred?

"Well," I say, "I'll let you get back to it. Thanks for the smoke. Tell Deborah I said good luck."

"Sure. What's your name?"

"Susan," I call out as I'm already down the hall.

"See ya, Susan," he calls out.

I let myself out as Deborah's kid finishes covering her tracks. Poor Fred.

As I walk out to Webster Avenue, I rack my brain to figure out what to do next. If Susan had the tickets to Miami and Deb is already in Florida, then I'm not the only one Mason is lying to. I just don't understand why Mason wasted so much time with me. Burying my case against Trovic doesn't seem like enough of a reason. Mason could have just dumped me, like a normal guy. I would have recovered from that.

Mason's up to something more, and I need to find someone besides him who knows what it is. I still don't have any clue about who else is working with him, and I still don't know what Fred had to do with it.

Who will talk to me? O'Connor says other cops are involved, but it doesn't sound like he's getting anyone to admit it. If I call Wade, I'll end up wasting another hour eating breakfast somewhere listening to the "you know better" routine. Dave Blake, Randy Stoddard . . . all the other cops who have potential are probably the ones who aren't talking to O'Connor.

Paul Flanigan has no potential. He's a rookie; Mason wouldn't bother with him. Anyway, he's the one who gave me Fred's phone records. He couldn't be involved. He helped me.

Which is exactly what I thought Mason was doing.

I find the nearest pay phone and call Paul. I'll take him up on that drink, if he's still interested. I could use one whether he knows anything or not.

31

thought you quit drinking," Paul says when I get him on the phone.

"I paused," I say. "You still willing to buy me a beer?"

"I think I owe you one, after last night."

"Meet me at Goose Island."

I'm at the front end of the bar, sipping a pleasantly bitter, much-needed beer, staring out the floor-to-ceiling windows. It's getting dark outside, and I anticipate Paul's arrival with every person that comes down the sidewalk. I hope Mason isn't following closely behind.

It's been almost an hour. I thought Paul would rush

right over here. I knew this was a long shot; I hope it wasn't a complete mistake.

If Paul is on the up-and-up, no one will find me here. Goose Island isn't a place anyone would look. None of the cops hang out here because it's so close to the station. Nothing against the beer; I used to make an occasional stop for a draft down at their old brewery off Clybourn until they started selling the stuff in bottles. I guess the novelty wore off when I knew I could buy a six-pack at Osco.

Wrigleyville isn't my kind of neighborhood anyway. This is one of our beats, and we all spend plenty of time here during night games around the corner at Wrigley. Even when there's no baseball, there's usually some drunken argument between aging frat boys over whose alma mater has a better sports program. One bar down the street caters to Michigan State fans. We've wasted a lot of time busting up fights just to listen to one burly Spartan or another whine about a fat lip he probably deserved. What kind of a dumb ass would throw punches over a college sports team?

The clientele here is pretty tame in comparison. The place opened a few years ago and nearly caused a community upheaval. The owners had to promise they wouldn't invite the sort of patrons who'd pee in their neighbors' yards. They advertise this place as a family establishment, and now the boys over on Halsted probably make more racket. There are a few places across the street that get rowdy without fail; but here, for some reason, it's always manageable.

That's why I picked the place. It's manageable.

I see Paul coming down the sidewalk dressed like an off-duty cop: everything is ironed and orderly, but he has absolutely no semblance of style. Still, he walks with an air of innocence I wish I still had. He obviously never killed anybody.

I move my stool and turn on the charm when he comes in and sits down next to me.

"Hi there," I say, keeping an eye on the front door to see if anyone else will be joining us.

"I hear you've got half the city looking for you. How come I'm the lucky one?" he asks.

"Because you're the only one who'd consider yourself lucky."

"What are you drinking?" he asks.

"Honker's," I tell him.

"Two Honker's," he says to the bartender.

I'd better pace myself.

The first round consists of small talk and getting-to-know-you-type stuff.

"You live around here?" I ask, since he arrived without gloves or a hat or a cab.

"I live right around the block," he tells me. "Isn't that why you wanted to meet here? Tell the truth. I know your MO. Have you been following me?"

"Just because I stalked my boyfriend doesn't mean I do it to everyone," I say. I try to laugh about it.

"I'm not worried," he says. "I've never had a problem with good-looking women being interested in me."

"Who says I'm interested? I'm here for the beer."

I think I'm doing a pretty good job of loosening him up. But if he's anything like Mason, he's doing the same to me. I don't want to play games, so I figure I'll just get to the point and ask him if he's working for Mason. I'm trying to find the best way to word it when Paul says, "So, I'll ask a stupid question. Do you like it when people call you Smack? I mean, I get it, Sam-Mack . . ."

"Actually, it didn't start because of my name," I tell him. A smile surprises the rest of my face. "Fred made it up. We arrested this guy for public nuisance. He was totally bat-shit, delusional, and at one point he just started freaking out—using all his strength to try to get away, screaming about how we were robots or machines or something. He came at me swinging, and my gut reaction was to slap him. The guy just stopped; he just stopped and started crying like a six-year-old. Fred lost it, he was laughing so hard. There I am on the street with these two men, and I'm trying to get them both to stop crying. 'Smack!' Fred kept saying, tears streaming down his face. 'You just smacked him!' he said. 'Look out, Rodney King!' He told the guys the story. It stuck."

"You think it's funny?" Paul asks.

"It's better than being called 'bitch-slap.' "

Paul laughs.

"So there it is. My persona demystified. Impressed?"

"Absolutely."

"You gonna buy me another beer?" I ask. I don't have all night, and the more I can get him to drink, the more I think I can get him to talk.

"If you'll demystify one more thing," he says. "Is Mason officially out of the running?"

I answer with another smile and then I flag the bartender. "Another round." Then I turn to Paul and say, "Try to keep up."

Over the next round I try the apology angle. I'm hoping Paul will feel guilty and fess up about Mason if I do. Or at least maybe he'll slip up.

"I feel bad for being such a bitch to you all the time," I say.

"I'm sorry I had to arrest you," Paul says. "You

looked like you had quite a night ahead of you until Wade and I interrupted."

"Yeah, trying to kill my boyfriend's wife just didn't do it for me. I was planning to spice up my Monday night with some random assaults. In high heels."

He tries to laugh about that, but he's having trouble. He's probably picturing me in that outfit. Or, he's working for Mason and I'm making him uncomfortable.

"I feel like I should explain myself, at least about Mason and me," I say.

"You don't have to," he says. "I know it takes two. I see the way he looks at you. It's not fair, you know. He already has one good woman. Why should he get two?"

He threw me there. And he's looking at me, looking for an acknowledgment with those big brown hopeful eyes. It's about the nicest thing anyone's said to me in a year. I grab my bag and fish through it for cigarettes. I realize I don't even know how to take a perfectly good compliment.

Paul hands me a matchbook from the bar, resigned to my silence. I suddenly don't feel like smoking.

"Have you ever been in love?" I ask him, Miss Shoe's words echoing in mine. And I thought she had problems.

Paul picks up his beer. "Once." He pauses a moment, toasting whoever it was, before he empties the glass. He can't be working for Mason. I can see his heart right there on his sleeve.

"I thought I was in love," I say. I want to spill my guts, but I don't continue. Instead, we both stare ahead at the beer taps in silence. Even though I don't know the first thing about him, just sitting here together is nice. Sitting here, Paul reminds me there are honest moments.

Of course he could be fooling me completely. These

are exactly the circumstances that made me fall in love with Mason: a real conversation, a vulnerable moment, a few beers. I have to stay focused. This is not a date.

"I think I'm going to get out of town for a while. Lick my wounds," I say, like I'm talking about the scabs on my knees.

"Where?"

"Florida," I say, to see if I get a reaction, but I don't. I tilt my head back to finish my beer.

Paul says, "Florida's great. You ever been to Naples?"

I keep my mouth shut so I don't spit out my beer and shake my head no. I swallow and slide off my stool.

"I'll be back." I head for the bathroom before he asks me anything else.

I stand in a bathroom stall and smoke. I know I should just be honest and ask Paul about Mason. But he could be here for information, just like me.

An image of Mason pops into my head. "Baby," he says, his warm grin tainted with pity, "you hit your head." He'd always state the obvious and then get me to tell him whatever he wanted to know. Building trust is the foolproof way to get answers. I flush my smoke and decide to press on with Paul. I haven't spent this much time with him for nothing.

Paul and two full beers are waiting at the bar. I wish myself luck.

"So," I say, sitting down with a new smile, "you know more than you'll ever want to about me, unless you want to talk about my *good* habits. What about you? Where you from?"

"Iowa."

"Why'd you come to Chicago?"

"Wanted to be a cop. My dad was a cop in Des Moines."

"Why didn't you stay in Iowa?"

"When you grow up in a place where you know everybody, it's hard to become someone they don't expect." He's got that right.

"How'd you end up in the district?" I ask.

"Dumb luck, I guess."

His answers are so generic I probably couldn't figure out what he had for lunch.

"You like it here?" I ask.

"I like it enough. I'm getting tired of being everybody's assistant, that's for sure."

"When I was a rookie," I tell him, "I fought my way out of that real quick. We had a guy, this junkie, who went ballistic when they uncuffed him. They were outside the station, letting him go. No one expected it. The guy was bouncing around, punching people, and really out of control. I was in the parking lot, getting Fred's jacket that he left in the car—I think just so I'd have to go get it—when this all happened. I came back to the scene and everyone's standing around this guy, doing nothing—even Fred—like the guy was a mountain lion or something. I walked over and took him down with one move. Nobody ever asked me to get him coffee after that."

"What did you do? Smack him?"

"You're hilarious. I'm a green belt. Kung fu."

"You think you could take me down?" Paul asks. From the look on his face, I think he'd be willing to let me try.

"It depends on how you attack me," I explain. "I learned a lot of specific techniques in training."

"Give me one."

"Okay . . . the overhead club."

"A club. A common weapon on these mean streets." Amused, Paul watches me swivel around on my stool.

"Say someone comes at you from straight on, with a club—a two-by-four, a beer bottle, whatever. You can deflect their strength by taking a step back, blocking the weapon with a moving hand to absorb the blow, and turning your torso at an angle that corresponds to the attacker's height."

"You're doing math? You're counting on an attacker coming at you with a certain weapon from a certain angle—what's your weapon, a compass? You think that works? You're no bigger than my sister, and she's in high school. I'm surprised you're still alive."

"You want me to demonstrate?" I ask.

"Maybe later," he says. But he makes it sound like that means later tonight.

I think I'm getting somewhere.

After four beers each and a lot of bullshitting, Paul finally gets up his nerve.

"Part of me wants to believe you're enjoying my company. The rest of me thinks you want to get me drunk and take advantage of me."

"What if it's both?" I ask, hoping I'm believable. If our whole conversation has been a game, we're tied. And he's good.

"One more beer and you probably could jujitsu me," he says.

"It's Shao-Lin," I correct him.

"Right," he says. He pushes both our empty glasses forward and nods at the bartender. "So you ready to head home and change into your killer outfit?" he says.

"Not yet."

Paul looks pleased.

* ◆ *

We end up at Paul's apartment, an upstairs studio in Wrigleyville that is, in fact, right around the corner. He turns on a lamp next to an oversized bacheloresque black leather couch. The first thing I take note of is a duffel bag full of police gear. It's on the floor next to a bench press with at least three hundred pounds on the bar. I also take note of the radiator below the window.

"You ready for the overhead club?" I ask.

"Sure, get me buzzed and then challenge me," he says, as he gets two Miller Lites from his fridge.

"No, really, I'm serious. I want to show you my moves. Come here, and come at me like you have a club in your right hand, over your head."

Paul thinks it's funny, so after he uncaps the beers, he comes at me with one.

I tackle him, I go straight for his gut, and we knock over the lamp. I straddle him in the pitch black and hear the beer spill all over the hardwood.

"Shit," he gripes. "My hip."

"Don't be such a baby," I say. "I told you I could take you down." I pull up his shirt to find the flesh of his midsection. I bite it playfully, and he scoots away, toward the window, like I hoped.

"Oh, you're dangerous!" he says, laughing a little anxiously.

I quit biting and start kissing, changing the mood entirely, but I'm trying to get closer to the weight bench and I'm feeling around for his duffel bag with my free hand.

"Oh," he says more softly. He pulls me up and kisses me. It's weird. He's tipsy, and clumsy, but passionate enough. I think about how inherently wrong this is, messing around with a rookie. But I also remember being in his position, and I was just as willing, so I keep kissing him.

I distract him further by undoing his belt. He starts to help me with it as I locate the handcuffs in his bag and open them.

"Yeah?" he asks, a little riled up by the sound.

"Yeah," I say, and close one of the cuffs around his right wrist.

"They do this in karate?" he asks.

"Kung fu," I correct him.

Then I pull his arm across his body and close the other cuff around the leg of the radiator.

"Wait. No," he says. "Sam?"

I climb off him, pick up the duffel bag, and take it out of his reach. Game over.

"Hey, what are you doing?"

"You have another light in here?" I ask.

"On the back wall."

I flip the switch and Paul is stuck on the floor, his pants half off, and his sense of humor gone.

"Very funny. Come on."

I light a cigarette and pull up a kitchen chair in front of him. I spin the cuff keys around my finger.

"Give me the key," he says.

"Tell me what you know," I say.

"I don't know what you're talking about."

"You know damn well what I'm talking about. Fred was killed to cover up something. Now his wife's gone. Susan Imes is in the hospital, Bruce Zahner and Marko Trovic are dead. Mason is playing the victim even though he's behind it all, running some drug deal. So fill me in. What the hell are you guys doing?"

"I've been working this case for almost a year," he says. "I'm not going to blow it now."

I try to act like I knew he was going to say that, but I had no idea. The cuff keys flip off my finger and across the room.

"You're IA?" Holy shit.

"We would have had Mason a long time ago if it weren't for you. You messed up Mason's plan, and you messed up ours."

"You're IA?" I still can't believe it.

"Damn right I am. You think I'd be spending all my off hours with Wade if I wasn't trying to get something from him?"

"You're with O'Connor," I say. A bunch of little incidents that should have clued me in are adding up in my head, totaling one big "duh."

"So why haven't you nailed Mason?" I ask, hoping for more details than I got from O'Connor's version. "We're running out of time here, Paul. I need to know."

"Then ask O'Connor."

"Good idea. Where's your phone? I'll call him up and invite him over here. I'm sure he'd love to see this." I reach over and tug at Paul's pants. "Come on. We can show O'Connor your hard-on."

He hangs his head.

"Paul. Let's hear it." I kick his shoe.

"Fred was working with Mason," he finally says. "They'd been extorting money from dealers for months, keeping them on the streets for a price. We finally convinced Fred to go state's once he got the idea that he was about to be passed over on Mason's list."

"So?"

"So Fred tells us about some heavy cash changing hands, and we plan to bust it up."

"Fred was trying to do the right thing," I say.

"Fred was trying to save his own ass. Didn't help with that wife of his pressing him to stay in with Mason."

"Mason set Fred up?"

"That's what we were trying to prove. Not much we could do, though, when Fred wound up dead and our only witness was Mason's girlfriend, who couldn't remember anything except seeing a dead guy. You can see our dilemma."

"I'm a woman before I'm a cop, is that it?"

"You're Mason's woman. That's a little different."

"What about the vest?" I ask. "Fred was wearing a vest. How come no one bothered to look into that?"

"The vest Fred checked out had a different serial number on it than the one that was submitted to Evidence. They're telling us it's a clerical error."

I remember the details of that night more clearly, now that my perception isn't skewed by anything but my own stupidity. I heard shots. Fred said he was hit. Why weren't there any bullets recovered besides mine?

"What about the autopsy? They could have found bruising where the first bullet hit—"

"—And called them ancillary wounds. Come on, Sam, you're going to tell me the details of the case make any difference when your boyfriend is the investigator? Where have you been?"

In love. Fuck.

O'Connor was right. Still, I want to know: "Why didn't your guys pull me in after Fred was killed? Why did you leave me in the dark?"

"Like I said, you're Mason's woman. We were waiting for you to make another move."

"So you thought I killed Fred, and that I did it for Mason?" I ask.

"No one thought you killed Fred. But we did think . . . well, actually it was O'Connor who thought that after Fred died and Mason gave you that nasty bump, you'd be bound to slip up . . . if you were involved."

"Mason . . ." gave me the bump? "Mason . . ." was the one at that house? Mason killed Fred?

"Yep," Paul says, knowing what I can't say.

Now the details become terribly clear. Crawling to Fred. Fred whispering, "You don't know what he can do . . ." I didn't know. Mason was there.

Firing. Blood in my eyes. I couldn't see. Fred knew. Mason was there.

"Are you okay?" Paul asks, his voice bringing me back to the room.

"Mason was there," I say. "He loaded another bullet into my gun and killed Fred."

"We haven't even been able to prove he was at the scene until well after the incident. His wife gave him an alibi."

"But she's in the hospital. She'll tell the truth now. She has to."

"We thought so," he says. "We were wrong. She's not saying a word. And whoever's been involved since isn't volunteering any information, either. I guess fixing a crime scene isn't exactly a résumé builder."

"Where's your phone?" I ask again. I get up and find a cordless on its station on the kitchen counter. I put my cigarette out in the sink.

"Who are you calling?" he asks. "Don't call O'Connor. Please, I told you everything . . ."

I ignore him and slip out the front door into the hallway. I punch *67 to block Mason's caller ID.

"It's Sam," I say when he answers.

"I've been waiting for you."

"To what, get out of jail? You set me up." I want him to know I'm not playing dumb.

"That's a matter of perspective, really." Smug fuck. "I'll meet you at your place."

"How do you know I don't have the entire Chicago PD there waiting for you?" I ask. I want him to think I'm willing to listen.

"Because I know you, Sam. And you know me. You

know I have an explanation for all this. And you know I love you."

I want him to think I believe him. I wish I did believe him.

"I'm leaving now," he says. "Sam?"

"I'll be there." I hang up.

I go back inside and put the phone back on its charger.

"Oh, shit, you just called Mason, didn't you. Oh, man, I'm in trouble." He squirms around and ends up sitting in the spilled beer.

I cross the room and take Paul's Bulldog .44 from his duffel bag. I wish I had more reassurance than a loaded gun.

"No, Sam, come on. Think about this," he says.

I stuff the gun in my boot. He knows I've thought about it. He knows I'm leaving. I go to the door.

"Sam, please," he pleads.

I turn around, because I have one more question. "Have you been hitting on me for the same reason you're hanging around Wade? To get closer to Mason?"

"That wasn't part of my assignment," Paul says.

"Good. If I make it out of this alive, I just might go out with you again. It was fun."

"Will you let me out of these? Please?"

"They're your handcuffs; you'll figure it out."

I leave Paul there to fend for himself. IA has been following two safe steps behind, and they won't catch up before I go face-to-face with Mason.

32

I hop in a cab and tell the driver there's an extra few bucks if he gets me to my place quick. We shoot down Lake Shore and pull up to my building in ten minutes flat. I keep my promise and give the guy a twenty on a seven-dollar fare.

When I get inside, Omar isn't manning the entrance. He must be on break. I use my electronic Marlock key to get through the security door in the lobby. I use my key for the elevator, too, and wait for it to come down from 13. It takes forever. No one gets off.

I'm anxious to get situated before Mason arrives. I don't exactly have a plan, but I have the advantage: I know the truth. I just have to get it out of him. If one of us doesn't kill the other first.

I open the door to my condo and start for my bedroom without turning on the lights. I stop in my tracks when I see a figure near the kitchen window.

"Mason?"

"You wish."

I back up and flip on the light. Marko's brother and the skinny Serbian kid with the medallion are sitting at my kitchen table.

"My name is Smitty. You remember my brother, you bitch?"

"I remember you," I say. Marko, plus thirty pounds, attitude apparently included.

Someone behind me locks the front door. It's the big, long-haired kid who scratched my car. And he has a gun. I don't make a move.

"You're the reason Marko is dead," Smitty says. "Fado," he directs the kid behind me.

The kid grabs my hair and puts his gun to my head, dropping me to my knees. I stare up at Smitty, trying to get a grip on the situation. I have Paul's .44 in my boot, but one of them will see me if I go for it. I wait for a chance.

"We know you're working with Mason," Smitty says. "You stepped in so you could blame my brother for killing that cop and take his share of the money. And all the while my brother was setting up shop for you in Miami. You used him and you got him killed."

"I wasn't involved. Mason set me up—" The words fight my gag reflex. My eyes begin to tear. Fado pulls my hair tight. I can feel the stitches tearing my scalp.

"You blamed my brother for your trouble. I want justice for what's been done. I want you and Mason to pay," Smitty says, his temper rising with him from his chair.

"I didn't know; I was stupid," I manage.

"It's not enough to take his life, but now you ruin the Trovic name?" the skinny kid with the medallion says, fueling Smitty's rage.

"Shut up, Josich," Smitty says, coming toward me.

Fado takes the gun away from my head and yanks my head back. I choke from the strain on my neck as Smitty gets in my face. "My brother has a little girl," he says. "That little girl loves him so much. I don't have the heart to tell her he's not coming back." His breath is hot and stale. "You and Mason killed my brother. Now we are going to kill you."

Fado lets go of my hair and comes around in front of me, putting his gun to the left side of my forehead. I can feel the metal of Paul's gun on my shin; I just have to get to it. I scan the area around me, searching for a distraction.

And there it is, right in front of me: Fado has an erection.

Smitty said himself that we don't speak the same language. But there's one thing that men around the world comprehend, and it's my only chance.

"Please, I'll do anything, anything," I tell Fado. "I'm begging you," I say, my eyes fixed on the bulge in his pants. "Anything," I say again. I hope he understands.

"Let's go, Fado," Smitty says from behind him. "Kill her."

"Hold on," Fado says. He looks down at me. "Anything?"

"Yes, please," I beg.

He starts to laugh.

Then he moves the tip of the gun he's got to my head slowly to my mouth.

"Suck it," he says.

I hear the kid with the medallion giggle.

"Suck it," Fado says again.

I have to. My jaw quivers.

"No teeth," he advises, showing me his.

I take the end of the barrel into my mouth. I open wide and try not to scrape the metal. I taste the gun oil and the powder residue and I feel the tip hit my uvula. I have never been so scared in my life. I can't breathe. I'm scared to breathe. I am two inches from the trigger. All I can see through the tears in my eyes is Fado's gold ring, tight around his bulging pinky.

I am afraid to move, but I am powerless unless I get this gun out of my mouth.

I bring my hands up, slowly, alongside Fado's hand and the gun. I move carefully, as though I am between his legs, back and forth, my eyes releasing tears. With my hand on his, I ease the gun out of my mouth. I put my lips around the tip, keeping it there, and I look up at him to show him I am brave and I am willing to do more.

"Fado," Smitty protests in the background. "Let's go."

"Relax, Smitty. You can be next. After me." Fado looks back at the third kid, exchanging a silent affirmation. Then he takes the gun from my mouth.

"Josich, take this. Hold it on her. Bitch can do something good before she dies."

Josich approaches on Fado's left and reluctantly takes the gun. He aims at me, but keeps his distance. Fado does not.

"You're good at that, aren't you?" Fado asks, touching my shoulder with a hand like a bear's paw. He undoes his belt. "You want to suck this?"

"Anything" is all I manage to say.

I unzip his pants, keeping my eyes on him. I try not to think of his dirty hair, the odor of his worn leather coat . . .

"I knew she was a little slut. Little cop whore. Fuck-

ing to get Mason's money," Josich says from somewhere behind him.

"Let's just do this," Smitty says.

"Shut up," Fado stops him. I can tell he wants this
more than the others.

"It won't take him long," Josich jokes awkwardly to
Smitty.

"I said shut up," Fado barks. He puts both hands on
my face and pulls me toward him. "This gun will go
off, baby."

I look him right in the eyes, and I hold my breath as
I reach into his jeans. Fado tilts his head back, in ec-
stasy at my first touch.

"Suck it," he says, as more of a suggestion. He likes
my hand.

I stroke him, and let him revel in the feeling, reach-
ing farther into his pants each time. I wait just long
enough to make sure he's totally off guard when I
reach in as far as I can and grab his balls and squeeze
them with all my might.

Fado screams as I let go and pull Paul's gun from
my ankle holster.

Josich asks, "What the fuck?" as Fado dry-heaves
in pain.

"Shoot her, Josich!" Smitty orders.

I spin Fado around for a shield, so by the time
Josich gets his nerve and shoots, he hits Fado in the
chest.

"Fuck!" Josich curses as I fall backward from the
force of the bullet that struck Fado. On the way down I
fire twice and hit Josich once. Josich goes down at the
same time I hit the floor with Fado on top of me. Paul's
gun slips out of my hands and across the hardwood. I
pull Fado's long hair back and try to get him off me,
but he's at least two-fifty, and he's not budging.

I'm pinned, and Fado's hair streams across my face. I know Smitty is still alive. I hear him approach, and then I see him pick up my gun. He stands over me.

"Fucking whore," he says.

Then he aims the gun at me.

"This is for my brother."

I shut my eyes and I hear a shot, but I don't feel anything. I wonder if dying is like my dream. I'm afraid to open my eyes.

Then I hear—

"Sam."

And suddenly Fado is lifted off me.

I suck in a critical breath and I open my eyes to see Mason.

He sits me up and takes me in his arms and I don't fight him. He just saved my life.

33

Less than an hour later, I'm in a dark hotel room on the near south side of the Loop. I remember this place: Mason and I came here spontaneously one night after dinner at Everest, drunk on rich food and champagne and each other. Lightning and thunder promised a storm that night, but we ignored good judgment and the one cab that passed and walked through the empty Financial District, his arm around me. I couldn't have complained about a single thing. When it started to rain, Mason and I ducked under an awning. He kissed me, and the next thing I knew we had a room here. I thought I was in heaven.

It's not as nice as I remember.

As far as I can tell, Mason hasn't called in to report

what went on at my condo tonight. It would be a stupid question to ask. Out the window, I imagine the city lights to the north look like a gigantic jewel box. To me, it's all a blur. The only thing that's clear is that I should already be dead.

Mason comes out of the bathroom with a towel. I lie on a thin, scratchy bedspread, my head propped on a thick pillow with a cover that smells of chlorine.

"Water's ready," he says. He's run a bath for me. As if the water will cleanse the memory of this night: the taste of Fado's gun, metallic like blood in my mouth; the vision of Smitty, eyes just like his brother's, standing over me, ready to take my life. Then Mason, out of nowhere, coming to my rescue, like a hero in a movie.

Except I don't count on a happy ending.

"Are you going to kill me?" I ask.

He sits down next to me, pulls me toward him, and puts the towel around my neck. I wonder if he's planning to drown me in the tub. I bend to him like a rag doll, my strength gone. I want to end this horrendous game. I have run out of strategies.

"It's okay, Sam," he says. "I'm not going to kill you."

"You might as well," I say.

"Everything I've done has been for you," he tells me, as though I should be ashamed of myself.

I knew he'd say something like that, but somehow, even after everything that's happened, I still want to hear his explanation. I want to know why he lied to me.

"I know you were the one who hit me over the head," I say. "I know you killed Fred. And you set me up."

"I was only trying to save your ass," he says, letting go of the towel. "You weren't supposed to be with Fred that night."

"But I was there. And so were you. You killed my partner, and you let me think I did it."

"Wade was supposed to be there," Mason says. "When you showed up instead, everything went to shit."

"Does Wade know about this?"

"Yes, Sam."

Wade, who I thought was a friend. He said he didn't want to act like my father, then he looked me straight in the eye and lied to me. Just like my dad.

"You and I both know Wade's been looking for a comfy way out of the job ever since he was shot," Mason says. "Problem is, he's a chickenshit. He talks a good game, but he's got no follow-through."

"You let me believe it was my fault," I say, and Mason nods. I can't believe I'm saying it and he's agreeing. I sit up against the headboard and it knocks into the wall, loose from too many nights of activity.

"I never meant for you to be involved," Mason says, brushing a long black hair from my shoulder—Fado's, I'm sure. "I know you, baby. You never would have gone along with us. We're taking money from drug dealers. It's illegal. It's crap." He puts his hand on my leg and I know he's about to lay it on thick.

"But I did it for you. For us, so we could get out of here."

It's twisted but I wanted him to say that. Though I know better, some part of my heart is still pulling for him. I tell myself that no matter how I feel, I have to act like I'm ready to hear more. I place my hand on top of his, but I can't look at him. I don't want to see the flicker in his eyes.

"Like we talked about, all those nights in the squad," he says. "Remember? You agreed with me: Our livelihood depends on criminals. We're not making a difference. We're just balancing the scales. You and I sat waiting for two weeks for some two-bit thief to screw up so we'd get a paycheck. We did some savvy detective work, arrested the guy, and in no time he was back on the street. So what are we supposed to do? Sit and wait for him to screw up again? It's futile. I'm tired of balance. I want the scales tipped in my favor."

"So you hurt the people you love?"

"I didn't want to hurt you, Sam. When I saw you come up those steps after Fred, God, my heart stopped. I had to think quick. I did what I thought was best—" He pauses when his cell phone rings. He checks the caller ID display and continues without answering—"I did what I had to do. I knew you'd be traumatized, but I thought we'd get through it. I never thought you'd come out of it with the crazy idea that Trovic killed Fred. That's when things went bad. When you started your Trovic campaign, the wrong people started getting suspicious."

"What did Trovic have to do with anything?" I ask. "He was a child molester. Fred picked him up for sexual assault."

"He was arrested for assault. He was never booked for dealing heroin. Or for being our contact for the guys we've been taxing." The thought of Mason working with a scumbag like Trovic makes the touch of his hand feel poisonous. I push him away.

"Trovic was never arrested because you corrupt assholes were keeping him on the street for cash," I say. "Then you killed him because he got in the way. And then Fred got in your way, and you did the same to him. And now I'm in your way. So what happens to me?"

Mason stands up, his patience waning, but I don't care. I have nothing to lose.

"How many of you are in on this?" I continue. "Is Sarge going to be the next one to blame me for something I didn't do? Is the chief going to pin the next homicide around here on me?"

"It doesn't go above me," Mason says, keeping his voice soft to remind me he's in control.

The leader of the pack. I should have known.

"I know my limits, Sam. I've been trying to get out of this mess for months. IA's on to us. My guys know it. We all want out. But we can't just quit. You don't just walk away from drug dealers. We needed a way to make a clean break from them without upsetting the order of things. Trovic offered me a deal that promised enough cash to go our separate ways, and I jumped on it."

"And Fred?" I ask. "He didn't?"

"You think Fred's so innocent. Fred was the one who hooked us up with Trovic in the first place."

"So why did he take the fall for the rest of you?"

"IA coerced Fred into taking a deal from the state's office." Mason sits back down, this time on the corner of the bed, and it bows like there's no box spring. "They had him in a pinch, and he was ready to fold. Fred arrested Trovic again and threatened to turn him in if we didn't call off the deal. I guess that was Fred's attempt to warn us."

"If you knew Fred was pinned, why didn't you call it off?"

"It was too late. Trovic was on his way to Florida the minute he posted bail. His bosses didn't want him to wait around like bait. A deal's a deal, they said, and the deal's going through, just as soon as Fred is no longer a risk. I tried to convince Fred to stay in with us. I tried to convince Trovic's bosses to hold off. They thought I was trying to play both sides, so they made me take care of Fred to prove I was legit. When it came down to it, I had no choice. It was Fred or all of us."

"Fred," I say, "and Trovic, and Bruce Zahner, and your wife?"

"I didn't kill Bruce," he says. "I hired him to follow you, yes. He was supposed to keep you out of the way."

"He was the one who went after Susan."

"He was framed. Trovic's family did it. To send a message. This whole thing went in the shitter when you brought up Trovic."

"Why did you kill him in the first place?" I ask.

"When we started this thing, it was understood: in or out, quiet or dead. As soon as Trovic went down south, he started bragging about his connection with the Chicago PD. I knew the news would make its way back up here before he did. Trovic dug his own grave, as far as I'm concerned. We had to get rid of him."

"That was your last-minute trip. That's why you couldn't go to Vegas." For some sick reason, I'm relieved he wasn't in Florida looking at real estate.

"I had it all worked out. He was MIA, and everyone assumed he'd found the wrong crowd down there. I had already retrieved the heroin, so his bosses didn't care where he was. We were going to kill Fred and do the deal and be done with it. No one got suspicious until you started blaming Trovic for killing Fred. His family thought he was on a cruise ship. They hold me responsible, and they've been after me ever since he turned up dead."

"And they came after me because they thought I was in on it."

"I told them you didn't know about Trovic; I told them you didn't have anything to do with it. I even asked Trovic's bosses to set them straight. But the bosses felt the situation had gotten out of hand and they wouldn't get involved. Then, when you got out of jail after Susan's accident, the family thought I'd sprung you. They were convinced we set this whole thing up."

"They killed Bruce. They tried to kill Susan. They killed your unborn child, Mason. And all of this for what?"

Mason's expression does not change.

"They killed your child," I say again.

"Susan will be okay."

"You blamed me." I won't back down now. "And you almost got me killed."

"None of this would have happened if it wasn't for you." He stands me up. "Once you were involved, I needed to keep you as far away from this as I could. I even had Wade try to steer you away. I needed you to hate me."

"It worked."

"It was on purpose. Trust me, Sam—all of this, the lying, the confusion, the death . . ." He pauses, and I know he's thinking about the child. "It's all been for us."

"How many of us?" I know if I actually say Deborah's name, I run the risk of blowing this. If he is taking her away with him, then I'm dead for knowing. If he isn't, I may as well be dead for suggesting it. I watch Mason's lips curl, as though he's suppressing the slightest grin. I know he knows exactly whom I'm talking about, but somehow he turns the grin into a polite smile, like he's talking to someone who's senile or mentally challenged. He takes my arm.

"You still think I'm cheating? I kept tabs on you. I know whose cell phone you've been answering."

It is useless to argue about fidelity. Neither of us can win.

"Who are you taking to Florida?" I ask.

"I thought we decided on California," he says. "Come on. Let's get you in the tub. It'll all be different in the morning." He leads me into the bathroom, and I let him. It would only take one sincere gesture, one honest look, to sway me, but I know he's incapable. I know he is holding something back from me, like he always has. I follow his lead. I may not get out of this alive, but it's the only way I'll ever find out the truth.

He helps me undress and eases me into the water. I don't find anything endearing about his efforts. His touch is like a stranger's. I pretend to be comforted, though I feel like he's settling me into a casket. "Different in the morning," he said. Like it's the same now.

"I have to make a call," he says.

I don't ask. I'm just glad he's leaving.

As soon as he's gone, I get out of the tub. The water is too hot for me, and unlike last time, I'm well aware of the grime in this place. Between the tiles. Around the sink. In the soap dish. I already feel dirty enough. I'm trapped even though this mess has nothing to do with me. Mason and his million-dollar deal that will ruin the lives of countless others. Fred and his willingness to gamble with lowlifes for extra cash. His materialistic wife, getting herself a real suntan, tipping her towel boy with Fred's pension. And Wade, and his pathetic attempt to get what he thinks he deserves. Greed. This is not because I accused a pedophile of murder. This is all because of greed.

I towel off and put my clothes on. I put my ear to the bathroom door and don't hear anything, so I carefully turn the handle and sneak out.

Mason is not in the room and I know he's in the hallway because the door is propped open by the dead bolt. I hear him talking; he's on his cell phone. I crawl on my hands and knees to get close enough to make out what he's saying.

"1079 at the Greyhound on Dearborn."

1079, 1079, what is that? He's definitely not calling

in the catastrophe at my place. 1079, the Greyhound station on Dearborn. I try to ingrain it in my memory. 1079, Dearborn Greyhound. 1079: That's police code for dispatching the coroner. Is someone going to die at the bus station?

"Yep, two o'clock . . ." Mason says as I crawl between the double beds and grab the hotel phone.

I dial fast and it doesn't go through. I scan the directions on the phone and dial 9 and then the number again. My hands sweat; my body is hot from the bath. The call goes through. It rings twice. I start to shake.

"O'Connor," he answers.

"1079 at the Greyhound on Dearborn," I whisper.

"What the hell does that mean? Where are you? We just got to your place—"

I hear the handle turn on the hotel room door. "Fuck—" I hang up as quietly as I can and push the phone under the bed. I may have knocked it off the hook, but there's no time to look, so I curl up in a ball on the floor and I begin crying uncontrollably.

It works. Mason doesn't notice that the phone is gone when he comes over and takes me in his arms.

"Shh, Sam, what happened to the bath?"

"Those kids were going to kill me," I sob. I'm actually crying because I almost was—and still very well could be—caught, but the effect is the same. Mason wipes my eyes.

"Come on, Sam, hang in there. There's one more thing we have to do."

"We?" I say defensively. I jump up from the floor and approach the door to get him as far away from that phone as I can. If it's off the hook I've got about thirty seconds before I'm fucked. Mason follows me.

"I have to meet Trovic's bosses. They still want to buy the heroin Trovic brought in before he died."

"But you killed him. And they hate you."

"A deal's a deal, so they say. They knew Trovic was a loser. They're not going to waste a perfectly good stash of black tar on a dead guy. They're giving me two-fifty up front, with over twice that in interest as soon as it hits the street."

"The street," I say. Where we try to stop it.

"You want to know which one?" he says sarcastically. "Truth is, these guys are taking it to the North Shore. Up to Highland Park. Out to Barrington. They say heroin is the new coke for rich high school kids."

"Well, that makes it okay."

"Come on, Sam, we're talking close to a million bucks here. This is the deal I've been waiting for. This will end it. And then we can walk away."

I want to argue but we have to go. Now. "What do you need me for?" I ask.

"Wade. He's bringing the H, but he's not leaving with the cash. Actually, he's not leaving at all. I need you there to make sure of it."

"Give me one reason," I say. I don't want him to think I'm agreeing too quickly.

"I'll give you two. Wade was the only one who could have told those kids that you were involved in this. He sent those kids to your place. He was willing to let you die for this money."

"And the other?"

"I saved your life," Mason says. "You owe me."

"One was enough," I say. I start for the door, to get Mason out of the room before he hears the phone, but again the effect is the same.

I open the door and get outside. Mason follows me out.

"This is a complete one-eighty," he says.

He's suspicious. So I go back to him and pull the

door shut at the same time I grab him and kiss him with all the passion I can muster. I don't think he hears the faint voice from inside the room: "If you'd like to make a call, please hang up and try again."

"Let's go. I just want to end this," I say. I don't have the same ending in mind, but if I don't go along with him he'll get away with murder. Again.

"I knew you'd come around," Mason says.

I don't know if I'm an accomplice or his next target, but Mason was right about one thing: This is the deal that will end it.

He takes my hand, trusting me, and we're on our way.

34

I stand outside a squad car waiting for Mason to un-
lock the doors.

"Get in back," he says, "and stay down."

I know I don't have a choice in the matter if I want
to be a part of this deal, but it would be out of charac-
ter for me to go willingly. I don't move.

"Come on, Sam. Trust me."

"Where are we going?" I ask. "I'm not hiding in
there all night."

We stare each other down until I give in and move
to the back door.

I get in the squad's backseat and watch Mason
through the cage. He puts his phone on its charger and

smiles at me through the rearview mirror. We drive off. He's got me right where he wants me, locked me in the backseat like a criminal. No wonder he took the squad.

"Where's the Navigator?" I ask.

Mason catches my eye in the rearview mirror. He knows I'm picking a fight. He answers me by adjusting the mirror so he doesn't have to look at me.

We drive south on Dearborn. I look back through the rear window. The lights on the Hancock are still green from Saint Patrick's Day last week. The city is alive with light. It would be a spectacular view if I were a tourist. Or a photographer. Or anybody else. I feel like I'm waving good-bye to home.

"Where are we going?" I ask.

He doesn't answer.

"Where is Wade?" I ask. "Are you sure he'll show up this time, or will I be tonight's stand-in?"

"I just told him where to pick up the stash. He has to come."

We cross Cermak Road, and I have this bad feeling that I shouldn't have told O'Connor to go to the bus station. I have this bad feeling if he goes there, the only person he'll bust is Wade. Then Wade won't show up. Mason and I will be empty-handed when we meet Trovic's bosses. We'll be in deep shit.

Mason turns right, and we drive down a dark row of tall warehouses. He pulls the squad into a deserted gravel lot just before we reach the expressway overpass.

"What is this place?" I ask. It's nowhere near the bus station. It's nowhere near backup.

"Used to be a shipyard. Stay down. I'm gonna look around."

I wait until he gets out of the car and I hear his footsteps move away on the gravel. Then I peek out the window. I can't see much. The only light comes from the moon. This looks like a place where business should be conducted during the day, if at all.

I eye Mason's cell phone. I can't get to it through the divider—no way my arm would fit through the grating. I can't open the doors—precautionary features in squad cars, of course.

I sink down into the seat and figure I should do what he says and lie low until he gives me the opportunity to do otherwise. I want to scream at myself. I'd rather think O'Connor could be on his way here than know he's headed in the wrong direction.

Mason's cell phone rings in the charger. Over and over. I feel like a monkey in a cage. I know the way out, but I can't get there. I could kick out the cage, it'd get me to his phone, but Mason would find out and I'd be dead before anyone could get here. Making a call isn't going to help me now.

I could break out the window and make a run for it, but that's not a viable option either. I am not running. I'm staying right here. I have to rely on Mason's trust in me to be his downfall. Does he really think I'm going to help him? Has he set it up so I have to?

The phone keeps ringing, like the person keeps calling back. He's not going to fucking answer. Hang up! The ringing is like a drill into my head. Into the wound Mason gave me.

The phone finally stops as soon as Mason appears. Of course. He opens the driver's-side door and releases the rear locks.

"Let's go," he says, "move it or lose it."

I run after him into the darkness. We go through an open garage door into a large open warehouse. The space is huge, and the wind blows through it like a sneeze—when it hits, the whole shell of the place shudders. Mason flips on a flashlight and shows me a foreman's dock in the center: a platform about fifteen feet up and eight feet around that a boss must've used to survey his crew. It's surrounded by empty unpaved ground.

"You're going to stay up there," he says, pointing to the dock. "Go on."

He shines the light on the only way to get up there: a rickety metal ladder.

"No way," I say. "I'll never get down."

"It's safe. You'll be able to hear everything from up there. All you have to do is lie down in the center and wait for your cue. Once the deal is made, you can jump off the fucking thing for all I care. Just as long as you shoot Wade."

He hands me a revolver. He waits a moment before letting go, but not long enough to indicate any insecurity on his part. I check the gun; there's only one bullet loaded in the cylinder. He's got this all figured out. If I shoot him right here and now, I wind up with an empty gun and a lot of explaining to do to some drug dealers. I don't think Wade will be much help.

"What if I miss?" I ask.

"You won't," he says. He takes the gun from my hands and shoves it in my pants. Then he leads me to a structure built into the side wall. He opens the door and pulls a string that turns on a naked bulb. The puny light casts huge shadows out the door and across the space.

"We're doing business here," he says. I look into what must have been an office, judging by the abandoned metal desk. Mason turns and puts his arms around me, over my shoulders, but it's not exactly a loving gesture. "I'm telling you, these guys would like nothing more than a reason to take out a couple of cops. Don't give them one." He lets go and spins me around to face the loading dock. "Now get up there and make sure you're out of the light."

I'm so fucking nervous that I do what he says. I hurry over to the ladder and start climbing. I don't know who Trovic's bosses are or what the hell I've gotten myself into, and suddenly Mason is the least of my concerns. I get up the ladder as fast as I can, counting the rungs—one, two, three, four, five, fuck! Six, seven, eight, nine, ten, eleven, that's twelve rungs to the top. From up here it seems like a lot more than fifteen feet off the ground. Another fucking jail.

Mason shuts off the office light. I drop to the floor of the platform and peer over the side. He shines the flashlight right in my eyes.

"I can see-ee you," he taunts. I move back. "Good. Shoot when I tell you to."

The sound of a car engine rumbles through the space like an airplane.

"That's Wade." Mason shuts off his flashlight and moves toward the entrance. I peer over the side again and practice my aim. I have the perfect shot at him just before he disappears into the darkness that hangs over the garage door.

"Bang," I say. But he's the only one with a shot here.

I cock my gun and lie back for all of two seconds before I know there's no way I can stay up here. I feel the ladder under my feet, twelve eleven ten nine eight seven six—then I hear the car's engine quit, so fuck it, I jump off and run for the edge of the building.

The only places I can hide are behind the office or outside the building. It was a terrible idea to have left that platform, but it's too late now. Voices echo faintly around the place: they're on the way inside.

I dart over to the farthest corner of the warehouse

and hope the light doesn't radiate this far. I lie on my stomach on the dirty ground. From where I am, I can see the entrance in the moonlight. I just hope no one can see me. I aim my gun. I'm ready to shoot if I have to.

Headlights flood the space from another vehicle entering the lot. I'm relieved when they don't fall on me. I won't be seen if no one's looking.

"Weapons in the trunk!" I hear a voice call out like a drill sergeant. I don't recognize it.

Then I hear footsteps on the gravel. There must be one, two three, four—too many people for one bullet.

"You check the place out?" a voice echoes through the space.

"Of course I did," Mason says.

"We're the cops, who do you think's going to bust us?" Wade says as I watch Mason, then Wade, then two other men come in through the garage door. No one laughs. Mason takes a suitcase from Wade and I can tell by Mason's body language that he's annoyed.

"You take care of your female troubles?" asks the man in a slick suit. The other man carries a briefcase.

Mason says, "I held up my end. Now you hold up yours."

Mason turns on the office light and they all go inside. I can feel the light on me, so I move toward a shadow on my left just before Wade, the last one inside, looks in my direction. He doesn't see me. He closes the office door.

The rest of the warehouse goes black, except for the faint light from the tiny office window. I'm safe for now, but I've gotta move because someone's bound to see me when they come out.

Just before I move, I hear more footsteps outside. I pray to God it's O'Connor and he followed Wade here, but when the figure steps into the warehouse, he's too huge to be O'Connor.

The man pulls out his gun and stands still for a moment, listening. Then he slips into the shadows to walk the perimeter of the place. If he makes it any more than halfway around, he's sure to discover me.

I get on my elbows and hold my breath. I aim in his direction. He's fifty yards away. I can't see him, but I can hear his footsteps on the sandy ground. Coming closer. Pausing. Coming closer.

I can hear the folds of his pants chafe.

The only thing I can think to do is pick up the first thing I find and throw it, to distract him, but that's my gun, so I sit there and hope if I have to fire, I won't miss.

He's coming closer. I have to swallow. I don't.

Just then, the office door opens. The man with the gun turns toward the light. He's so close that I can see the tattoo on the side of his neck just below his ear: a knife that bleeds the word TRUST. He must not get much of it.

"We good?" the man asks, and pivots, starting toward the office.

I'm in the light like he is, but I see a place only five feet to the left that's still shadowed, so I roll like a log with my gun still pointed at the guy.

I'm hidden just as the man who had the briefcase comes out of the office with Wade's suitcase and gives a thumbs-up. He joins the tattooed man near the loading dock.

"What the fuck is that platform?" the tattooed man asks the other, indicating my original hiding place. They study it for a moment.

"Beats me," says the one with the suitcase. The tattooed one approaches it and jiggles the ladder. He puts his foot up on the second rung like he's going to climb, but as soon as he puts his weight on it, the whole fucking ladder comes down at him. He jumps out of the way and the ladder crashes to the floor.

"You fat-ass." The one with the suitcase laughs at him.

The commotion brings all the men out of the office.

"Let's go," says the third man, the guy in the suit. Evidently the one in charge.

Wade walks the men to the edge of the garage while Mason stands there, looking up at the platform, grinning. That bastard.

"Nice doing business with you," Wade says, waving the men off.

"Fuck off, pig," the tattooed man says.

Wade lights up a cigarette and watches them go. Mason goes back in the office.

Their car engine rumbles and I finally have enough nerve to swallow. I release my grip on the gun and wipe my hands on my pants.

The car pulls away and the lights fade. I'm waiting for Mason to come out and say "Shoot," but I get the feeling that wasn't the plan after all. Maybe he wanted me to think I was going with him until he was sure he'd get away. Then he'd leave me there, stuck on the platform, to deal with Wade's dead body and a dirty gun. Another crazy story to tell the authorities.

I watch Wade put his cigarette out, bend over, and pull a gun from his ankle holster.

So maybe Mason is right about Wade.

But he's wrong about me.

35

I creep to the edge of the office door and drop to the floor. When I peek around the corner into the office, I see Mason counting a stack of money from a briefcase full of more stacks. The briefcase is sitting on the empty desk up against the far wall, so Mason's back is turned. Wade stands behind him, about ten feet away, gun in hand.

"This is it," Mason says. "We're set."

Mason starts to close the briefcase, but Wade says, "Leave it." Wade clicks his gun safety, and as Mason turns around I duck out of sight.

"Brilliant, a backup gun. Why didn't I think of that?" Mason says sarcastically.

"Only one of us can walk out of here, you know that," Wade says.

"I know that, Wade. It's not gonna be you."

"I'm the one with the gun."

"But you have no spine, Wade. You want the money, but you're not willing to go all the way for it. I made it so easy for you; all you had to do was ride with Fred and make sure he went into the house, and you couldn't even handle that."

"You were sending me to the slaughter," Wade says. "You got rid of everyone else who was in the way of that cash; why not me?"

"You gutless fuck. I've spent every second since that night covering up for your mistake. You think I planned to wait until the last minute to take you out? After all that trouble?"

"You had to," Wade says. "You couldn't have done this without me. You've been stringing me along just like everyone else. Deb Maloney's the only one smart enough to know she was getting hosed, and that's probably because she's more greedy than you. I'll bet you even let Sam think she was going with you, right up until those kids killed her."

"Funny you should mention that," Mason starts, but I don't let him finish. I step into the doorway with my gun aimed at Wade's back. Mason sees me and I know he's surprised, even if he doesn't show it.

"There's a gun pointed at the back of your head, Wade," Mason says.

"Don't move," I say.

Mason won't stop smiling. I should have said "Don't smile."

Instead I say, "Wade, did you send those kids after me?"

"It doesn't matter what I say now, Sam. You never listened to me anyway. I tried to warn you—"

"Sam. Shoot him," Mason interrupts.

"She should be aiming that thing at you, not me. You're the one who wanted to kill her. But I suppose you convinced her otherwise."

"Put down the gun, Wade," I say.

Wade looks over his shoulder at me, sizing up the situation. He turns, his gun pointed, but not aimed, at me. His eyes plead silently for reprieve.

"Give me the gun, Wade. We don't have to do this," I tell him.

Wade doesn't budge. "I have to do this," he says. "I'm not going to jail."

"You said yourself you choose your battles. Don't pick this one," I say.

"Listen to me for once," Wade says. "The other day, I . . . I was trying to tell you, you're a good cop, Smack. And you also have a good heart. But please, don't let it get in the way—"

"Hey, Wade," Mason calls, and Wade closes his eyes like he knows what's coming. I take a step to the left and see the tiny pistol in Mason's hand. It's a Mexican standoff, but Mason's the only one without a gun pointed at him. "She's not listening."

At the sound of gunfire, Wade's eyes open and set blankly on me. Then he falls to the floor.

I am frozen there. A pang of regret hits me in the chest so hard that I want to drop to my knees and sob. But with Wade out of the way, I'm aimed at Mason. I don't move.

And neither does he: he's aiming at me. Now it's a real standoff. Mason smiles.

"Let's get out of here," he says. But he doesn't drop his aim. Neither do I.

"Put the gun down," he says.

I don't.

"Come on, Sam, this is what we wanted," he tells me, motioning to the briefcase, still open and full of cash. "The money, getting out of here . . . we're on our way. You and me." He lowers his gun and steps toward me.

"What about Deb?" I ask, maintaining my aim.

"Baby, I had to keep her close, right to the end. I let her think what she wanted, to keep you out of trouble. I let her think she had control."

"Were you having an affair?"

Mason smiles that unbelievable smile of his, like the question is preposterous, even though the answer is even worse.

"She got what she wanted, and now so are you." He tucks the pistol in his pants and moves toward me. He tries to take my gun, but I don't let go, so instead he moves my arm out of the way, pulls me to him, and kisses me.

It only takes a moment before I kiss him back. This is what I wanted so badly. Not the money. Not the escape. Just this. I would have traded everything for this.

He pulls away and looks at me, and his eyes cross just a little. I knew I was in love with him the first time he looked at me this way.

He tries to back away, but I won't let him go. I want to hold on to this moment. I want to remember what it feels like to let my heart get in the way. Because I will never let it happen again.

He kisses me and I can't help myself. I loosen my grip on the gun and hear it clank when it hits the floor.

While we kiss, I feel Mason's gun press against my waist. It's then I know that something will always come between us. This has to be good-bye.

"Come on, baby. We can't stay here all night," he whispers between kisses.

I reluctantly let go of him. He looks at me with those eyes one last time, and though he doesn't say he loves me, I know it's not on purpose.

I don't say I love him either.

He goes to the table and tends to the briefcase, and to what I expect is his final farewell to me. He takes a moment to put the last part of his plan in action, but I have finally accepted that I am not in on it. Not in the way I'd wanted.

As he turns, his aim is off. I am no longer standing there waiting for him. I won't give him a clean shot. I'm on the floor, with Wade's gun pointed at him. Before Mason can react, I fire and hit him in the arm.

Mason falls hard to the floor, gun in his hand, evidence of the truth. Like a toddler whose reaction is delayed, Mason doesn't know whether to laugh or cry. He just looks at me.

"I only trusted you because I didn't trust myself," I say.

He holds his breath as he tries to prop himself up on his good arm, straining to point his gun at me with his bad one.

I stand up with Wade's gun, my hands trembling, tears again blurring my vision.

"Drop the gun, Mason. Drop it or I'll kill you. I swear I will."

He lets the tip of his pistol rest on the floor, but only because his arm is losing strength fast. He sits up.

"You can't kill me. I love you. Don't you love me?" He waits for me to answer.

I lower my gun. I keep my eyes on him as I feel around Wade's coat for a radio. My fingers are numb as I turn on the power and turn down the squelch.

"All units. I need backup. Officer down, a block from I-90 at an abandoned shipyard, cross street unknown, due south of Cermak," I report, my voice shaking. "Dispatch immediately, all units. Officer down."

I watch Mason reach for his gun with his left, unwounded hand and try to aim. He's testing me one last time.

I don't hesitate. I shoot him again, and this time I make it count. He falls backward, his gun thrown from his hand when my bullet hits him in the crotch. Painful, but not fatal; I won't let him off the easy way. He's going to have to suffer through the rest of this life.

"Repeat. Officer down," I say into the radio.

"They can't help me, Sam," Mason says.

"I wasn't talking about you."

I take Wade's handcuffs off his belt. Mason lies on the floor, clutching his groin and clenching his jaw. I cuff Mason's wrists. Then I stand over him.

"You think this hurts?" I ask. "I'd break your heart if I could."

Mason writhes in pain, unable to craft a comeback.

I light a cigarette and wait for backup, like I should have the night Mason killed Fred.

36

The barrage of squad cars and ambulances are a welcome intrusion when they finally arrive. I don't recognize any of the officers because I'm out of my district, but I'm glad. Everyone at my ward would probably feel sorry for Mason. These cops treat him like any other criminal.

I'm leaning against one of the squads and smoking a cigarette when O'Connor comes up.

"Nice of you to stop by," I say.

"Nice of you to cuff my co-worker to his radiator," O'Connor says.

"He was getting fresh," I say.

"I'm sure. Green belt, huh?"

The coroner shoots O'Connor a look as she wheels Wade's dead body across the lot.

"Been keeping her busy," O'Connor says. "Been keeping *me* busy. We have a lot to explain."

"No, we don't," I say. "He does." I watch a paramedic roll Mason on a stretcher to the back of an ambulance.

"You're gonna make it, man," I hear the medic tell him.

Mason stares me down and I look away. He knows there's a part of me that didn't want it to end this way, but I'm not going to give him the satisfaction of acknowledging it.

"I spoke to your sergeant," O'Connor says. "Of course your presence is requested immediately at the station."

"Lucky me," I say, and toss the last of my cigarette into the dirt.

"Give you a ride?" O'Connor asks.

Captain Jack takes charge at the station so I can get in and out as fast as possible. The advisers must have learned something from our previous meeting, because while I give my statement, the jittery one sits with his legal pad and scribbles every word as it comes out of my mouth. His monotone partner sits quietly next to Sarge and listens like he should have the last time.

Once I'm finished, Sarge takes me to his office and sits on the corner of his desk to give me the here-on-out. He says I'll be asked to testify against Mason, and that I'll have an affirmative defense. He says I have to stay on med leave, and "actually" go to counseling. He also says he's ninety-nine percent sure I'll be reinstated.

I say I'll watch out for that other one percent.

◆ ◆ ◆

It isn't until Sarge lets me go that I realize I have nowhere to go. I wander out of his office and down the hall like a senior on graduation day. I wonder if this is the last time I'll set foot in this place.

O'Connor is waiting for me on a bench at the end of the hall.

"I figured you'd still need a ride," he says.

"I don't know where to go," I tell him. "I made one hell of a mess."

"I know," O'Connor says, standing up. "I'm on the clean-up crew. Come on, I know a place."

On the way out, some of the overnight patrollers gather at the entrance and give me a round of applause. That's about as candid as a group of cops can get. O'Connor smiles at them, acknowledging each one for the gesture as he escorts me down the steps. And then, for the first time, he smiles at me.

O'Connor drives me to O'Shea's, where Marty has a seat waiting for me. The place is crowded, but I like the fact that life goes on in here.

"Just like home, right?" O'Connor says. "But with decent coffee." He sits me down at the bar, though he doesn't sit himself.

"There's an empty room upstairs," Marty says, serving me a bowl of chowder and a Budweiser. "If you need to set up camp for a while."

"Thanks, Marty."

"Don't thank me," he says and hands me a key. "This guy's the one doing dishes for your keep."

"Told you I'm on clean-up," O'Connor says.

Marty winks at me before he takes an order at the other end of the bar.

"Don't worry," O'Connor says. "It was a mess

worth making." Then he squeezes my shoulder and leaves me to enjoy my chowder in peace.

The room upstairs isn't bad, though it's musty in addition to the faint smell of smoke and grease coming through the air vents from the bar. It's unfurnished except for a twin bed and a broken pinball machine that used to be popular downstairs. Now, the machine is covered with bar towels packed up in plastic ties from the laundry service, standing in for a shelf. I guess every game gets old sometime.

I turn up the space heater and flip off the light before I strip to my underwear, settle into the bed, and pull the covers up to my nose. The window glows neon with a beer sign, which I know from the outside says SPECIAL EXPORT ON TAP. Never had a nightlight quite like this one before.

Never had a night quite like this one before.

I thought I was a good cop. I thought I'd stop people from hurting each other. But the truth is, there are no laws for preventing the hurt I feel. There are no answers that can justify the pain of losing a loved one. And I don't know of any rules a person's heart can follow.

I close my eyes and hear a few drunks downstairs getting more drunk, carrying on about whatever they momentarily decided to be their honest-to-God truth.

I drift off to sleep, thinking they might as well be right.

Keep reading for a thrilling excerpt
from Theresa Schwegel's next novel

PROBABLE CAUSE

Coming in hardcover in December 2006
from St. Martin's Minotaur

The store's alarm doesn't startle anyone. Two blocks away, in a rehabbed three-flat on Washtenaw Avenue, an underwhelmed DePaul professor hears it. He momentarily loses his place in a *Tribune* article, skims through something about the mayor's unfair hiring practices, yawns, and skips to the METRO section, assuming the alarm is part of whatever movie-of-the-week his wife is watching downstairs on TV. Downstairs, it doesn't matter what's on TV, because his wife is already well into a bottle of average cabernet and the first stages of sleep, dreaming of being appreciated.

A block away, at the intersection of Lincoln and Foster, a taxi driver hears the alarm while he waits at the light. Sirens all sound the same after ten years driving this route: bau, bau, bau, bau; whup-whup-whup-whup-whup-whup—*whatever*, the driver thinks. The sound is mildly irritating, like any red light. He steps on the gas and makes a right for Lake Shore Drive.

On the sidewalk in front of the store, a homeless woman wanders and, believing the alarm is a signal from her God, is confused as to why there is no church. No church, just Lucky Mike's Electronics: neon-yellow signage over a locked-up storefront, its windows and door fortified top to bottom by steel curtains. The woman moves on, ready to tell any other living soul her predicament.

A decal on Lucky Mike's blacked-out door declares security courtesy of WESTEC: area office located exactly 9.2 miles from the store. There, a little red light blinks on a console, summoning some dispatcher to get off his ass for the third time this shift and send a car. He finishes his pastrami on rye. The dispatcher is used to false alarms.

Seven and a half miles from the store at Spiaggia restaurant, Officer Ray Weiss probably wishes he could hear the alarm. It'd be a nice way to ditch the horrendous dinner date his mother guilted him into making. Monica has already ordered an appetizer and a twenty-dollar glass of some kind of wine she couldn't pronounce, and now she won't shut up about the shopping on Oak Street. She says "eww" in some kind of baby voice when he cracks his knuckles. Weiss tries to act interested in her and decipher the menu at the same time, but he's never heard of half the items, and every one costs more than both his shirt and tie. He orders something with sweetbreads, expecting, well, sweet bread. He's twenty-three. He wants a burger. He wants to get out of here and catch bad guys.

No, the store's alarm doesn't startle anyone, but Jed Pagorski thinks he can feel the adrenaline coming out of his ears. In the alley behind the store, his hands are slippery in his gloves as he jimmies the loading dock's heavy garage door. "Noise" Dubois is over his shoulder, watching, making sure Jed doesn't slip up. *It's the heat of the night,* Jed thinks; that's why he's sweating. Can Noise tell?

"Rent-a-cops will be here in ten minutes, tops," Jed says.

Noise's look says: No shit.

Too late to back out now, Jed thinks. Not that he would. He slides one leg underneath the door, then the other, then his torso, the weight of the door held by his twitching arms like a stacked bench press.

Ten minutes. Less.

"Hold this fucking door up for me." *Be in control,* Jed thinks. *It's all under control.* Noise's fingers appear in front of Jed's nose, healthy pink nails against black skin. Underhanded, Noise holds the door.

As soon as Jed slides through, the garage door hits the pavement like a guillotine.

Nine minutes, no counting.

Jed pulls a flashlight from his belt, turns it on, and sweeps the space with light. Layout looks like the map Noise penciled on a napkin at Hamilton's earlier tonight: a doorway behind opens to outside and runs ahead to the showroom; inventory is there to the right; alarm keypad is mounted on the wall, over there.

Nine-one-zero-one-six, Jed repeats in his head, the code memorized easily, after so much practice. The gloves prove difficult as he disables the alarm. The siren stops; his ears ring in the silence. He thinks he hears his own heartbeat. He remembers to breathe.

Jed hears the car pull up out back, just like they

planned. One of the tires crunches broken glass in the alley. Car door slams. *Seven minutes,* Jed thinks, *to be on the safe side.* To be out of there with no trouble. He approaches the door to the right of the loading dock and presses his ear against it, waiting for the signal. He turns off his flashlight like a conscience. He waits, counting backward from ten three times over, and again, the numbers steadying his concentration.

Jed smiles. He's in it: he's in the game. And he won't get caught—can't, really. He smiles, notices his jaw is clenched. He's so god damn tense he wishes he'd taken Noise up on that drink back at Hamilton's. Sweat trickles through his brow and into his eyes and he wonders, *where the hell is Noise?*

Be in control. It's all under control. He grips his flashlight like a weapon in his right hand and reaches for the door with his weak left. He turns the lock, it clicks; he pulls the handle down and inches the door open to get a look outside.

Before he can make sense of it the barrel of a gun slips through the crack. The muzzle stops an inch from his face. He drops the flashlight and turns to take cover, but the door is pushed open quickly and with so much force that Jed can't get his feet set. He tumbles to the floor and covers his face with his forearms like a little girl would.

Noise doesn't say anything. Just holsters his gun and stands there, shaking his head.

"God damn, Noise, what the fuck?"

"Is that a question?" Noise swipes Jed's flashlight, then helps Jed to his feet. Through the open door Jed sees the car, trunk open.

Five minutes left, no time for Jed's answer.

He follows Noise into the showroom. The only light comes from a flickering EXIT sign just above them; the front windows are blacked and reinforced, shielding the merchandise from bad reflection during the day and undue interest at night—a security measure, back-fired. Noise shines the flashlight over surround sound stereos, home theater systems, the digital projection packages. He stops, focuses the beam of light on a 48-inch Sony plasma television.

Jed can't see Noise in the dark so he asks, "That's it?"

"It's a nice TV."

"I know, but that's all we're taking?"

"You think we should load up the backseat? Strap a big screen to the hood?"

Jed knows better than to ask stupid questions. He knows that. He also knows he has to be the one to lift the TV. Sometimes he thinks they only want him for his muscle. *Suck it up,* he thinks. *One TV, maybe three minutes and one fucking nice TV,* and he's in no matter why they want him.

Noise disappears as Jed disconnects the control box from the screen. He can't carry both at once, so he takes the box first, out the back, down the steps. He sets it in the trunk like it's his mother's favorite porce-lain figurine. Noise sticks his head out the back door, uses Jed's flashlight to inspect the job.

Jed hustles back up the stairs past Noise, says, "I know," assuming Noise's pursed lips were about to squeeze out a customary *Be careful.*

Jed goes inside, and he can see the finish line now, his vision narrowed in the showroom. He hoists the 48-inch screen under his right arm and negotiates his way through the dark, out the back. Noise isn't there, but there's no time to wonder where he went.

Jed hopes Noise won't harp on him about the screen's scraped edge. Forty-eight inches happen to be a perfect fit for the trunk, except he didn't know that when he gave the screen a little too much elbow grease on the way in.

Jed shuts the trunk and closes his eyes, sealing his fate in the trunk: He is one of them. Finally. And with at least a minute to spare.

"Jed." Noise's tone is far from congratulatory.

Jed looks up: Noise is standing at the top of the steps, holding a VHS tape. *Be careful.* Jed had mocked him, instead of checking for cameras.

"Surveillance. Man, Noise, I thought—"

"Don't tell me what you thought. Tell me what you know."

Jed's answer comes out like a reflex: "Cover your ass."

Noise stops short of a nod. His body seems to tense from the inside out. Jed watches him, waiting to maybe get yelled at.

A car turns into the alley, shining its high beams on the men. Noise tucks the tape in his jacket and remains on the steps.

"Shit," says Jed, thinking he fucked this up somehow, took too long, and now they'll have his ass. He leans over the trunk, his arms spread, head hanging, like he's ready to get frisked.

The driver pulls up, gets out, says, "What is going on?"

"Mr. Lukas?" Noise comes down the steps cautiously, gun drawn, held close to his leg. Jed is afraid to turn around.

"Yes," the driver says. "What in the hell happened?"

Jed can feel the rush in his veins. He stands up, reaches into his jacket, waits for his cue.

"Well?" the driver asks.

Of course Noise doesn't say anything.

Be in control, Jed tells himself. *It's all under control*. Then he turns slowly, arrogantly, and produces his badge. "I'm sorry, sir, it seems there's been a burglary."

2

A serious-looking white woman grips a knife, her eyes glaring at the camera, her skin tinged orange by the TV's poor color calibration. "To a police officer," she says, "this dagger is a potential weapon." She palms the handle, presents it for a close-up. "But to a Sikh man, this is a *kirpan*, a sacred symbol carried as a sign of spiritual devotion." The camera zooms out to reveal she's standing in Lincoln Park, next to a Sikh. She smiles at him like he's retarded, then hands him the knife. He bows slightly and steps out of the frame. She notices his turban is casting a distracting shadow, so she moves to the left. "How can we ever understand one another?" she asks the camera. Then she pauses, takes a step forward, and says, "If strength comes from knowledge, cultural sensitivity is muscle."

Ray Weiss cracks his knuckles, looks around the briefing room cautiously, like he's cheating on a test. He's trying to get a read on the other beat cops, to see if anyone else thinks this is complete bullshit.

As the woman starts in about how Saudi Arabians mean yes when they shake their heads from left to right, Field Training Officer Jack Fiore whispers an undecipherable though predictably vulgar comment to his colleague, Noise Dubois. Next to Weiss, Officer Gary Anzalone rocks on the back legs of his metal chair, his iffy balance providing self-entertainment. Across the room, Jed Pagorski is sound asleep. All the guys in between pretend to watch the monitor, their eyes glazed over by real life.

Weiss looks at the District 20 beat map on the wall to his left, though he's studied it so often he sees it when he closes his eyes. To his right, he glances at another ineffective use of space: a corkboard tacked with familiar and otherwise useless information: Beat events, CAPS information. Memos about crystal meth pushers in the LGBT community. Sex offenders, Most Wanteds. Weiss wishes the room had a window. Anzalone beats him to a sigh.

On the TV, some guy in a pinstripe suit says, "With security concerns paramount in current times of turmoil, it is critical to have strong elements of trust and understanding between our law enforcement agencies and the communities they serve." He's probably from the State's Attorney's Office, Weiss figures, since his statement sounds rehearsed and the camera caught him on his way out of the courthouse on La Salle.

When the orange woman returns, pamphlet in hand, Weiss is reminded of the information the stewardess gives you before you fly: great in theory, but when your plane is falling out of the sky, you're going to be shitting your pants, not locating your flotation device. Just like if some Latin King puts a gun in your face—you aren't going to be concerned with his personal space or his religious rights. Weiss looks at his watch. Twenty minutes 'til his four o'clock shift.

"In a city as diverse as Chicago," the orange woman says, "we have many different cultures that view the police from varying perspectives." The Sikh steps up behind her, followed by a black woman, and an Asian couple. A Hispanic woman joins them, holding a vacant-eyed baby; a Hasidic Jew brings up the rear. It's a regular rainbow coalition, Weiss thinks.

"As police officers," the woman says, "you have the responsibility to understand those perspectives to better serve and protect our communities. You earned your badge; now earn their respect." Cue the feel-good music.

Sergeant Flagherty turns on the overhead lights; Weiss' eyes adjust. Flagherty looks like he used to be fat and he walks like he still carries the weight. He goes to the VCR and shuts off the tape, triggering static noise that jerks Jed from sleep. He wipes drool from the corner of his mouth, runs his hand over his buzz cut, tries to focus. Fucking guy, Weiss thinks.

Flagherty picks up a Magic Marker and scrawls on the Dry Erase board: SENSITIVITY. From the back corner of the room, Johnny Giantolli groans like he does when he's imitating his wife.

"We have to do this, guys," Flagherty says, his pronunciation heavy on the *a*.

"We do this," Walter Guzman says, two seats over from Weiss, "and I still got to spend all day in court with some spic who says I arrested him because he's

Mexican." Everyone laughs—even Jed, who just yesterday spent the better part of their workout insisting that Guzman was Japanese. Sure, he has Asian features, Weiss agreed. But what about his name? And the time that guy from the twenty-fourth called him "Galtero"? What about the picture of the Virgin Mary in his locker? Nope, Jed insisted: Guzman's Japanese. Look at his hair. The shape of his eyes.

And now Jed sits there, his big mouth fixed in a contagious, stupid grin, like he knew all along. Weiss wishes he could let himself off as easily.

On the board under SENSITIVITY, Flaherty writes the word SPIC.

"Guzman's only sensitive about his sexual preference," Giantolli says.

"You'd know, you faggot," Mark Sikula says. Weiss thinks he sounds angry, but Giantolli's his partner, so who knows. In the front row, Sikula doesn't turn around.

Flaherty writes FAGGOT on the board.

"Sarge, what's the point here, huh?" Guzman asks. "We don't need a seminar on how to piss each other off."

"It's city-mandated. The department has suffered some serious blows lately. With all the trouble in the twenty-third, cops getting killed—"

"The twenty-third: your old stomping grounds," Fiore says.

"Did you know that woman cop?" Giantolli asks Flaherty. "Was it her fault?"

"It's complicated."

"Leave it to a woman," Fiore says.

Flaherty ignores him. "We've got problems on the southside, too: racial profiling, police brutality. The press is up the mayor's ass about all this, and he's got enough on his plate. He wants this nipped in the bud, ground level. So the superintendent is cracking down on corruption."

"With a videotape?" Guzman asks.

"They should be showing us *National Geographic,* the fucking animals we deal with," from under Sikula's breath.

"I'm just following orders," Flagherty says. "You should all give it a try." Flagherty turns back to the board and adds ANIMAL to his list.

"This is ridiculous," Giantolli says. "I need a cup of coffee. Or something I can hang myself with."

"Hey Flagherty," Fiore says casually. "Why don't you write *nigger* up there."

There are other black cops in the room, but this was clearly intended for Noise, who is sitting right behind Weiss. Noise Dubois, given name Innis, is a quiet, observant cop—his nickname a testament to his aural acuity, not his mouth—but when he speaks, he always has something to say.

So far, he hasn't. Nobody has said anything. The air in the room is as still as a dead man.

Finally, Flagherty says, "Look, guys. I think the point is made." He puts down the marker, addresses Noise: "None of us is immune to insult."

Weiss hears Noise's chair slide across the linoleum, Uh-oh.

Flagherty swallows hard. He's fairly new to the district, and he isn't quite standing up straight yet. Weiss is pretty sure Noise isn't about to help him feel welcome.

"This whole exercise has been an insult to my intelligence," Noise says, each word like it's capitalized. "Some woman talk-show host, telling me to be nice. A group of model citizens pleading for my understanding. I'm not in the job to make friends and didn't come to work today to sit here and talk about racial epithets. Because you know what? When I get out on the street, I'd rather be called a nigger than a dumb cop."

Jed puffs up his chest, nods, proud. He looks over at Weiss, probably hoping he shares the sentiment.

"And I do believe the street is where I'm needed," Noise says. Then the door at the back of the room opens, and closes, and Noise is gone.

The collective exhale in the room is heavy with whispers from the guys in the back. "Fiore was right, that certainly made it interesting," Giantolli says.

Flaherty goes to the podium and reorganizes his papers, and most likely his thoughts. "Enough," he finally says to the chatter, though he waits for it to die. "As a result of last night's shit storm, you might want to take notes." He reads through his own: "Stay in your beat. Notify the watch commander if you so much as think about crossing Lawrence Avenue. And, gentlemen, let's try to skip the confusion about who's doing whose paperwork." He looks right at Jed. "I don't want any more fuzzy interpretations of investigational protocol. Read your manual on downtime if you're unclear."

Weiss knows why that last bit was directed at Jed: last night Jed and Noise tripped a burglary alarm and swiped a TV. Jed was supposed to seal off the perimeter for the detectives once he secured the so-called crime scene; instead, he let the store owner into the building, which screwed up everything. Not everything, exactly, since no one got caught. The screwup, as far as Flaherty knows, is in the paperwork.

The theft was Jed's "initiation." Weiss doesn't know if all cops go through it and he doesn't know whom to ask; all he knows is that he's supposed to be next. He feels the burrito he had for lunch turn in his stomach.

"Giantolli and Sikula," Flagherty says, "at twenty-two hundred hours I want you to join the 2024 beat car, backing up the guys in the twenty-third. They got a concert letting out at the Aragon, and they're expecting a bunch of potheads from the suburbs."

"Rock on," Giantolli says.

"Anything else?" Flagherty asks the rest of the guys, half of whom are already out the door.

Weiss has so many questions, but he never asks; given enough time, he thinks, the answers always present themselves. He can only hope they are the right ones.

"Weiss," Fiore says with a *V.* The German pronunciation sounds commanding, which is obviously the intent. He jerks his chin toward the door. *"Andale."*